# THE MIRACLE OF SHIH SHENG KANG

The chanting of Shih Sheng Kang stopped as the monk's voice failed. Twisting, he saw from the corner of his eye what had been watching him. Two serpent forms regarded him with intelligent, meaningful scrutiny. They swayed toward him. Their motion and their eager eyeing suggested more than his mind could accept.

The candles winked out in a twisting draft. The full moon reached in, riding the wind. It lighted the serpent forms, played with the sandalwood smoke.

"Sing, Monk. Sing for us. Sing your blessing."

The serpent forms became translucent, misty. They rose from their supporting coils. These coils began to fade. As they thinned into gossamer and smoke, new figures took shape, becoming the solid bodies of women—young, beautiful and bare!

# THE
# Devil Wives
## OF
# Li Fong

## BY E. HOFFMANN PRICE

A Del Rey Book

BALLANTINE BOOKS • NEW YORK

For Jade Lady,
*to whom I bow three times.*

# CHAPTER I

UPSTREAM, a thousand miles or more from the sea, mist blanketed the Yangtze, muffling the voice of the river and all night sounds, whether of beast or bird or insect. The valley slept beneath a gray blanket.

A gray veil hid the lower slopes of the nearby hills. Their rocky heights reached into the glamour of haze lighted by a rising moon. They became islands in a sea of gray.

Near the crest of a headland towering above the river, a point of light winked from the dark masonry nestled among overshadowing trees. The deep note of a bell stirred the stillness. Though subdued at last to a murmur, it persisted, clinging as if the music had life of its own, and loved that rich life.

A second note, full-throated and majestic, in its turn slowly died to a whisper; a third and final was followed by the clanging dissonance of quick blows against the bronze.

*"Gate, gate, paragate, parasamgate, Bodhi, Svaha!"*

Although the voice tried bravely for resonance and failed, it did not quaver. The man intoning a Sanskrit *mantram* did his best. He hoped that the spirits of the Ancestors would be pleased. This was the fifteenth night of the Seventh Moon, the festival in honor of the dead.

Trees for centuries untended embraced the ruined monastery in which the monk, Shih Sheng Kang, was speaking to all the lonely and forgotten dead. The walls, riven by quake and time, had scattered half their substance, strewing the first court with blocks of masonry. Roots thrust paving slabs out of their beds. Beams had fallen, dropping tiles from the curved eaves to lie among accumulated rubbish.

The space in front of the shrine, which faced the main entrance of the monastery, had been neatly swept. A path, clean and smooth, led to the left; an-

1

other, to the rear of the shrine and deep into the further courts. Beyond these were storerooms, rows of cubicles for monks, and a lecture hall.

The wavering flames of two candles brought golden highlights from the gilded faces of three human-size figures which sat on lotus-blossom thrones. In the center was the most ancient of ancient, Amitabha, Infinite Life, Infinite Light. On the right sat Compassionate Kwan Yin, and on the left, Mahasthama, Buddha of Wisdom.

The placid faces had been dusted and cleaned.

In a censer of bronze, corroded beyond polishing, a cluster of coals glowed. Shih Sheng Kang set aside the baton which he had padded with turns of well-worn cloth. Since there was no cushion in front of the altar, he had laid out the remnant of a mat.

Stepping to this, the gray-robed monk put palms together and bowed. Dancing candlelight modeled the contours of his clean-shaven head. In a continuous motion, he placed knees, hands, and forehead on the mat. He rose, paused, made a second kowtow, and finally a third. This time, remaining on his knees, he picked a sliver of sandalwood from the table, raised it to his forehead, and put it into the coals. With his left hand, he fed a second sliver to the fire. Again with right hand, he put a final bit of wood into the bowl. Fragrant smoke rose to the height of the candle flames.

On the altar, Shih Sheng Kang set a tiny bowl of rice and two sprays of foliage from the courtyard.

There should have been a shrine for the Ancestors, apart from that of the Buddhas, and a votive tablet, just outside, in front of which he would have put incense and a spoonful of cooked rice. This would have been for the spirits who wandered unhappily, the lonely ones who had died childless and for whom there were no rites. Shih Sheng Kang was improvising. He was both celebrant and congregation.

There was neither drum nor "fish head" with which to beat the cadence. However, in the rubbish he had found a single-stringed fiddle. The bow was usable. He plucked the frayed fiddle-string, took up a twist of the peg, and drew the bow. He swallowed, blinked, licked his lips, and lowered the bow.

2

The loneliness had not oppressed him, nor had the desolation. However, he was now certain that he was no longer alone. There should have been the chirp of crickets, the twitter-cheep of bats, the stirring of birds, the scratching of field mice. The small creatures who lived in the ruin had left, disturbed by his cleanup. That they had not returned, after a dozen hours, was neither right nor natural.

Shih Sheng Kang's wrinkled face puckered. He closed his eyes so that his ears would sharpen until he could hear what he now knew was lurking. Apprehensively, he leaned forward, not breathing.

He would now welcome one of those Taoist priests whose specialty it was to drive away devils and unfriendly spirits.

"*Na-mo-o-mi-to-fu!*" he intoned in Chinese. "I take refuge with Amitabha!"

Resolutely, he faced toward the alcove and bowed the fiddle. Its quavering was somewhat short of music, but the attempt to play distracted him from his uneasiness. Presently he was doing well with the single-stringed instrument. Its voice became sweet, plaintive, happy in a sad, compassionate mode. *They* would know that someone remembered them.

Although Shih Sheng Kang's qualms subsided, he had not been the victim of his imagination. In the shadow fringe, eyes regarded him. More than reflecting the candle flames, they had an inner glow of their own. There were two pairs of eyes.

Light was mirrored by reptilian scales.

Slowly, two serpents emerged from the debris. They disturbed small pieces of rubbish. The frail sounds were masked by the moon-fiddle's voice. Shih Sheng Kang chanted as he plied the bow:

"*Though I were cast on a mountain of knives,*
*None could hurt me.*
*Though dipped in a lake of fire,*
*I would not burn.*
*Though hurled into Hell,*
*I rise to Heaven!*
*All hail, Compassionate Kwan Yin!*"

Whether drawn by the scent of sandalwood, or by the warmth of the monk's cooking-fire, or by the voice of the fiddle, the serpents came to the very edge of the circle of brightness. One was white, the other green; the scales of each were iridescent. Neither was more than seven yards in length.

Each coiled and, so supported, extended perhaps a third of its length, erect as a monk sitting in meditation. They swayed, elegant and graceful, keeping time with the chanting.

The monk's voice failed. Twisting, he saw from the corner of his eye what had been watching him. They regarded him with intelligent, meaningful scrutiny. This was more disturbing than a serpent presence. They swayed toward him. Their motion and their eager eyeing suggested more than his mind could accept.

"Two sing-song girls, moving with music, like snakes. They've been eating herbs, grass, leaves—they're not girls, not snakes—"

Terror made him ply the bow and finger the string. A voice within him spoke in blurred, half-shaped words. The snakes were speaking to him. This he could no longer doubt, no longer deny. They addressed his mind. They made no sounds.

"Sing, Monk, sing . . . for us . . . sing your blessing. . ."

He regained voice:

*. . . though Hell opened to take me,*
*It could not hold me . . .*
*Hail, Compassionate Kwan Yin."*

The candles winked out in a twisting draft. The full moon reached in, riding the wind. It lighted the serpent forms, played with the sandalwood smoke, and fanned the embers of the cooking-fire.

The fiddle called to the heart, singing of grief and hope and joy, of misery, and of the release from misery.

The serpent forms became translucent, misty. They rose slowly from their supporting coils. Those coils began to fade. As they thinned into gossamer and smoke, new figures took shape, becoming the solid bodies of women—young, beautiful, and bare. Far from driving devils away, he had summoned a pair, a menace deadlier than what he had hoped to expel with music and *mantram.*

4

Terror shackled him. He could have escaped from snakes. Flight from devils was something else.

The one who had been green came in small, quick steps to Shih Sheng Kang. She kowtowed. She caught the edge of his robe and cried, "Master—all these centuries—"

The monk's cramped throat tore free in a tremendous yell. He staggered, recovered, jerked clear of the woman's grasp. He stumbled and lay for a moment, clawing the pavement. He almost regained his feet, only to crumple and roll as he fell. His eyes stared at nothing. His bared teeth bit air, until he ceased gasping and went limp.

The one who had been green cried, "Mei Ling! We're human! This one helped us change—oh, what happened?"

Mei Ling, who had been white, dropped to her knees beside the monk, buried her face in the gray robe, and sobbed. "Our first human friend! Oh, our father—we killed him—frightened him—oh, you're not, you can't be dead!" She shook the monk's shoulder. "Meilan, let's do something—maybe it's not too late."

She thrust Meilan aside and rushed to the hearth.

Meilan said, "Elder Sister, there's no help. I touched him. I went to pay respects, thank him—it's my karma, my fault, not yours."

Mei Ling shook her head. "This is ours. You and I, we start our new human life under a curse."

# CHAPTER II

Mei Ling and Meilan sat close to the little fire, which they had fed with chunks of shattered beams. They drank tea and divided the bit of rice left from the monk's final meal. By eating human food, they might make their newly formed bodies more permanent.

Each regarded the other in wonder and in perplexity. Each saw in the other the problem that both faced. They were thinking, "After all our many lives, all these many centuries, we've won human form, which is so very hard to win. What do we have to do—what can we do?"

As yet, neither could recall the details of incarnations, though each sensed that long ago she had been human, or nearly so. Each, shoulders hunched and shivering, was less concerned with bodily discomfort than with her growing awareness that she had within her a soul-wisdom, the essence of all the experience in earlier forms and in those realms of spirit-without-form. Mei Ling and Meilan knew more than they could realize at once.

Mei Ling brightened. "We'll have to learn what we already know!"

"I'm all in a muddle, Elder Sister," Meilan replied. "I know what you mean, though you might tell me a thing or two. But just sitting here is no good at all. That holy monk is dead—his spirit will be annoyed; he'll make trouble for us. There are things we have to do."

"He'd never harm anyone. He came to bring peace to the unhappy dead. But you're right, he ought to have honorable burial. Very important human custom. Gravestones on the hill, remember? We found our way among them." Mei Ling frowned. "Somehow, I *knew*, then."

"About burial?"

"More than that. About coming to this place."

"For me to win a curse!"

"Each human life has its curse," Mei Ling said, "Part of the payment for human form. Gods and spirits can't ever become Buddhas. They can't become really immortal, the way our benefactor will."

Meilan's thinking was for the here and now. "We can't eat snake food any more. We might work on farms or fishing boats. Or carry wood to market."

Mei Ling stretched from the waist, drew her hands along her body, and cupped her breasts. "We've got to get something to wear. It's human custom—" She shivered. "Funny how I notice the cold!"

Meilan's somber eyes twinkled again. "Some boats are tied up along the river. Clothes are hanging out to dry. I'll steal just enough for us. One small extra curse is nothing, when I already have a big one."

"I've been remembering," Mei Ling resumed, very slowly, and closed her eyes for a moment. "Travelers used to stop at these monasteries to sleep and eat. Troubled people came to sit and face the wall, to wait for peace to overtake them. Others came with friends to talk and laugh and have picnics.

"Each left more than prints in the dust. See where our benefactor cleared two paths." Mei Ling gestured. "One that way and one to the further court."

"What for?"

"Maybe to fix the place for travelers again. Maybe for sitting and facing the wall." Taking a candle from the altar, she got it burning again. She wrapped the ragged mat about her. "I'm going to look. You light joss sticks for this holy monk. And more sandalwood."

Meilan, studying the hairdo of the Kwan Yin painted on the wall, gave a strand of her own hair a tentative twist. "See if you can find pins like hers," Meilan suggested as she turned to feed the censor.

When Mei Ling came back, she had an armload of salvage secured in the ragged mat. Meilan meanwhile had done her hair in a high twist and a loop. A bamboo chopstick served as a pin. She knelt as Mei Ling dropped the bundle. Both sneezed when dust billowed up.

There was an adze, rusty yet serviceable. An alms bowl of wood. A monk's razor, which would never shave unless a smith restored the corroded blade. A quilted jacket. A ragged tunic. A pair of cloth slippers. A yellow robe, made of the traditional patches stitched together. A string of *cash*, and a *tael* of silver. The former was greenish, the latter black. There was a book, a writing brush, an ink stone, and the stub of a stick of ink.

Meilan snatched the quilted jacket and wriggled into the grimy garment. "You take the tunic. It's longer. More dignified. Here's the other chopstick for your hair."

Mei Ling slipped into the gray robe and twisted her hair into a knot at the nape of her neck. "Now he

7

won't be offended," she said, glancing at the monk's body. "*Aiieeyah!* If only we'd realized!"

"It's my fault, Elder Sister."

"I'm accepting the benefits," Mei Ling said, "so I have to take my piece of the karma. But the first thing to do is to make a coffin and dig a grave."

She opened the book. Between the hard covers was a single strip of paper, many yards long and folded, page after page, in pleats.

"This may give us some advice."

"How can you read?"

"Something tries to make me remember." Mei Ling folded the pages and set the book aside. "While we do other things, it will speak to me."

"Devil-spirits don't read—snakes don't read—never could!"

"They don't speak human talk, either, but we do." Mei Ling got to her feet. "The soul remembers what it heard and couldn't understand. Maybe we were human and wasted our lives and became devil-spirits and then snakes. There must have been a remembering to bring us here, to eat the right herbs, where the right monk was chanting the proper *mantrams* and *sutras.*

"Let's get water and wash the body—do what's suitable for respectful burying."

At daybreak, they found a spot outside the wall, enclosed by the gnarled trunks and great spread of trees. Secure from lowland observation, they took turns with the adze to loosen earth and with the bottom of a broken jar to scoop and throw it out.

During pauses to rest and to ease their blistered palms, they looked down at the distant fields where buffalo pulled plows. In other quarters, men wearing mushroom-shaped hats plodded in the watered squares set out with rice. Again they looked down at the broad Yangtze, with its fishing boats and square-nosed *sampans.* There were houseboats moored to pilings. These floating homes rose and dropped with the swell set up by close-passing barges.

There was much more to their world than this—but this offered all that they could handle, for the time . . .

Toward sunset, they had completed the coffin. Since they could not groove and notch the ill-assorted planks to fit them together, they assembled the pieces in the grave. This done, they lowered the frail body.

"Three coins," Mei Ling enumerated, "and chopsticks, and a bowl, and that yellow robe. He can pay his fare across the Three Rivers and begin making his alms rounds again."

After placing these essentials and the monk's rosary of one hundred and eight beads with the body, they laid the cover planks into place.

With scoop and a wooden slat, they pushed earth into the grave. Mei Ling tugged a block of masonry from the debris and set it up as a marker. Meilan brought rice and some stunted peaches from the scrawny tree in the courtyard.

"A present for Hsi Mu Wang," Meilan said. "The Goddess will give him immortality. Just in case he isn't reborn as a Buddha."

"Younger Sister, how you remember what you don't know!"

Meilan gestured, an arm-sweep which included river and fields and distant villages. "When we begin meeting people, there'll be too much, all at once. I'm scared and worried!"

There remained only two handsful of Shih Sheng Kang's rice and a little tea. The candle stubs would last no more than a few hours.

After drinking their tea and washing the dishes, Meilan watched Elder Sister open the book. She sat, eyes closed, and nodded as she fingered three copper coins.

"What are you doing now? What—"

Mei Ling gestured for silence and did not answer.

Meilan draw back into the shadows beyond the circle of light. For some moments she watched Elder Sister, who was trying to remember. Then, as if she herself had begun to recall, Meilan retreated toward the courtyard and picked her way into darkness.

Relieved of the disturbing presence, Mei Ling unfolded the book. In addition to elegant calligraphy, the most formal characters, there were patterns of square figures. Each square was composed of six lines, some solid, some broken: except that the first, called *K'hien*, contained no broken lines, and the second, called *Khwan*, contained no solid lines.

Crossing her legs, she seated herself in the way of the figures in the shrine. She arranged her hands correctly, then her thumbs. Her lids drooped until the long lashes joined. Her breathing became slower.

The joss sticks shed an inch or two of ash, but Mei Ling did not stir; nor had she moved when, three quarters of an hour later, the final crumb of incense glowed on the bamboo fiber stem.

Mei Ling was not startled when Meilan returned with a compact bundle of blue cloth. She gestured and leaned forward to pick up the three coins lying near the book. She flipped them and noted that all had fallen with the inscription side up.

"All three are *yin*, and it is six," she said aloud. She tossed the coins again. Again, she saw that no *yang* side faced up. And thus it was, throw after throw, until the hexagram was completed and she consulted the book. In it she found the diagram, the pattern which corresponded with the numbers the coin-faces had symbolized.

"Our way is the Receptive, the Way of Devotion. You and I are *yin*, we are the earth. We look to *yang*, the light, the spirit, the sun, for balance and for guidance."

"*Aiieeyah!* That's what we've been doing!"

Mei Ling smiled. "Our benefactor, *yang*, spirit and light. That's how we started."

"Male and *yang*!" Meilan exclaimed happily. "We'll marry a rich landlord, or a magistrate, or even a merchant if we can't do any better."

"*Yin* goes with things as they go," Mei Ling resumed. "By devotion and serving, we'll become *fully* human again, instead of just in the body."

Meilan digested the judgment of the Oracle Book, the *I Ching*. "You figure things out for us. I'll be your maid, and in that simple way start my serving. And when you marry a high official, I'll be his concubine."

"You might wait until we find someone to serve."

"It won't take long! You're beautiful and talented and you know things; you're likely to be a governor's Number One Wife!" She slid a bundle toward Elder

Sister. "Here's my first bit of serving. I found these things on a houseboat wash-line down there."

"I'll wear some of these things," Mei Ling said, "and I'll share the karma with you. The Book says to go south and west, but I'm going to compromise. We came out of the western mountains, so let's go east and see what happens." She paused and eyed Meilan for a moment. "Any objections, Younger Sister?"

"Why did you fool with the book, if you're not going to follow it?"

"Using your judgment and accepting risks is part of being human! And the *I Ching* isn't supposed to give you any hard and fast rules. You've got to use your imagination. Maybe I'm leading us into a lot of trouble!"

Meilan shrugged. "Better than being a snake! Let's try it."

# CHAPTER III

HOUSE servants joined Li Fong's fellow apprentices to swell the chorus of quips that began as he stepped from the courtyard and into the back room of Mr. Sang's drug store. This was the fifteenth day of the Fifth Moon and Li Fong's first holiday in two years. He was dressed, indeed somewhat overdressed, for the occasion.

Instead of blue cotton jacket and trousers to match, he wore a gray silk robe and embroidered shoes. The handle of his folded parasol was trimmed with an agate knob. In every detail, he appeared to be a first- or second-class graduated scholar, eligible for a post in the Imperial Civil Service.

"*Aiieeyah!*" a mocker screeched. "When you see the Viceroy, put in a good word for me."

"He says he's paying respects to his Exalted Ancestors!"

"He really means the new whorehouse at the Tiger Head Gate!"

Li Fong whisked a fan from his flowing sleeve and made a stately pass. "Please do not kowtow. I, too, used to be an apprentice."

With a grin and a wink, he stepped from the cluttered workroom and storeroom and into the shop where Mr. Sang sat at his tea table in a corner of the open-front drug store.

The entire room, perhaps twelve feet square, had side and back walls fitted with hundreds of little drawers and shelves on which stood jars and jugs. Each contained herbs, roots, dried blossoms, or one of the animal or mineral substances required for prescriptions. Among the latter was realgar, a tiny crystal of which, when dissolved in wine, gave immunity to snake bites. Better yet, a cup of such wine was useful in discovering whether a woman was human, or whether she was a serpent-spirit masquerading in a human body. In such case, the impostor would at once revert to her original form.

Li Fong bowed to his employer. Mr. Sang set down his cup and folded wrinkled, slender hands. On one finger he wore a ring of green jade. A bracelet of mutton-fat jade peeped from the sleeve of his black tunic. After a moment of arranging himself, he inclined his head slightly to acknowledge the courtesy of a Number One Apprentice who was neither too casual nor too obsequious.

"Thank you, Learned Master, for this holiday which I do not deserve."

"Attention to duty entitles you to rest." The old man dipped into his sleeve and took out a small red envelope with an inscription in gilt. "When you have paid respects to your Ancestors, you may take time to drink wine and enjoy yourself."

Li Fong bowed. He retreated a pace and bowed again. He paused in the entranceway and made his final bow. Protocol taken care of, he merged with the pack peddlers, the surging stream of shoppers, the farm woman with baskets of vegetables balanced on their heads.

Slender and erect, Li Fong picked his way, savoring the bouquet of fruit and spices, the garlic odor of sausages frying on a vendor's portable stove. The cosmetic sweetness exhaled by a red-lacquered sedan chair carried by a pair of coolies evoked a vision of the woman concealed by the drawn curtains. She could be the frail and wrinkled first lady, the *tai-tai* of a wealthy householder—though Li Fong preferred to fancy that this was a sing-song girl on the way to her hairdresser.

This fifteenth day of the Fifth Moon was a happy relief from the tiger claws, the snake livers, the roots and herbs and barks that he pulverized twelve hours or more every day. Li Fong inhaled so much of the pungent, bitter, fragrant, reeking dust that the taste of it tainted the rice gruel and vegetables he ate with fellow apprentices and servants in the compound of Mr. Sang's house.

The death of Li Fong's parents had interrupted the education which they had hoped would qualify him for the Imperial Civil Service. Although Li Fong's apprenticeship offered worthwhile prospects, he liked to fancy himself a scholar.

His smooth, tawny-pale skin would have made Li Fong seem boyish but for the grave and thoughtful cast of his lean face. His nose, although by no means conspicuous, was sufficient to take command of his features and organize their lines and pattern. There was sensitivity combined with forcefulness, and the promise that the years would blend all into dignity, presence, and—distinction.

Inwardly, Li Fong was neither as self-assured nor half as arrogant as his carriage suggested. Women tried to catch his eye; from the corners of his own eyes, he was aware of them, but he kept his gaze straight ahead.

There was so much he had to learn about women. The first step in such an apprenticeship would be sing-song girls and flower-boat girls, since there were no serving maids in his present home who were accessible. They had neither time nor inclination, as he reckoned it, for anyone who worked for meals and a place to spread his sleeping mat.

Once he had cleared the cavernous gate which faced the hills and fields and the groves which girdled West Lake, some three miles beyond Hangchow, Li Fong relaxed and let his shoulders slump a little. At times he paused to savor the breeze which had kissed so many peaches and pears, jasmine and magnolia blossoms. Had there been a companion, he would have laughed in happiness and delight.

Pavilions and tea houses nestled among pines and willows. The sound of flute and stringed instrument invited him, and so did the voices of gaily dressed girls who lounged outside the wine shops. Once past an alluring group, he paused to open the gift envelope which Mr. Sang had given him.

It contained silver. This, added to the holiday gift which his sister Moutan and her husband had handed him, made the invitation difficult to resist. Before his thoughts went too far, he reminded himself of the Ancestors and the duty he owed them.

Ahead, he saw the principal ferry, which would take him directly to the farther shore. It was moored in a break among the willows. The rippling lake twinkled in the sun. Light gleamed from the lotus pads which dotted the water. It was a long time since he had enjoyed such beauty!

He was about to hail the ferryman when two women cleared the farther clump of willows. The sight of them made Li Fong feel that, until this very moment, he had never seen a woman.

They were almost of an even height, although the lady seemed taller than her maid. To say that she walked would not be accurate. Li Fong discarded that word and groped for one which could describe her elegance of motion.

The shimmer and shift of light on her pale blue tunic told him of an exquisite body, subtly curved and eloquent. Her face was sweet and grave, and of a radiant kindness that left him with no thought of outward beauty.

Li Fong wished that he could share the thoughts which evoked her shadow of a smile, a smile which peeped from within and drew back again behind curtains of reserve. Her hair was arranged in coils at either ear, and the maiden-fringe came nearly to her eyebrows. Not married and not a sing-song girl. A lady of good family. For Li Fong, this set up a fatal barrier.

The maid, more solidly built, moved as if she had devoted much time to imitating the mistress. This was a lively, sparkling wench whose flashing glance missed nothing and no one, shifting from the grizzled ferryman to Li Fong and thence to a passerby. Despite the prominence of cheekbones and the line of jaw and chin, her features were neither squarish nor heavy, and rather harmonized with her solid structure. The dance of eyebrows and the flare of nostrils made it plain that she relished all that the day offered; and if there were twice as much, nothing would go to waste—neither of her nor of it.

Her hair was arranged in the mode of the mistress. This set Li Fong wondering.

The lady's voice, as she bargained with the ferryman, was music. She spoke the local dialect, yet something about the lilt and the tones aroused his curiosity. "From the uttermost west," Li Fong told himself whimsically. "From the Mountain of the Gods."

The maid joined in the haggling. The boatman made a gesture of acceptance and turned toward the square-nosed craft. The maid detained him, then came to Li Fong.

"Elder Sister, Miss Mei Ling," the wench began, "begs pardon for thoughtlessness. Too late, I told her that you had been about to engage the ferry."

Li Fong's glance shifted and came to focus on Mei Ling's maid.

"Ah—thank you—she is very kind—but—well, I was not—I was just—uh—looking at the water——"

"Lovely, isn't it! That's what Elder Sister and I have been doing, and what could be nicer than crossing the lake?"

"Oh, yes, beautiful—ah—have a pleasant ride."

"The mistress would be happy to share the ferry with you. The boatman is already paid. Please be our guest. Do use the honor?"

This was his lucky day—except for the horror of facing Miss Mei Ling and confessing that he was an apprentice, not a scholar who brushed elegant characters and composed exquisite verse.

"Thank you. Please tell Miss Mei Ling that—ah—I must meet my cousin. We go to pay respects to the Ancestors." He gestured. "He will come from over there. I do not yet see him—but it is time——"

Li Fong turned and followed the fringe of willows.

His day had been glorified, only to be blackened by his own stupidity and shyness. He finally convinced himself that ferrying across West Lake with two such women would not be conducive to a mood correct for showing respect to his deceased parents.

Through a rift in the willows he glimpsed the ferry. There was a twinkle of blue silk in the shade of the canopy. The ferryman, sitting astern, sculled the boat toward the distant landing.

"Mei Ling," he mused, "moves like mist, or spirits, or flowers touched by the breeze. She moves even when she stands still, and that is exceedingly strange."

# CHAPTER IV

MEILAN followed Mei Ling along the shore. There were benches and tables among the blossoming peach trees. Nearby, the red-lacquered columns of a pavilion supported a tile roof with upsweeping eaves.

The serpent-women paused, looking at picnic groups, hearing their voices and the cries of the vendors who offered *won ton* and roast duck and roast pork, cakes and candied lotus root. For a moment the two gazed about, happy and glowing, drawing breaths of total contentment. Then they faced each other.

Mei Ling's smile faded. Fiercely, she caught Meilan's arm.

"We should have stayed home! And cleaned that rat's nest! *Aiieeyah!* Look at them, lolling around, strolling around. It makes me so lonely I could cry!"

Meilan said wryly, "They're used to being people."

"Let's get away!" Mei Ling made a sweeping gesture. "All these, they belong to someone."

Once clear of the willows, they paused to scan the nearby hills. They watched the flecks of color moving about along the crest and toward the groups of gravestones which dotted its length.

Mei Ling pointed. "That one could be the nice-looking scholar. No, over that way—see?"

"He was going to meet his cousin. That one in gray—he's alone."

"Anyway, he has ancestors. Human ones."

"Let's pretend we have."

After a moment, a dark one, Mei Ling brightened. "Imaginary ancestors. That would be a good start. For imaginary women. Go get something from the peddler. Offerings and things to eat."

Meilan lost no time in getting cakes and dried *lichis*, as well as sticks of incense, a packet of gilt-paper coins, miniature paper shoes, jacket, trousers, and a tiny paper bird. She wrapped the lot in her scarf and went with Mei Ling toward the ridge.

Near the crest, they found a grave long unvisited. Only a trace remained of the paint which had once filled each ideogram chiseled into the sandstone slab. There were no remainders of former offerings. The absence of grass and weeds indicated that the soil had been treated to prevent any such growth. Someone who knew himself to be the last survivor had done his best to maintain the grave after what would be his final visit.

Mei Ling and Meilan kowtowed three times. Turn and turn about, they thrust joss sticks into the cracked earth and laid out "spirit-money" and the miniature paper things that would cheer the deceased. For good measure, they added three *lichis* and three rice cakes.

"Revered Ancestor," Mei Ling said, "your son could not come to pay respects. He sent us to speak for him. May you be pleased with the best he was able to do." She glanced along the ridge, right and left. "There's no one we can borrow fire from. Too bad we didn't have the incense lighted."

Meilan had a handy solution: "Elder Sister, use the magic you had before we became snakes. You told me how—"

"I didn't tell you everything! No, I won't call the Fire Dragons to light the joss sticks and burn the offerings. The fire-magic is only for extremes. I can't use it a second time. Calling the Lords of Fire is the last magic."

17

"You mean, it would kill you? It's deadly dangerous?"

"There are very few who can call the Fire Dragons a second time. It's an awful magic. I'll tell you more when I remember. Anyway, what we've just done helps us stay human."

"Human!" Meilan echoed. "*Aiieeyah!* What a year of it! Being servants—farm workers—wood carriers—just about everything but flower-girls! Straw sandals and rags, till you found that money. Elder Sister, that was magic, wasn't it, knowing what was buried under the tiles?"

"That was only our good karma. Let's eat."

As they ate, they looked out across the valley and down at the picnic groups. Voices raised in the shouting and laughter and screaming of wine-games blended with the wail of flute and fiddle. Tears trickled down Mei Ling's cheeks.

"Wherever we went, we didn't fit. We didn't know what to say to people. Our thinkings and rememberings weren't right. Maybe we're too much like that good-looking scholar who shied away from us."

Meilan's eyes twinkled maliciously. "Dirty and ragged as we were, back there in that last village, we got more attention than we wanted. Supposing we'd not escaped before they sold us to that whorehouse keeper, how would you have liked *that*?"

Mei Ling grimaced. "One look at that flower-boat and the drunks who stumbled aboard was more than enough!"

"The experience might have made us a bit more human," Meilan said speculatively. "Or if we'd turned back to serpents, do you think we could have got back again to human shape?"

"*Aiieeyah!* Hush! Sometimes I think you're still half devil!"

"But could we?" Meilan persisted. "We—anyway, I'd like to know, just in case. Remember, we heard some odd things about snake-women making love. Well, that money changer in Hangchow was rather nice. The first man who noticed me when you were around. They never look at *me*!"

"They do, too! He was awfully helpful, and so was

the furniture man he sent us to. I wasn't sure I liked him or that either of them had any family we'd want to meet. Everything is *family*! I never realized what we were getting into. That scholar is the very first nice human." Mei Ling sighed. "What did we do to scare him away? What did you say?"

"He didn't hear a word I said. He was too busy looking at you. His family would see through our story, with our imaginary background."

Again Mei Ling glanced along the ridge. "This is our lucky day. He's done paying respects and he's leaving the graves."

Meilan twisted about and shaded her eyes. "He was telling the truth; well, half of it anyway. No cousin with him."

Mei Ling drew a deep breath. "Maybe his imaginary cousin set you thinking of an ancestor for us."

"He may be married," Meilan suggested. "But he might want a concubine."

"He's not married or he wouldn't be woman-shy. He'd have fallen over his own two feet, getting into the boat. We'll see more of him."

"Do we have to trail him all over Hangchow?" Meilan wondered.

"We won't have to. Just get rid of our parasol."

"What's that got to do with him?"

"He has one. And it's going to rain."

"*Aiieeyah!* Elder Sister, use magic and make sure."

"No. Let's pray to Compassionate Kwan Yin. Promise her two tall, red candles and a *catty* of sandalwood."

They bowed to their adopted ancestor and made their way down the slope. Mei Ling glanced at the gathering clouds. Presently a raindrop splashed her cheek.

"Two new robes for her image, and two *catties* of sandalwood! *Na-mo-o-mi-to-fu!* He's going over that way, not to the pavilion."

"You mean, he's afraid he might meet us there?"

"No, Younger Sister. There's a small boat, see it? It won't be crowded. The one near the pavilion will be jammed."

They changed their course. The breeze became chilly. Larger drops fell, and clouds darkened the sun.

"Hurry, Sister! He's closer to the landing than we are!"

## CHAPTER V

ONCE he had put those fascinating women behind him, Li Fong ascended the slope. Presently, nearing the granite headstone of his parents and his grandparents, he glanced down toward the knoll to his left. Two flecks of color caught his eye: one was pale blue, the other green. These, and a metallic twinkle, and the sheen of silk were moving among the ancient markers.

"What ancestors does she have *here*?" he wondered. "*What* is she?" was his next query, instead of "Who?"

Laying aside his parasol, he took flint and steel and lost little time lighting joss sticks and touching off a string of firecrackers. They popped, smacked, crackled, adding the smell of niter and sulfur to the incense fumes. Li Fong kowtowed three times. He set out his offerings and burned "spirit money." For moments he knelt, choking, gulping, sobbing outright, as he blinked away new tears which followed earlier ones.

Someday, he said to the deceased, he would be an important official and give them cause for pride. Until then, he wished them well-being and exalted rebirth.

A raindrop breaking against the back of his hand aroused him from his reverie and his happy-sad memories of the final years of his parents and their pride in his accomplishments at school. He kowtowed once more, to take leave. He backed away a pace and turned to make his way toward West Lake and the day at hand.

Beyond the nearby and overshadowing gloom, the sun gleamed on distant groves and pagodas. There was a small boat, well away from the one which docked at the cluster of pavilions. This one was his best chance to avoid a drenching and reach the sunny distance. He did not notice the two figures, far off, one blue, one green, moving down the adjacent slope.

The raindrops were larger. Lightning blazed blue against darkening clouds. Li Fong kept his parasol headed into the twisting wind which attacked from the side. Moving crabwise, he outwitted the treacherous gusts and kept his parasol from being torn to shreds.

The ferryman, a knotty-legged fellow wearing a mushroom-shaped straw hat and knee-length pants, was looping a line about the stump near the landing. Still cocking his head, he darted forward to secure the bow. This done, he eyed Li Fong.

"No crossing," he declared, on the verge of hostility. "Storm!"

"That's why I want to cross. Too much storm."

"Nice for you, under canopy. Me, I stand outside. Too much wind. Too much work. You wait."

Li Fong fingered some coins. "No storm on far side."

The ferryman considered. "Five times fare."

Li Fong bristled. "Maybe two times."

"Five times."

This was robbery. Pelting drops dug into Li Fong's tunic. He'd be soaked before he could, as a matter of principle, beat down that retired pirate's extortion.

"Devils eat you and your turtle-fornicating boat!"

"Devil-dung on your father's grave! Five fares, or swim across."

Then Li Fong saw two women lurch into view. Their parasol was turned inside out and torn apart. Apparently they had been darting from one clump of shrubbery to the next, not coming into view until within a few paces of the landing. Li Fong and Mei Ling stood face to face, for the moment too busy eyeing each other even to blink in the rain.

Lightning blasted so near at hand that the thunder came right on its heels. Not a twitch from either. They didn't hear Meilan's cry of fright.

The maid pounced forward. "Let us go in your boat."

She had concluded that Li Fong had paid his fare for that trip, and accordingly was entitled to cross alone or to invite as many as the boat could carry.

21

"Five times," he resumed, turning away from Mei Ling and thrusting coins into the man's hand. "Hurry, help the mistress aboard."

He followed his guests amidship, to the shelter of the bamboo canopy. Huddling along the center line, they escaped the downpour which wind whipped in from the side. The ferryman cast off and poled his stumpy craft away from the pier.

"Should get seven times," he grumbled, and Li Fong could find no argument. Wind coming now from astern drove rain against the boatman until his hat dripped like the eaves of a house. His jacket was soaked.

The lake became choppy. Hammering rain raised jets of water. Wind whipped these into low-flying spray. Far off, sun played on groves, pagodas, villas. Kneeling, Li Fong thrust his parasol against the wind to shelter the women snuggled against him.

"Lower the side curtains!" the ferryman yelled; he muttered something about the obscene stupidity of passengers. "Make 'em fast; I've got my hands full. You might as well swim, this way, you blockhead!"

He did have his work, sculling against wind and wave.

Li Fong disentangled himself from the fascinating female huddle.

"Meilan," said the mistress, "take the parasol. Don't let it blow overboard!"

Li Fong secured the curtains. A lurch of the boat tumbled him between his guests. Their combined efforts to help him regain balance prolonged the exciting confusion. Happy inadvertence, as the three wallowed and tumbled and groped, told him more about the feminine body than he had ever dreamed. There was a long moment of nuzzling cheek and throat—though in the confusion he couldn't be sure whose—and a ripe handful which he could have released somewhat more promptly—

Laughter and gasps, as the tangle developed, reassured Li Fong. His awkwardness had given no offense.

Breathless, flushed, radiant, Mei Ling regarded him as Meilan disengaged herself and edged away—at least an inch away—on the crowded bench. Raising hands to pat her hair into place, she accented curves which now had new meaning for the shy apprentice.

"*Aiieeyah!* It was lucky! If you hadn't haggled with the man, we'd be out in the rain. Where's your cousin?"

A gesture disposed of the imaginary kinsman. "From the graves, he went that way."

The promise of sunlight beyond the shore was fulfilled. The squall died down. Rain no longer whipped the lake into myriads of tiny jets. The passengers had escaped with a sprinkling which evaporated, giving Li Fong a whiff of perfume as dizzying as the third or fourth cup of wine.

Glancing from mistress to maid, he sorted out his touch-memories. Mei Ling's fascinating litheness—she didn't have a bone in her body!

Then came a moment of regarding each other, not so much in appraisal as to digest that moment of body-to-body closeness. Each knew that the other had responded. And as Mei Ling's breathing subsided, she asked, "You're a scholar?"

"No." He gulped his distaste and nerved himself for confession. "I am Li Fong. An apprentice in Mr. Sang's herb shop. If my father had lived, if my mother's illness hadn't taken all we had, I would have completed my studies."

"And you would be secretary in some *yamen*?"

"Maybe, in another few years, yes."

"But now you'll be a *doctor*?" she glowed. "How very wonderful!"

"Mmm . . . someday, and that might not be too bad."

"Li Fong, being a healer, that is splendid! So many you could bring back to happy health. If there had been a good doctor, your parents might still be living."

"It's not quite as fine as it sounds," he said dubiously, although his visit to the graves did give force to her words, and meaning all new. "Most of my time, I mix potions for old men who have young wives."

"That makes them happy, doesn't it?"

"I wouldn't know about the wives or the concubines or the sing-song girls, but the old men don't look it. They're always greedy and anxious."

"How much worse it would be if you couldn't mix potions for the elderly. How old are you?"

"Almost twenty. Twenty, next moon."

"Only a year older than we are," she said happily. "Meilan and I."

"Where are your Ancestors? You're from far away."

Mistress and maid exchanged a glance, swift and sidewise. "Kwangan, in Szechwan Province," Mei Ling answered. "My parents are dead, and so are Meilan's." She sighed. "Father was a magistrate. Debts ate up the house. We came to Hangchow a few weeks ago, to live with a branch of the family we would see only every third or fourth or fifth year, at New Year's reunion. We rarely heard of them otherwise.

"Anyway, we were pretty much set back, finding not one of them left. The caretaker had got tired of waiting for his pay, as nearly as we could learn, and he left. You can imagine what happened to the house!"

"I'm not as alone as you are," Li Fong said. "But my sister and her husband and their little son may be moving to Kwangchow. They've had their problems."

"Otherwise, you're entirely alone?" Meilan inquired. "Not married?"

"An *apprentice* with a wife?" he mocked. "Sister Moutan's husband paid Mr. Sang to accept me as an apprentice."

His glance shifting from Meilan, he saw that Mei Ling's expression had become thoughtful. Perhaps she was pondering the next question to be raised, though she had touched all the basics.

Now they were nearing the pier. They regarded the sun, quite low, which dappled the green with bands of light and shadow. The inviting loveliness of the scene darkened Li Fong's heart, brought him back to reality. They'd be parting, and he didn't even know where she lived.

He squinted at the sky as he followed his guests ashore. "Better take my parasol," he suggested. "There's likely to be another squall, and not a sedan chair in sight to get you home. I'll pick it up in the morning . . . or any time you would prefer."

24

"But you're not dried out yet," Mei Ling protested, "and we're all of us a bit chilled. Come with us. I'll make a bowl of soup, and we'll sit by the fire."

## CHAPTER VI

THEY had walked no more than a few *li* when Mei Ling pointed toward a villa half hidden by towering trees. The place was well away from the city wall. Such isolation was dangerous, unless one had armed retainers to repel prowlers. River pirates, for instance, would at times venture inland to loot and kidnap, then would disappear among the hundreds of houseboats moored along the Yangtze.

No gatekeeper came out of the gatehouse to admit them. Meilan leaned against the heavy door. The hinge squeal made Li Fong shiver. He had followed them into the first courtyard before he recovered sufficiently from amazement to exclaim, "You left the door open—don't you know—you *must* be strangers!"

Meilan worked the ponderous bolt into its socket.

"When we're away," she explained cheerily, "there's nothing worth stealing. And if someone really wanted to get in, it would be easy to get over the wall." Her eyes narrowed, gleamed fiercely. "Even easier for me to get to work with my meat chopper!"

"You're deadly!"

Behind his whimsy, he meant precisely what he said; just as her words had been a literal statement of fact.

She laughed, and ferocity vanished. "Only with nasty people!"

The limbs of trees outside the grounds overhung the wall. Its twelve-foot height, crowned with spikes, was no real protection. Trees within, long untended, mingled their branches with those outside.

Stucco had cracked and dropped, exposing the bare brick of the front. Although the outer court and the canopied corridor which skirted the left of the house were not littered, the garden had had only the skimpiest attention. The silence disturbed Li Fong.

He followed mistress and maid into the spacious reception hall. He got glimpses of apartments which opened from the left and from the right of the tall, red-lacquered columns. Judging from the absence of scroll-paintings and art objects, the place had been looted, though not thoroughly. Dark, substantial furniture remained.

The inner court had been swept. There was no rubbish in the pool. A corridor, formed by columns and canopy, skirted the court on three sides. To his right was what appeared to be the Great Book Room, the master's study. Gathering dusk kept him from getting more than a vague sight of the furnishings.

From this court, Mei Ling led the way into the next sitting room. Again, apartments opened from left and from right. Whatever lay beyond would be a collection of minor apartments, smaller courts, pools, garden areas, servants' quarters, storerooms, utility sheds—a miniature village when fully inhabited and staffed.

The odors of a kitchen mingled with the scent of cosmetics, the exhalation of women's garments, the lingering fragrance of incense. He felt more at ease. The place was run-down but not uncanny.

Slanting ruddy rays came in through windows at the eaves. These retained only shreds of the oiled paper which had once covered the ornately patterned framework. When Meilan came in with lighted candles and then brought in two oil lamps, further perplexities were exposed.

The nondescript couches and chairs were new, and not in keeping with the ancient carved woodwork with its tarnished gold leaf and time-seasoned lacquer. Several pieces of original furniture remained in the room, shoved into corners to get them out of the way. The brazier and tripod of wrought iron were new.

Li Fong wondered at the disappearance of an entire family as important as the former residents of this villa had been. If Mei Ling's kinfolk had vanished during his years of living in Hangchow, he would have heard at least gossip. Whatever had happened, it had been more than three or four years ago.

All this nagged him until candlelight glorified the magnolia-blossom tint of Mei Ling's cheeks and throat and brought to life the jade ear-pendants and pearl necklace. His apothecary's nostrils told him that the mistress exhaled the perfumes of wealth, and so did the maid.

Meilan, moreover, was quite too well dressed. "She isn't wearing the lady's castoffs," he decided. "Wouldn't fit. Not the way that gown fits her."

Though she was beautifully shaped, Meilan could not have got into Mei Ling's gown without popping every seam. An odd business, this equality of dress and adornment and perfumery.

After kindling charcoal in the brazier, Meilan quit the room. Presently, the odor of herbs and spices drifted from the kitchen.

"She makes vegetable-herb soup," Mei Ling remarked. "Very tasty."

"You don't look like Buddhist nuns. You haven't cut your hair."

"Yes, we eat no meat, no fowl, no fish. But we are not nuns. Not even *upāsikas*, but a little dedicated, of course. Moderately dedicated. A monk saved our lives. Out of gratitude, we do not eat any living thing. That is to pay our debt. Meilan, heat some wine!"

"Yes, Elder Sister."

Li Fong beamed. "Not Buddhist nuns!"

"Not even *upāsikas*," Meilan said, in a voice which made him recall that exciting moment when the lurch of the boat had at once furthered acquaintance and shattered formality.

On the nearby tabouret was an old book. The hexagram patterns of solid and broken lines identified it.

"You understand the *Book of Change*?"

"It was my father's. He loved it."

"You use it?"

"Today we went out because it said we would meet someone important."

"An uncompleted scholar who escaped from a drug store."

"Li Fong, your future is richer than you think."

"Today, yes. Today makes all the rest of my life poor!"

"No, tomorrow will be better than your past."

Invitation and promise; more than he could believe, yet nothing for him to deny or doubt. His inner shackles fell apart. He slid caressing fingertips along her shoulder, barely a fleeting touch, yet enough for her femaleness to make him tingle all the way to his ankles.

"Tonight," he said after long silence, "most of all?"

His audacity amazed him. His heart rose and choked him. Time stretched on and on as he waited for her eyes and the shadow-smile at the corners of her mouth to warm into acceptance or to solidify into rejection.

Mei Ling looked over her shoulder and gestured. Meilan was bringing cups and a jar of wine. She poured for three and drank with mistress and guest.

"I've never tasted anything like this," he said, and let Meilan refill his cup. "Please tell me?"

"It's not thousand-day wine!" Mei Ling laughed softly. "Drink up!"

"If it were, I'd be late to work."

"Unconscious for one thousand days, you would miss so much life . . ."

Voice and eyes renewed their promise.

Meilan brought in three bowls of soup. It was spicy-hot, Szechwan-seasoned, something new to Li Fong. There was a faint bitterness, an undertone of tart sweetness, a contradiction of tastes, and with all this, a substance which he could not imagine in any meatless broth. In calling this a vegetable soup, she had either misspoken herself or had whimsically underplayed the surprise, leading him to expect the somewhat pallid things usually served at Buddhist festivals.

Again, Meilan filled his cup.

"Elixir of Immortality!" His face seconded the applause of his voice. "Essence of that fantastic fable, the *Mushroom of Life*. Liquefied!"

"The wine, or the soup?"

"Both," he answered, trying to read his fortune in Mei Ling's eyes.

There would be no answer until Meilan finally withdrew.

Unfortunately, the maid stood by with the wine jar.

Li Fong began to wonder whether he should propose

a wine-game. The loser's penalty, on each play, was to toss off a cup. With only a little connivance, the mistress could make sure that Meilan lost every play.

This inspiration bogged down. He was so drunk that he couldn't recall his brilliant plan. The candle flames danced in pairs. The outlines of mistress and maid shimmered, blurred, and coalesced. At times there was only one woman, and that one was also two women. The heat of the brazier added to his confused well-being. He sat back, looking into his cup.

Mei Ling's face shimmered, faded, drew far away. She floated into the distance. He tried to get to his feet. Without even making the first move, he knew that he could not follow her ... pure disaster ...

She became a spindle of glamour in the farther shadows. Whatever tomorrow's fortune, this night had expended itself. Even if he dared the venture, he would not be able to find Mei Ling in this maze of desolation and darkness.

And now Meilan had him by the arm. Once he came out of his cozy stupor, she urged him to his feet. Somewhat to his surprise, he could stand straight. Despite the blurring and the contraction and expansion of the candle flames, he was not dizzy. With guidance through the maze and to the gate, he should have no trouble finding his way home.

His thoughts were pointed, purposeful, and reasonable. "Give Meilan a present, and she'll be my go-between ... the proper, polite way ... stupid, thinking of speaking directly ... what crazy-wine-thoughts ... going to sleep with her ... crude impropriety of a farmer ..."

"Too late for going home," Meilan said, cutting into his reflections. "Better wait till daylight. There can be danger outside, robbers at night."

She guided him into an adjoining room, warm and musky-fragrant. Dust tickled his nostrils as he lurched between the parted curtains of an ancient bed. Something he was going to tell Meilan ... about a present. ..

Before he could retrieve his lost thought, Meilan had something to tell Li Fong:

"Mistress says I will sleep with you."

She set the candle on the table. Since her night had been fully planned, she had only to seat herself and await the next move. Meilan was far from sure whether or not he had understood her words . . .

## CHAPTER VII

UNTIL Li Fong thought to run his fingers along the quilted mattress, he was sure that he floated in the air, adrift in space. It was curious, but no harm done, none at all, particularly since there was neither dizziness nor nausea.

No harm, either, in the odd aftertaste of the wine, or of that unusually filling and nourishing soup. Bitter-tart-spicy-hotness was in his blood. It permeated his body until even his toes began to tingle. Most puzzling of all was that taste perception was no longer restricted to his palate. There were moments of savoring wine and soup through his fingertips.

Meilan was taking off his damp shoes, which she set on a table near the brazier. He didn't understand her cozy murmuring as she helped him out of his tunic. Nothing required understanding. Indeed, he now had all knowledge of everything, and this was not confined to brain-mind. His hands had intelligences all their own. They needed no directing. Without any regard to him, they plucked the fastenings of her gown, plucked ever so daintily and reached into its warmth. Those versatile fingertips smelled her fragrance. Nostrils, developing new talents, tasted her smoothness. Li Fong was far too fascinated by these oddities to wonder at them.

She murmured, snuggled up against him, then wriggled free of her garment without ever quitting his embrace. She left him for long enough to snuff out the candle flame. For a moment, after she had shed her innermost garment, her body mirrored the brazier glow.

Li Fong wondered at the just perceptible dappling of her skin. It was like watered silk with a shadow pattern of scales. As she turned from the coals, he reached out and slid his hand slowly along her body, in a caress which rounded the curve of her hip and at last found a spot for lingering and fondling. At the moment of her gliding into the gloom of the curtains, he had lost his gift of seeing by touch and he had lost those other contradictory senses. All these lesser gifts had been lost in the greater knowledge which awaited him.

Her body twined about him, and her lips made small flutterings along his throat and shoulder. Meilan's eyes were self-luminous. He looked into immeasurable depths, yet it was also as if he stood apart in space, watching himself stroking her hair and the curve of her back and the sleekness of her thighs.

The all-knowledge awaited him, that concerning which he had wondered half his life. This he knew, yet he could not quite believe, and some feeling akin to awe restrained him. Finally she whispered something which he could not understand, but he knew what she meant.

Entering the land of wonder, Li Fong marveled that he was neither tense nor unbearably excited, neither clumsy nor impotent, nor any of all the awkwardnesses he had feared, the embarrassments which had always lurked to make him doubt himself. Li Fong, the Witness, was pleased with Li Fong, the Lover, knowing that both were pleasing Meilan. Her nails dug deeply into his back. Her legs tightened the embrace. Witness and Lover and serpent-mottled woman became one—

Her cry startled Li Fong, shocked him, dismayed him. She choked, sobbed, lay panting and trembling until her body spoke again, and she drew him closer. The fire of her flesh blazed anew, and now her murmurings had meaning. He was gentle then with the newly opened realm of wonder, until frenzy seized him and her at once, and they would have perished, each knew, had not each extinguished the other's fires.

They lay for a long time, inhaling each other's breathings and stirring at times to come closer together.

At last her breathing told him that she had fallen asleep. Li Fong slipped from her relaxed embrace. He would lie awake for hours. For the first time, he knew himself as a man and marveled that Meilan could sleep so readily after realizing herself as a woman.

He recalled the apprentices' yarns and what Mr. Sang's customers talked about while waiting for him to grind and sift a prescription guaranteed to arouse any but the walking dead. He understood now what the sage had meant in saying, *"He who knows cannot tell—he who speaks does not know."* Li Fong pitied the old men and the young men who did not know and did not even suspect that they did not know.

"Mei Ling," he mused, "gave her to me for her first time. A prize for a rich old man . . . why give her to me?"

Two women, living in an isolated, run-down villa, eating odd food, drinking strange wine . . . Silence and mystery combined to disturb him.

A sage had said, *"When the sun is at high noon, midnight approaches."*

When luck is too good, the opposite is close at hand.

The bed of coals was ash-filmed. The room became chilly. He slid beneath the coverlet. Meilan did not stir. He could barely hear her breathing. It was as if she had expended herself in that devastating embrace which had drained Li Fong to emptiness. Her utter passiveness invited exploration, while he could relish without desiring.

This was wonder of a new sort, to lift the cover for a look and then find refuge beneath it for fondling and probing and tasting and smelling and imagining depths plumbed without seeing . . . and fancying what they'd do the next time . . . experiencings he had never imagined, a nirvana of un-desiring—a new knowledge of the everlastingly new . . . and everlastingly ancient. . .

Li Fong, neither awake nor asleep, nor any longer engrossed in fondling a passive body, reached far into the darknesses and mazes of that strange villa. He was akin to the blind swordsman of the opera who fought and won. He did not need eyes. He could see with his mind. This ancient story of blades and sorcery no longer puzzled Li Fong.

Someone . . . something . . . moving . . . some-where . . . not friendly . . . raiders from the river would be reckless, noisy, quick . . . this was too stealthy . . . this was danger insidious . . .

Getting to his feet, he slipped into trousers and jacket. He decided against putting on his cloth-soled shoes. Somewhere, something scratched and scraped. Not a rat, not a mouse. Not the scurry-patter of any rodent. A human prowler was at work.

Midway across the reception room, more than half of which was touched by long blades of moonlight, he stopped. A chill trickled down his spine. He tried to swallow the dryness in his throat, but could not. There came an urge to yell and run. Doing neither, he finally overcame panic. Before he did so, he was in a sweat; but the violent trembling which followed was not as bad as what he had conquered.

An ancient chair stood on three legs. The fourth lay in a corner. He hefted it. It was heavier than it looked. It was comfortable to his grasp; well handled, it would kill a man. Li Fong was armed, ready, and eager. Eyes narrowed, taut lips exposing his teeth, he set out to stalk and strike.

Moon patches brightened his way. The furtive *scratch-scrape* guided him across an inner court and to the entrance of the Great Book Room. A faint glow warned him. He tiptoed into the study.

In the far corner sat a lantern of paper, containing a candle. A man crouched, his back toward Li Fong. His shoulders moved in accord with the *scratch-scrape*. The man hitched himself to the left, cocked his head, and set aside a paving tile. He straightened, then hunched forward, elbows and shoulders moving as if he were trying to lift something difficult to grasp.

Li Fong stretched his legs in a long, silent stride, then a second. His presence, the force of his purpose, warned the intruder. About to close in and smash the averted head, Li Fong had to check himself and correct his balance.

The prowler, flinging himself aside, had landed, crouching. He gripped a long and heavy knife. His teeth glinted in the lantern glow. Sweat gleamed on his flat face. He was afraid and dangerous. A greasy-looking fellow, desperate and venomous.

He lunged, slashing instead of thrusting.

His balance regained, Li Fong was as poised as a dancer. He pivoted, at once avoiding the attack and whipping the chair leg down on the burglar's head. The man crumpled. He lay on his face, mumbling and wheezing. Instead of finishing him off as a matter of security, Li Fong exhaled a long-contained breath. He relished the instant of triumph, the power to kill or to spare. For a scholar and drug pounder, he had done very well.

Li Fong saw that two tiles had been pried from their bed. They had covered the broad mouth of an earthenware jar. Up to the neck, it was full of tarnished *sycees* of silver and gold pieces; gems twinkled from among the coined metal.

Clout the fellow again for good measure? Better twist some of Meilan's garments into cords and secure him. This was Mei Ling's house and her problem. Disposing of a corpse could be awkward.

Li Fong did not make much progress in his cogitations. Too late, he knew that he had company. His senses warned him, and he turned. The man lunging for him wore a black robe and a Taoist hat. He was unarmed. He moved with assurance. He was perfectly poised. Li Fong was not. Turning from a flat-footed clown to face a pouncing tiger demanded an impossible change. This was for a professional, not a novice.

The man shifted.

The chair leg, which should have flattened the peaked hat, did not even knock it off. The newcomer's *kung fu* attack dropped Li Fong to the tiles with a numbing crash. The Taoist rolled, his motion unbroken and continuing into the next phase.

Li Fong clawed for the knife.

The enemy's boot to the solar plexus was paralyzingly perfect. Though conscious, Li Fong was unable either to breathe or to move.

The intruder picked up the knife. He wasted only a glance at the man who lay face down, muttering, mumbling, and still not recovered from Li Fong's blow. Wagging his head, he regarded the exposed treasure, then dismissed it as business which required no immediate attention. Li Fong was the problem.

The Taoist, expert at his craft, was aware of Li

Fong's helplessness. He fingered the blade as he pondered. Apparently he had a choice of solutions, each of which deserved consideration.

Li Fong was now fully aware of his danger. The second intruder could not afford gossip.

Despite its lines and angles, the man's face was essentially benevolent and devoid of malice. He would never needlessly kill anyone. On the other hand, without having spoken a word, he had made it clear that however he regretted it, he would never shrink from necessity.

The flame within the paper lantern was dimming. Shadows changed shape. The darkness above the overhead beams reached lower and lower. As he lay helpless, so helpless that he gave up all hope, Li Fong saw what came down from the gloom.

A serpent was reaching out of the darkness. The coils which twined about the beam were lustrous and gleaming. The yard or more of body extended until a second yard emerged. The unwinking eyes, the beautifully twinkling head, came ever lower.

Deliberate, elegant, gracful; gleaming silver-white and terrible in its purpose. For the first time, Li Fong realized the splendor of a great serpent. The Taoist sensed that cogitation on harmonious killing was outmoded. He might have been warned by Li Fong's glance, his change of expression. Neither was able to follow that which lashed out.

The python locked the Taoist's arms to his sides and snuggled its head against his head. The snake let go the rafter and, in a blur of motion, enclosed him in constricting coils. The blade clanged to the tiles.

The man could not cry out. His face became gray, then bluish, and finally, purple. No bones cracked. The serpent began uncoiling and looking about. Before Li Fong could react, the silver length glided out of the room, leaving him alone with two disabled enemies.

# CHAPTER VIII

STILL gulping air, Li Fong snatched the heavy blade. His first impulse was to finish off his assailants before they recovered. The power to choose life or death had lost its charm. However, and quite aside from his innate aversion to killing, something checked an entirely reasonable impulse.

The first intruder twitched and mumbled and slobbered. The Taoist's face was still bluish-purple, yet he was recovering. Li Fong considered the chair leg. If he were to strike too hard, the fatality would be accidental and bloodless.

The arrival of outside counsel relieved him of decision.

Meilan, wearing only a jacket not long enough to impede her legs, bounded into the room. She gripped a kitchen chopper. The sight of two subjects was confusing. In her fury, she didn't know which should have the first cut.

"Son of a dog-fornicating mother!" she screamed, and pounced for the first intruder. "Kwong Chi, eater of turtle-dung—"

"Wait—don't!" Li Fong croaked. He caught her arm.

"All right, you chop him! And the other one, too!"

"No. Get cords, anything. So I can tie them. Quick! I'll watch."

"*Tie* them? Are you crazy?"

"You know that one." He pointed. "Kwong-something-or-other. Get cords, hurry; I'll tell you later."

Though unconvinced, she raced away.

Li Fong regarded the burglar. The blocky man, Kwong Chi, was getting to his knees. His eyes were not yet in focus. He wobbled and lurched to the tiles before Li Fong had to knock or cut him down.

The Taoist's attempt to regain his feet ended in a gasp and a grimace of acute pain, as if cracked ribs were stabbing him. He slumped, made a desperate effort to support himself on his elbow, and succeeded, for a moment. This was sufficient for him to regard Li Fong, and to marvel.

Li Fong flicked the chopper. "If you are friendly and helpful, I'll not slice your throat before you can do any more *kung fu*."

"You stopped that crazy woman—you didn't want her to kill—"

"I still don't. And the snake was friendly. But don't push your luck."

However much he was in command, Li Fong was relieved when Meilan came back. The Taoist felt otherwise. She brought rattan withes which had secured a bale of merchandise.

"This will hold them." She snatched the chopper and squatted within easy reach. "One move, and there'll be nothing big enough to tie."

Li Fong got to work. The withes were still flexible and cruel as wire. Once done with the Taoist, he secured Kwong Chi. The captives were so tied that if they fought their bonds, they would cut or choke themselves to death.

"Now what shall we do?"

"Call the mistress. Let her decide. It's her business, her house, yes?"

"I can't call Miss Mei Ling. She was sick last night and took some sleeping opium. Why do you suppose I took her place?"

He nudged her into the court and said in a low voice, "We've got a tiger by the tail. You called the chunky one by name—the one I caught prying up the tiles. Who are those fellows?"

"Kwong Chi? He's a money changer. He must have thought we were rich, so he came to rob us."

Li Fong considered this and its implications. "Then we can't turn them over to the magistrate. By the time the law got through with them and us, you wouldn't have much left. Particularly not if some of your relatives got wind of what you found."

"That's why we've got to kill those turtle-children," she declared earnestly. "We could bury them in the back courtyard."

"Women are always practical," he conceded. "But I've got an idea. Go get a piece of charcoal and some paper. I'll have a few words with Kwong Chi and that priest."

He went back into the library and regarded the prisoners.

"Kwong Chi—and you, Reverend Nobody—tell me how you got the idea of looting this house. Maybe I won't slice you."

Kwong Chi said, "Those ladies brought me some old, old money, silver all black, gold all tarnished. They were dressed like farm women. I was sure they'd stolen it. I still think so. I came to look. I was afraid I'd get into trouble if I ever tried to sell the old money. Safer to get a reward from the real owners of this place."

"Just a little prowling, and you found the tiles they'd loosened and tamped back into place. You came to steal the lot. You don't know who owns this house."

No rebuttal.

Li Fong dipped into the hoard. He came up with jade, and rubies, and sapphires beneath the first stratum of silver and gold. Apparently, Mei Ling had no more than skimmed the top layer to buy clothes and household gear and cosmetics. He turned to the prisoners.

"You know too much about this place. You, Kwong Chi, didn't just blunder upon the right tiles. You had a shortcut. Tell me, *now!*"

His tone was a threat.

"I consulted him—Reverend Chang Lu. I asked him to make a divination—tell me where the treasure was hidden. Also, to pick a lucky day for the searching."

Li Fong eyed the Taoist diviner. Chang Lu said, "That is true. I consulted the *Book of Change* and read the hexagrams. I consulted the spirits. I'm a master of divination."

"Having the heart of a thief, you followed this fellow."

"I followed," Chang Lu declared earnestly, "to help him, in case he wasn't able to use the words I gave him. As you said, this is a large house. The words of the book are symbolic. Things could be most confusing."

"I didn't need your help!" Kwong Chi snarled. "You were going to rob me."

"That is not true," the priest protested. "You promised me a share. I had a right to see what you found. This young gentleman might have killed you if I hadn't got here in time. I risked my life, and you aren't grateful."

Meilan came back, bringing paper and a chunk of charcoal. She also had a candle to take the place of the stub that was dying in the lantern. Once he had fresh light, Li Fong made for the court and beckoned for her to join him.

He wrote a few characters on a piece which he tore from the sheet. He wrote on a second piece and on a third.

"Can you read?"

"Not well, but I'm learning."

"Then listen. Take one prescription to Mr. Wang's herb shop. Another to Mr. Sang. Another to the Home of Superlative Health and Eternal Felicity. If you can't find these places, try somewhere else. Don't answer any questions. Just play stupid."

"Then what?"

"Bring me what they give you."

"Why not get everything in one place?"

Li Fong sighed. "Elegant and fascinating lady! Must I explain myself whenever I say a thing? If you bought all this in one shop, someone would be interested enough to follow you and find out what's going on."

"Oh. I hadn't thought of *that*. Why don't you go? You understand such things. I don't."

"Charming and beautiful woman! With no questions, you would have been halfway there! First, if I left you alone with those clowns, you'd kill them. In the second place, each apothecary would be wondering too much. I'm known in every shop in town. I'm Mr. Sang's Number One Apprentice."

Li Fong stepped back into the library.

"Your chances have improved, moment by moment," he announced amiably. "Please wait. I won't be long."

"You're notifying the magistrate?" Kwong Chi croaked. "I beg of you—just listen—we'll not run away—we'll wait—"

Li Fong smiled. "Between His Excellency and a squad of guards from the *yamen*, we'd all be left empty-handed."

Chang Lu brightened. "It is wise to avoid extremes. Your insight delights us. We will be waiting for your pleasure."

"Your patience delights me," Li Fong assured him, and went back for a word with Meilan.

"I wish I knew more about your plan."

He sighed. "If you did, you'd be as muddled as I am. It's sunrise already. By the time you get to town, the shops will be open."

He went with her to the gate. Glancing about, he noticed the rope dangling from a limb overhanging the wall.

"That's probably how they got in," Li Fong remarked. "One more thing. Did you deal with any money changer except Kwong?"

"No. He gave us such a good rate."

"Mmmm . . . that simplifies things a little, but not too much. These fellows have friends. Each one probably gabbled enough to give grounds for guessing, if these fellows remained missing. Then we'd be investigated, and too thoroughly. We might not live through it."

Meilan grimaced in dismay. "I hadn't thought of that. But if we don't kill them, what shall we do?"

"Meilan, Lovely Orchid, First Woman, there is a way."

Her eyes widened. "Your *first* woman?"

He nodded.

"My first lover."

"I knew." Li Fong took her in his arms, held her close, and kissed her. "Better run along now." He slid the heavy bolt from the socket. "How'll you let me know when you come back?"

"There's a hidden door in back. Anyway, I could climb the tree and slide down the rope."

# CHAPTER IX

BACK in the second reception room, Li Fong paused to get his bearings. He and Meilan had gone *that* way . . . Mei Ling had stepped through *yonder* doorway when she left him alone with her maid . . .

Regardless of indisposition and Meilan's evasions, he had to intrude. Whatever sedative Mei Ling had taken, she would probably not be in a stupor. Before Meilan returned, Li Fong wanted all the information he could get. There was more to this than disposing of a pair of burglars.

Several rooms he dismissed with a glance. Presently he came to the entrance of a suite which invited him with its familiar fragrance, its odor of female elegance. He paused at the threshold, cocked his head. He heard no stirring behind the curtains, nor the sound of breathing. That was odd, particularly for the drunk or the opium-drugged when they were emerging from stupor.

"Sleeping opium," moreover, should by now have worn off.

He regarded the tall, ornately carved cabinet of camphorwood, all packed with shimmering garments. There was a three-panel screen of sandalwood lattice, and a dressing table; a tabouret inlaid with mother-of-pearl; chairs of rosewood and a settee to match.

He tapped on the jamb. "Miss Mei Ling."

No answer. Venturing in, he got a better view of a room beyond, one which Meilan probably occupied. The bed curtains were drawn. Armoire doors, half closed, exposed garments ranging from austerely serviceable to things amazingly luxurious for a maid. There was no dressing table. Apparently she shared Mei Ling's facilities.

Li Fong stepped to the bed and scratched the brocaded curtains.

"Miss Mei Ling! This is urgent!" He raised his voice. "Serious trouble. Please answer."

Total silence. She might be dangerously drugged. He yanked the curtains apart. The bed was empty. Beside it were blue and gilt slippers, and near them, the muddy shoes she had worn that afternoon.

He turned to the dressing table. Scattered among the cosmetics were bangles, pendants, bracelets, rings, hairpins. Something was lacking. He groped, frowned, fumbled in his mind. Then came the answer: *no miror*.

He quit the room and shouted, "Mei Ling!" She might be in the bath alcove. "Come out! Robbers!"

No answer. Too much house, too little time.

Li Fong went to the kitchen. It was still warm and savory from fire and wine fumes and food. He scooped up a bowl of embers and snatched the tongs and bellows. Tucking a slicing knife under his arm, he hurried to his prisoners.

Deliberately, he set the fire bowl on the floor and plied the bellows until the embers glowed and sparks flew. Carefully, he chose a coal and slowly passed it for Kwong Chi and Chang Lu to inspect. His amiable smile was more menacing than any scowl as he returned the fire to its bed and fingered the kitchen knife. It was a chef's delight, honed fine, for slicing both tough and delicate.

Kwong Chi sweated conspicuously. Chang Lu's face tightened.

"Perhaps you'd like to tell me where the mistress is?"

"She's opium sleeping," the Taoist declared.

"Maybe she was. Now maybe she's walking in her sleep?"

"We don't know—I—I came in—right here," Kwong Chi stuttered.

"She isn't in bed. She's not in the bath. Not knowing she was opium sleeping, you strangled her and hid her. Where?"

The Taoist said, "I followed this burglar. I moved, made no noise. This took time. How can I know what he did before I came in?"

"I was in her room long enough for you fellows to cook up a story."

"We weren't speaking," the money changer protested. "He came to rob me. He's no friend."

Talk which postponed burning or slicing encouraged Chang Lu.

"You know I didn't have time to harm her," he pointed out. "You caught him, and then I came in—too much happened—how could I have time for finding the mistress and strangling her? I doubt he did. Why didn't he kill you and the maid? Why just the mistress?"

Li Fong smiled amiably. "I'm asking *you*." And his glance shifted to the fire.

"I beg leave to speak for your benefit, Young Lord. If she's really dead, you're in this as deeply as we are. Killing us now would harm you. With only you to explain this business of an evening with two women just come to town, the magistrate would hold you accountable. We three shouldn't be enemies."

Li Fong nodded. "We met on such friendly terms."

"Danger makes one impulsive," Chang Lu pointed out earnestly. "Turn us loose, after you've divided the treasure into three parts. By sharing our discovery, each is rewarded for tonight's dangers. We'll get out of here before the maid comes back. You divide, you be the judge."

Kwong Chi cut in. "These women are strangers in town. They asked all kinds of questions when they came in with very old *scycees* and Indian and Persian gold. I knew they'd stolen it."

"You told me all that. And how Reverend Chang Lu picked the lucky hour for the job. Does it still seem lucky?"

Chang Lu's face darkened at the mockery, but he was a fighter.

"Young Lord, you are in worse danger than we are," he declared with disturbing reassurance.

Li Fong swallowed his growing unease. "Your danger is right now."

"When that girl wanted to kill us," the priest continued, ignoring the interruption, "you stopped her. I am grateful. He is grateful. I recognize a keen mind, great

43

foresight. Daring, yet prudent. Purposeful, yet humane. Like the Great Men of Old."

Li Fong fingered the knife and realized that the longer he temporized, the less he would achieve. He was losing ground. "Where is she?"

"You will thank me for my insight. For my occult perception. The mistress has not been harmed."

"When the maid comes back, we'll search the house."

"Let me tell you about that one. She's a devil-spirit who got into human form. You were sleeping with a snake-woman last night."

"You don't know a thing!"

Chang Lu resumed, "No man, young or old, would have slept alone, not with that woman in the house. And if you had been with the mistress, you wouldn't be wondering where she is. She would have followed you, just the way that one did."

"Snake-woman!" Li Fong chuckled. "Another drum-song!"

"Let me sing without a drum," Chang Lu proposed. He chanted:

*"A traveler returns from pilgrimage.*
*He meets a beautiful girl alone by the road.*
*She is weeping. She says bandits killed her parents.*
*He takes her home and lives with her.*
*She gives birth to a son, a splendid boy.*
*One night she changes into a white snake.*
*First she eats their child.*
*She kills the father.*
*She drinks their blood to win*
*Another thousand years of immortality."*

Li Fong grimaced derisively. "After what happened to you when that household snake gave you a shaking up, you would have snakes on the brain! Try something better."

"Don't mock me. I told Kwong Chi that this would be his lucky day. It is exactly that. And I tell you again, you slept with a snake-woman. I can tell by the science of reading lines of the face. Go to someone who reads palms. He will tell you the same. Make the most of your good luck—turn us loose—I'll protect you against these devil-spirits. I'll recite *mantrams*. I'll give you medicines to cure spirit-poisons."

"Carry on with your drum-song," Li Fong told him. "Waiting for that girl gets tiresome."

# CHAPTER X

When Meilan returned, Li Fong's first question was, "Where's the mistress? I've looked all over, and I can't find her."

"She probably woke up, thought of something she wanted, and slipped out through the escape gate. She thought you and I would be sleeping late and didn't want to disturb us." She eyed him sharply. "What happened while I was gone?"

"Nothing. I wanted to talk to her before I asked those burglars some questions. They told me things that I wanted to check with her."

"What did they say?"

"Heat a small pot of water and listen."

Li Fong summed up the stories of the prisoners, except that he skipped all the nonsense about serpent-women. Meilan said, "That's pretty much the way it must have started." She handed him the three little packets. "Here's the stuff you ordered."

Li Fong pulled the bench toward the kitchen table. "See if you can find a board for rolling noodles. By the way—" He pointed "There's your jar of money and trinkets. You ought to find a new hiding place."

"We'll see what Elder Sister says," Meilan answered over her shoulder as she rummaged in a locker. She found a slab of marble not much larger than a paving tile. "Will this do?"

After dusting the smooth surface, he set to work with the drugs, which had been powdered at the shops. Meilan watched intently as he blended the ingredients, using a knife as a spatula.

Once the mixture was uniform, he divided the heap into halves; one of the halves into quarters. Finally, a quarter was divided. He put one of the portions into a bowl of hot water. From time to time he stirred the potion with a chopstick.

"I'm glad Elder Sister didn't hear the rumpus in the library," Meilan remarked. "And it's lucky she isn't here now."

"Why is that?"

"She's too kind-hearted. She wouldn't let you go on with your plan."

"What do you think I'm going to do?"

"You've mixed a slow poison so they'll die a long way from here."

Li Fong chuckled. "Beautiful and talented lady, your mind is keen and subtle." He glanced about. "Those jade cups are just right. Yes, and heat some wine. Good wine."

He fingered the rims of the translucent cups. One was chipped. Two were flawless. The fourth had a flat spot. Meilan nodded as she fingered the blemishes he pointed out.

Setting the cups on a tray, he spooned three drops of the infusion into each of the perfect ones. "No mistakes, now! Don't taste either of these. Be sure you can feel the chipped spot or the flat spot before you drink." He picked up the tray and the slicing knife. "Bring the wine jug. We'll play a drinking game. Remember, we're friends, all four of us. Be sweet."

"*Taijen*, Number One Master, you're wonderful! I'm loving you more every minute."

She followed him into the room where the prisoners lay.

"You have convinced me," Li Fong said, "that I should not have you . . . ah . . . disappear. But before I set you free, you must make a solemn promise never to trouble these ladies again."

"*Aiieeyah!*" Meilan cried fiercely. "You can't believe a word they say. If our Lucky Silver Dragon Snake hadn't been guarding you, they would have killed you."

"Please," Li Fong protested. "We'll exchange solemn promises. We'll swear an oath. We'll forgive them their errors. That is the enlightened way of the Sages."

"Scholarly Young Lord," the Taoist said, "we

solemnly swear to forget, and to act as if we'd never heard of these ladies, or of their wealth, or of you."

The money changer contributed his bit: "You can believe us! We were tempted. I am a poor man. I make such a small discount on each deal. Ask the mistress if I didn't give her a special rate."

"I'm sure you did," Li Fong agreed. "So I'm going to cut the bonds from your wrists. Once you've drunk a glass for oath-solemnizing, I'll free your ankles."

"We promise, we swear," they chorused.

Li Fong sawed the rattan until it parted. Moments would elapse before either could flex his paralyzed hands.

"You swear to make no trouble for any of us. You won't tell your wives, nor concubines, nor any flower-girls, nor any sing-song girls, nor anyone at all. You won't tell any magistrate or anyone else any lies about us, anything true, or anything at all."

The prisoners beamed happily.

"I've not cut the throat of a white fowl," Li Fong continued. "But you're in the presence of gods and spirits and devils just the same as if we'd made blood sacrifice and dropped blood into this wine. You say this and call gods and spirits and devils to witness?"

"We say this and we call gods and spirits and devils to witness."

Li Fong tured to Meilan. "Pour wine." And when she had done so, he continued, "Do you promise with me, when the four of us drink?"

He took a cup. She took a cup, but scowled. "If I ever have a chance, I'll chop them fine enough for crab bait!"

Li Fong regarded the prisoners. "That is too bad. I'm sorry."

The priest was not worried. "We deal with you. Let's drink."

Eagerly, they extended shaky hands to snatch the cups which Li Fong tendered. Meilan relented sufficiently to say, "All right, I promise with you, but it's just for this time." She eyed the intruders. "If you ever make any trouble again, you won't live long."

They drank. Li Fong commanded, "Fill them up

47

again, Miss Meilan. Let us now have good will, harmonious fraternity, with this cup."

She poured, and again the cups were drained.

"Benevolent and enlightened young Lord," Chang Lu suggested, "while your hand is still steady, you might free our ankles."

Li Fong cut the bonds.

The captives flexed their legs and massaged their ankles. Presently, they were on their feet. Neither could quite believe that luck could be pushed so far.

And then Mei Ling stepped into the room, stately, elegant, serene. She glanced at Meilan. "We have guests? Mr. Kwong, I'm sorry I wasn't at hand to welcome you. There is something to discuss?"

"Only a trifle. Miss Meilan attended to it." He gestured. "This learned person, Reverend Chang Lu, was walking with me—he has no interest—"

"*Tai-tai*, I pay respects," the Taoist said. "Respects before leaving your distinguished presence. Please forgive my discourteous haste. My being here is an intrusion. This is my friend's business. I beg leave to depart at once."

Li Fong caught Mei Ling's eye and made a small gesture, which he hoped would add force to his words. "If I'm not too presumptuous, I'll go to the gate with these gentlemen."

"Please be kind enough to go with these distinguished visitors to the gate." She bowed to the burglars. "Thank you for calling."

Li Fong took each by the elbow, helping him through the main hall and across the garden. After sliding the bar and fighting the hinge, he said, "We have sworn an oath. If ever I catch either of you, or anyone you know, annoying these ladies—"

Priest and money changer regarded him. They blinked, frowned.

"Uh—mmm—*oath*?" Chang Lu demanded. "What oath?"

"Ladies?" Kwong Chi echoed. "Where? What's all this?"

"Who owns this run-down rat's nest?" the priest went on. He eyed his accomplice. "Well, who are *you*?"

Bewilderment eyed bewilderment. Responding to Li Fong's gentle nudge, each went toward the trees which fronted the wall.

He watched them cross the green and go in the direction of the West Gate. They neither stumbled nor wove, but their gait was that of men bemused. They glanced about, as if seeking and not finding any landmarks. Neither appeared to regard his companion.

"They don't remember they ever were together" flashed through Li Fong's mind. His smile was whimsical as he closed and barred the gate. "If Meilan and I had taken any of that potion, we'd forget all and have to start over again . . . which might be nice . . ."

He found the women in the kitchen, huddled about the pot of treasure. Meilan's voice dominated the exchange. "I told him we ought to kill those dung-eaters! He's a schoolboy, but he's so domineering! What could I *do?*"

He cut in. "Miss Mei Ling. Miss Meilan. Please hear me."

Mei Ling said, "Little Sister told me so much that I understand nothing."

"If we don't get out of here," Meilan raged, "we'll have the Thieves Guild, every soldier from the *yamen*, and the magistrate, too, trying to jail us—rob us—rape us—"

Li Fong spoke into the inevitable pause for breath. "Miss Mei Ling, rape is a most detestable crime. But humanity is at times overcome by beauty. Honesty is overcome by displayed wealth. In spite of all the temptations in your home, I have committed no crimes. Please relax."

Mei Ling glowed. Meilan eyed him warily, divided between suspicion and hostility.

"That slow-poison business! They'll talk all over before they die!"

"But I didn't give them any poison."

"Why didn't you? You idiot!"

He ignored the question. "You were amazingly subtle, pretending to fight the idea of making a covenant, with oaths and promises. That's what made them gulp the wine. Making me look like a half-wit was an inspiration. You still don't know what I put into the wine."

"Well, what?"

"Something to make them lose their memories." He repeated the talk of the guests as they departed. "Thy'll have a time finding the way home. I doubt that either can remember his own name."

"How wonderful!" Mei Ling exclaimed. "Now we don't have the karma of killing."

Meilan brightened. "No corpses to dispose of and no one wondering why two men disappeared. Old Master—"

"Younger Sister told me how brave you were," Mei Ling resumed. "Let's have a bowl of soup, and then I think you ought to rest. You're all worn out, more than you realize. Let's have wine, and then you'll sleep till it's time for us to talk. We still have problems."

Mortal weariness made it easy for him to agree. "Let's have wine, and a happy hour."

# CHAPTER XI

"Is he sleeping?" Mei Ling asked when Meilan returned to the reception room.

"As if he'd drunk a jug of thousand-day wine!"

"Lucky he kept you from chopping those fellows. Sometimes I think you're a devil and a barbarian!"

Meilan grinned impishly. "That shows I'm becoming really human." She parted her robe, baring her legs to the hip. "Look—not a bit of those shadow marks that had us so worried."

Mei Ling nodded. "Last night did make you a real woman. I wasn't sure what would happen. I'm glad I was right."

"Try it yourself and find out." Meilan stretched luxuriously, and then suddenly frowned. "You wanted me to risk it first!"

"Don't be that way!" Mei Ling patted her shoulder. "You're always looking to me for magic. If sleeping with Li Fong had caused a setback . . . well, I should have skipped nothing to make things right again."

"*Aiieeyah!* You mean, if you'd been first and your human form went all wrong and you were a snake again, I would not be able to help you?"

"Something like that."

"Maybe we can tell each other a lot." Meilan pondered. "You must have had quite an experience last night. Was it painful or squeamish, going back to snake-form? And how about returning? *That's* what's been worrying me ever since we set out. How did you do it last night?"

Mei Ling closed her eyes and drew a deep breath.

"I woke up. Something troubled me. I heard sounds. I was confused and afraid. I rushed into your room, to find you alone. Sleeping. Then . . . real danger—deadly—Li Fong facing a knife. I can't tell you, I still don't know . . . but something like the way it was in the old monastery, only going the other way, and with desperation that killed my wits. The first thing I knew, I was coiling up a column and to a rafter."

"You're really in love with him, to be hit that way."

"Probably I'll be more so when I'm really human."

"How did you turn back? That's what I've got to know."

"It just happened. Once I had that Taoist monk throttled, I got away as fast as I could. I was terribly worried about turning back. Just suppose I *couldn't!* And all the worse, after meeting Li Fong!"

"Didn't you *do* something? Eat some of that herb we brought along?"

"I can't remember! I must have gone blank. I hid in a rubbish-cluttered room, and when I came to my senses, I wondered how I'd got there. Too happy to be human again to do any remembering. It was like a dream—right when you wake up, you could write down lots of things. By the time you wash and dress and eat a bowl of *congee*, you've forgotten almost all."

Meilan snatched at Mei Ling's jacket, parted it, eyed the smoothness of breast and shoulder. "Maybe the pattern's a shade stronger. Next time there's danger, I'll change back, if you tell me how."

"I haven't asked you about your experience last

night," Mei Ling said. "No matter how you tried, nothing you could say would mean anything."

"How do you know?"

"From your presence, Younger Sister. Though maybe it's in your eyes. Much has happened to you. You're somehow not the same. Then you were frightened and you grabbed the chopper, instead of turning back."

"Probably I'm not in love with him, the way you are. I was just killing mad and did the natural thing."

"I'm glad it's that way with you," Mei Ling said. "I've been wondering how you felt about him. So I'll marry Li Fong. You'll always be with us."

Meilan caught Mei Ling's hand. "*Aiieeyah!* I'm happy about that! I did my share of wondering this morning, while I was trotting around from one drug store to the next. And there's something else."

Meilan frowned, groped.

"Tell me, I'll understand."

"I'm always nagging you about magic and wanting answers, when I ought to know as much as you. We started out together a thousand years ago, or two or five thousand. Sworn sisters."

"And before then?"

"I can't remember."

"I couldn't either, not at first. But it is coming back. There were many lives before then, with so many mistakes that I finally ended in that devil-spirit world where you and I met, to start all over again. I had new remembering just the other day."

Mei Ling went to the lacquered cabinet and took out a piece of chalk and a wooden sword with cross hilt and straight blade.

"Where did you get it?" Meilan demanded, eyeing the ornate carving of the hilt, and the symbols incised into the blade.

"Thieves market, while you were haggling about the price of a pot."

"What's it for?"

"It's peachwood."

"Peachwood. So you really are going to work with magic."

"I hate to, but there's no getting away from it. This

time I'll try to be right-minded. In those long-ago lives, the wrong magic put me into the devil-world. But this will be for self-defense, not malice."

"In case Chang Lu gets back too much of his memory?"

Mei Ling nodded. "He's a disgrace to his calling and to his Ancient Master. Quite a few Taoists are practicing an evil magic these days and forgetting the noble work of the Great Men of Old. Where this whelp got into trouble, another one might take his place and do us real harm. So I'll make a spirit-sword and a *tulku*—that's a thought-form—that will protect us. And one thing more right now."

"Yes, Elder Sister?"

"Do not tell Li Fong. But always make sure that he leads and we follow. He is *yang* and we are *yin*."

"Which is the greater, the stronger?"

"Neither can exist without the other," Mei Ling answered. "There is neither greater nor lesser. Each comes out of the Tao, and each goes back into the Tao, That-Which-Is-All. Give him his way, even when he may seem to be wrong. We do need his protection. Also he needs ours, but he must not suspect it."

Mei Ling drew a circle on the floor. She took the stumps of joss sticks from the burner and thrust the wooden sword into the sand.

"Get seven joss sticks and light them. Then go to the market and get some things for the wedding banquet."

"How many guests?"

"For the three of us. We'll meet Sister Moutan later—and her husband and their son."

"For just us, we have everything we need. And I want to watch what you're doing. Otherwise, how can I ever learn?"

"We need a mirror. Get one, without looking into it. Above all, if you just have to glance at it, don't let anyone see your image."

"Buy something without looking at it? Whoever offered it would make a point of showing me how good it is."

"You figure that out when the time comes. And get a cover for it. For me, for us, the covered mirror." She

53

sighed. "How long it has to be that way, I can't even guess. But someday it will show a human image."

"I can get the mirror later, while you talk to Li Fong."

"I need silence and alone-ness. Even then, it's going to be hard to pour my thought into the sword, make it come alive. Harder yet to give my thoughts a shape firm enough to move around and do as I order."

"You can make such a thing?"

"The lamas in Tibet have always done it. Now leave me alone! I don't want a *tulku* that will ask questions and argue every time I speak!"

Once alone, Mei Ling seated herself in the circle, crossing her legs in the lotus posture. She sat very straight and drooped her eyelids until the lashes joined. Her breathing became slow, scarcely perceptible, and in an unvarying rhythm.

At last, when the day's thoughts were drowned in the Ocean of Universal Mind, she began to chant. Her hands moved in cadence. With each gesture, her fingers changed from one figure to another, each finger-arrangement and hand-shape a symbol of power, a *mudra*, an evocation.

She was not sure what the words meant. Sometimes she was certain that they had no meaning whatever. The forgotten knowledge returned, telling her that it was the sound, the vibration, not the meaning, which was the source of power. Her gestures were *silent*-sound, the *shape* of sound. They amplified that which the ear could not hear.

Not quite right . . . start over . . .

Finally, when the tone was exact, the stately *mudras* gained force. Without changing her voice, she altered the effect by correcting each *mudra*, harmonizing vibrant silence with vibrant sound.

At last Mei Ling's voice became as something from outside, as well as from within. Surges of power made her body tingle and become as the lute of a thousand strings. Cosmic forces began to pluck the strings. They would tear her to shreds, destroy her, if there were any flaw in her bodies, visible or invisible.

The fumes of the joss sticks had been rising, straight, unwavering. Presently the smoke began to curve outward, as if following the contours of invisible substance gathering about the upright sword. Substance beyond the eye's perception was concentrating in the half-circle outlined by the sticks of incense. The invisible shape became broader, taller.

The sword rose from the bowl of sand. Its ascent was slow, as if, after being submerged in fluid, it had been released to rise and surface. It made its way toward an invisible level. Point and hilt interchanged positions. The blade moved as if a hand brandished it in cadence with Mei Ling's chanting. Her face was drawn, tense. Sweat gleamed on her forehead. She had gone far enough. Next time, the guardian entity would be solid and visible.

She made a flashing gesture, clapped her hands, and cried, "*Svaha!*"

The sword dropped, knocking over several joss sticks. Incense fumes now rose in straight threads.

Mei Ling tried to rise, but wavered, toppled. An outthrust hand supported her for a moment, but failed. She rolled, stretched her legs, and lay gasping. Finally, when her breathing became normal, she sat up and regarded the peachwood sword. She reached for it.

A thread of blue fire crackled, lashing out as her hand approached.

She jerked back as if she had touched red-hot iron.

Mei Ling grimaced ruefully and muffled her fingers with a silken kerchief. She picked up the sword, held it without discomfort, and then put it into the cabinet. Later she would find out whether the power she had chanted into the peachwood remained, or whether it had dissipated. She had also to learn the difference between the sword's effect against human opponents and against invisible enemies, intangible ones who could be conquered only by ceremonial magic.

The night's doings had justified the premonition which had prodded her toward the ancient arts she had resolved not to practice. Although Chang Lu had not resorted to occult methods, he had recognized Meilan as a serpent-woman. Even if his memory were to be permanently obliterated, one who was his equivalent might well have a similar sensing and set to work, to make the most of a chance for profit.

55

There were philosophical Taoists as benevolent and holy as Lao Tzu and Chuang Tzu. Others were healers, operating out of good will for all creatures. Among those who were magicians and alchemists, the aim of some was to learn the secrets of nature and immortality. Others devoted themselves to transmuting base metal into gold. And, all the worse, there were some who favored such short cuts as converting someone else's gold to their own use.

In any event, Chang Lu had sufficient mastery of the *Book of Change* to follow a hint and describe all too accurately the location of a treasure hoard.

Though depleted and weary, Mei Ling was encouraged by her success in reviving her old skill in magic. Three times she kowtowed to the east. It was time now to get back to the important business of being a woman.

# CHAPTER XII

QUITE aside from aches, bruises, and total depletion, Li Fong had been entirely willing to drink his wine and quit his companions. Experience had to be digested.

These were puzzling women. Neither appeared to have any awareness of metropolitan life, such as would be a matter of course for anyone of an official's family. Radiant femaleness could go just so far in keeping him from asking himself questions which he could hardly pose to them, concerning details which simply did not fit.

No mirror on the dressing table, and nothing at all on Meilan's table. Apparently each attended to the other's make-up. Though exquisite, the effect was not quite Chinese. He recalled that there were civilized and elegant women in far off Turkistan and in India.

"That Taoist bastard and his yarn about snake-women," he cogitated. "It originated in India . . . Meilan did have an odd pattern under her skin . . . might have been that peculiar wine I drank . . . cool specimen that Chang Lu, neck under the knife and thinking up a story and the idea of dividing the loot three ways and bailing out . . ."

His imagination always got back to Mei Ling's loveliness and the promise of her voice and her eyes, yet his fancies remained the dream substance that they had been from the start. There was something strange, something different, about Mei Ling. To kowtow would be more natural than undressing her.

Li Fong's thoughts pursued each other until they and he were at last subdued by exhaustion. His sleep was troubled by flashes of Taoist steel, never quite parried with a table leg, yet never driving home. Never a silver serpent's intervention. . .

He was startled when Meilan, seating herself on the edge of their bed, aroused him. The room was dusky now, and only a little sunlight reached in. The presence and the fragrance of First Woman brushed aside all cogitation. He laid a hand on her thigh and sought to draw her to him. She edged away and twisted out of his half-enfolding arm.

"Elder Sister sent me to tell you something."

Her tone, so remote and level, prodded him to entire wakefulness. It set up a tremendous barrier between him and this woman whose ardor he had aroused, and who had opened a realm of wonder for him. Dismayed and bewildered, he got to his feet and reached for his tunic.

Meilan, meanwhile, was pouring tea. She had arranged the scene before rousing him. She gestured to chair and table, inviting him. Then she said, "Elder Sister says that we three are linked by karma—by danger we have shared, by things we have done, by thoughts we have together."

He regarded her perplexedly. Her manner, her aloofness, and then those words—somewhat like presenting an Imperial Proclamation to declare that around noon, the sun would be near mid-heaven. And commanding that it be so!

"Elder Sister," Meilan resumed formally, "sends me as go-between, for the politeness of things. She would send someone more fitting, but there is no one else. You and she are to marry. That is her wish."

Li Fong felt as if he had swallowed a jug of *kao li-*

*ang*, been clubbed with a mace, struck by lightning, and booted into an abyss, all in an instant. Meilan meant what she said. This was no game.

"She—wishes—to—marry—*me*—"

"Who else? She loves you."

"But—but—I can't even afford a wedding banquet. I haven't any family except Sister Moutan and her husband, and they're poor."

Meilan laid fingers against his mouth. "Miss Mei Ling—Elder Sister—she has more than the treasure pot. She understands herbs and every other kind of medicine. She is all-compassion, all-love, for all living creatures. She is the Shadow of Kwan Yin—but, alone, she can't do what she might if she had a husband."

"But—but—"

"Quit blinking and gulping like an idiot! Don't be silly. The moment, the first little moment you saw her, you fell in love with her. She was beautiful, too wonderful to be real. You wanted to kowtow instead of to tumble her into bed."

Li Fong swallowed a mouthful of air. This wench was a mind reader.

"But when you finally noticed me, your first wondering was about how I'd be, all spread out and eager."

Li Fong achieved a new high in meaningless facial twistings and blank looks. He groped, "But—listen— you and I—last night—"

"That was last night! You don't suppose she'd want a clown who had just read about it in books? Or looked at sing-song girls and did nothing but write poems about what he imagined it would be like?"

"Well, I was your first lover," he flared up, "and nothing much wrong with you that a second time wouldn't correct! Nothing missing at all!"

Meilan shrugged. "There always has to be a first, or there couldn't be a second. Nobody is asking you to marry me. Elder Sister told me to sleep with you, and I did, and it was really awfully nice, and what has that to do with marrying Miss Mei Ling?"

Callous, matter-of-fact brutality shocked his poetic soul. This wench was practical to the very center of things!

"But I'm only an apprentice."

"You blockhead, she'll buy a drug store, and you'll run the business. What a life! She loves you—I can't imagine why!"

"I can't quite believe—anyway, you and I—"

"You won't remember me very long. Just a couple of times with her and you'll be like those drugged burglars, as far as I'm concerned."

"There is something else."

"You do take a lot of pleasing! All right, what is it now?"

"At the gate—you remember—we spoke of the next time."

Meilan's square-faced ferocity became a lovely glow. "We'll have that. There will be a time."

"Well . . . that's not all."

"Now what?"

"Before you tell Miss Mei Ling—" He gulped. "I want to look at you."

'What are you doing now?"

"I mean—get out of that dress—so—uh—I can see—"

"Just to refresh your memory." Meilan sighed resignedly. "Anything for Elder Sister's husband-to-be." With three lithe moves, she slipped out of her garments. "Farewell look? What a lovely compliment!"

She turned slowly, arms moving to harmonize with her motion, and eyes aglow as she regarded him. Taper light danced and flickered, bringing golden highlights from her smooth body. There was not a trace of the serpent-scale pattern. She cupped her breasts and swayed her hips.

"Nice? Well, she's nicer."

Meilan snatched a handful of garments. "If there ever was a matchmaker who had to do *this!*"

"Every one of them I ever heard of was an old, revolting bitch, usually a retired whorehouse keeper."

"That's what I should have been, and you'd have made up your mind sooner."

"You may tell Miss Mei Ling that I am too happy even to believe my good fortune. I accept gratefully and I bow three times."

Meilan dressed almost as quickly as she had stripped.

"Wait for me in the sitting room. I will tell her and bring her to meet you. Don't worry about what to say or do. She'll be in as much of a silly flutter as you are."

He followed Meilan into the room where they had first shared that strange wine. This was all wrong, marrying without consulting his sister and her husband. This was not polite. Reduced to sheer disbelief, he sat there and hoped that the Ancestors would be pleased.

Meilan finally stepped into the room.

Three paces behind her, and in the shadows, Mei Ling followed. She wore a red gown, long ruby ear pendants, and a chaplet of red gardenias. Meilan stood aside and addressed Li Fong.

"Sir, it is my honor to present your bride, Miss Mei Ling."

The lovers looked at each other, neither having the sense to move, or speak, or even to bow, each to the other. Mei Ling's face changed in a flash of dismay. She brushed her cheek. No veil!

Li Fong croaked, "I forgot—no wedding present—"

Meilan said, "If you must be formal, give her your parasol with the nice agate handle. Wait a moment, I'll light the wedding candles."

She touched flame to the pair of tall red candles on the table. She recited lines from the Qalama Sutra, stating the five major obligations, concluding with those which bound man and wife.

"Face the east," she directed. "Over that way—the sunrise spot."

Li Fong turned, Mei Ling with him.

"Bow to Heaven and Earth."

They obeyed.

"Bow to the Ancestors."

"Uh—which way?"

"You ask more questions than I do! Anyway—the Ancestors are everywhere!"

Again the two did as she directed.

"Now bow to each other."

Still moving like marionettes, Li Fong and his exquisite wife bowed to each other.

Meilan poured wine. Li Fong gulped half and waited for Mei Ling to taste her cup. Then each poured wine into the other's cup, and after this blending they drank again.

"You two still look dazed," Meilan said, and filled three cups. "Sit down and get used to the idea."

Mei Ling settled back in her chair. "There is something we forgot."

"What did I do wrong now?"

"Nothing, Younger Sister. We forgot something important."

Li Fong glanced about apprehensively. "Should we do the ceremony over?"

"No, Old Master," Mei Ling answered very formally. "But I had—and now *we* have—an obligation to Younger Sister. I have my own home, and so we must find her a husband, to give her a home. It is an old custom—"

"That's something I have not yet found for you, for us."

Mei Ling smiled. "There's another way. You may accept Younger Sister as your concubine." She relished, for a moment, his look of amazement, then went on, voice warm and affectionate, "Meilan and I are sworn sisters. We can't ever part."

Li Fong's voice sounded strange in his ears, as if another were speaking. "My wife's first request—I wish to honor it—if Younger Sister accepts—"

Meilan refilled the cups.

"Before Heaven and Earth and the Ancestors, I accept."

They drained their cups. Mei Ling and Li Fong stood looking at each other, question and wonder intermingling. They turned to Meilan.

"You two are forgetful! The wedding banquet, remember? Always a banquet, first."

# CHAPTER XIII

THE coals in the brazier slept beneath a blanket of ash. The flames of oil-floated wicks remained alert, however, making the brocaded bed curtains twinkle. Mei Ling, bestirring herself, drew a deep breath and stretched languorously. Li Fong's arm welcomed relief from its slender burden. During long moments of wakefulness, he had been asking himself whether he had really pleased his bride. He had feared to move, lest he disturb her.

Mei Ling's drowsy smile and her eyes and her voice reassured him. She murmured, "I do hope that I give you a son."

"We fired joss sticks for the Immortals, for the Ancestors, and for the Buddhas and Kwan Yin."

With a quick move, he set feet on the floor.

She caught his arm. "What—"

"No harm in lighting more incense. Just to make sure. And maybe the wine is still warm."

He fired a joss stick. Mei Ling joined him at the little shrine. "Let me offer it," she said, taking the fuming incense. "For my prayer."

"Each, then," he compromised, and touched another to the lamp flame.

Side by side, they faced the shrine with its images, its flowers, its bowl of rice and pyramid of pomegranates. They touched their foreheads to the floor; with formal gestures, they placed the incense in the holder.

Mei Ling got two cups of wine, the little jade cups. Li Fong restrained her. "*Tai-tai,* Number One Lady, wine is not fitting to offer to the Buddhas. For the others, yes, but not for Shakayamuni."

"My Old Lord is such a whimsical man! Would the Compassionate One wish Eight Immortals and the Ancestors to be thirsty?"

"I thank them all for this talented lady."

Each raised a cup to forehead, lifted it high, and set it on the altar. Then Mei Ling nudged him aside and put the bronze jar near the coals.

"Now that I've waited on Them, I'll wait on my husband."

"If it's warm enough for Them, it's good enough for me." He gestured and seated himself on the edge of the bed. "We forgot to strike the bell."

"They don't need that to let Them know we've made an offering." Mei Ling smiled impishly. "Meilan might wake up and think I needed help."

"She said—remember when she led us to this room, so very formal and stately?—that she would watch the house, chopper in hand, and anyone who disturbed us would lose more than his memory."

Mei Ling added charcoal to the brazier. She tested the wine with her fingertip, then set cups and jar on the tabouret. As she turned to join him, he checked her with a gesture, then flipped back the folds of her robe.

"Too late now!" Mei Ling mocked. "You've got to like what the broker arranged for you."

He was not surprised to see the serpentine tracery that showed through her skin. Until this moment, he'd forgotten to look. He whisked the robe back about her.

"All beautiful! I owe her an extra present. But I knew, that first sight of you, at the lake."

"Strange, having a wife? And so soon!"

"It will take time, to become really real."

Mei Ling filled the cups.

"There's so much for us to talk about."

Li Fong added, "And think about, *tai-tai*."

She regarded him intently. "Meilan told me that you'd already done a lot of thinking."

"We're in for trouble," he declared grimly. "The sooner we get out of town, the better. Why not move back to . . . to Kwangan, your old home in Szechwan, where your father's family lived?"

"*Aiieeyah!*" she cried in dismay. "He left too many debts!"

"We'll pay off; I mean, with profits from the shop."

"They can wait."

"The Ancestors are unhappy when debts are neglected."

"I know, I *know*! Please," she implored, "humor my notions."

The pot of treasure would pay off the most extravagant official's debts and still leave Mei Ling wealthy. There might have been a scandal, something she did not want him to learn. Once she'd borne a son, Mei Ling would be so self-assured that nothing her father had done would embarrass her, as far as Li Fong was concerned.

"How would you like Soochow?"

"I'd love it. Maybe Sister Moutan and husband would like Soochow?"

"If they could afford the move, yes."

"We'll keep them from any loss. I'd feel a lot less cut off from life if they were near us. We'd have some family with us."

"You know that you have them. They don't know that they have you. Not yet! But that banquet, let's put it off till we're all in Soochow."

"Much better," Mei Ling agreed. "Then we'll have thirty-three courses, and invite the magistrates and important merchants, and give presents and send cooked meals to all the monasteries."

"*Tai-tai*, with all respect, only nine courses. No important men, nothing conspicuous. And save the monasteries until later."

Mei Ling smiled contentedly. Li Fong didn't suspect that his Number One Lady had baited him into asserting good sense and clinching it with his own words.

As Mei Ling turned from refilling the cups, she saw Li Fong eyeing the joss sticks and their lengthening ash.

"Impatient?" she mocked, affectionately feigning malice. "Can't wait long enough for the Gods and the Ancestors to smell all of a stick of incense!"

He threw up his hands in mock despair. "If I say, *can wait*, you'll tell me that I don't love you. If I say, *cannot wait*—"

Her laugh cut him short. "I'd remind you that rape is a most detestable crime! You said so yourself, remember?"

"Woman, you forget important facts. Consider," he said very judicially. "Wine—food—incense odor—we

64

enjoy these, and the Gods and the Ancestors enjoy them with us. True, is it not?"

"Yes, Old Master, very true. They enjoy *what's on the altar*."

"So we've been depriving Them, all evening, of something very important!" He regarded her, his glance concentrating on very important areas. "I wonder if anything would happen to Them if—" Li Fong made the most dainty, grazing-fingertip caress. "If we burned two hairs, or even a paper picture—"

She slapped him, right and left. "You devil! Mocking Them!"

"Hear some reason, *tai-tai*. When I burn picture money at their graves, they spend it in spirit-land. When I offer wine, they sing and play wine-games."

"So a brush drawing of *it* would give the Immortals and the Ancestors—"

"Yes, they'd have ecstasies."

"You lout, there are two female Immortals, and how about Kwan Yin, and how about Tien Hou, the Queen of Heaven?"

"My keen-witted Old Lady. But awfully absent-minded. The females would share your pleasures and the males would be envious."

"And," she retorted, "be tempted to commit the most detestable crime! I'll have nothing put on the altar, not even a picture! There would be too many disturbances in the spirit-world."

"Your beautiful body would disturb Heaven and Earth?"

"You mean it wouldn't?" she challenged. "Tired so soon?"

"I know little of Earth and less of Spirit-Land. Now, you may remember, there are immediate and unpleasant things to talk about. I will hear whatever you have to say, no matter how many joss sticks burn out."

"Well, take your hands away and try to listen."

"Look!" He gestured. "Hands far away. And now I drink wine."

He set down the empty cup and resumed. "What's really on your mind? We've decided to go to Soochow to live. But there's more. Perhaps so much that I should light another joss stick. Tell me?"

Her smile was as beautiful as the full moon rising through river mists.

"I've been wondering . . ."

"Yes, *tai-tai*?"

"How did you like your concubine—how *do* you like her?"

This quirk of female curiosity left him gaping. "Um . . . ah . . . the best concubine I ever had. But wasn't it odd to give me a Number Two Lady before we were married?"

"Of course it wasn't! I told you Meilan and I are sworn sisters."

"If she'd told you I was dull and revolting, you would not have married me. From first sight, I knew you were wonderful."

Her glowing eyes and the lengthening ash of incense teamed up.

"You haven't noticed that I have a contrary streak?"

"Well, no, not yet. And nothing has to make sense."

"I don't blame you for wondering." Her eyelashes fluttered, and she drew a deep breath. "All my life I've wondered what *happened* to a woman. What *really* happened. I mean, did she become somehow different, a new self? So Younger Sister—"

"Did her duty, and found out about being a complete woman? To tell you."

"We've been talking too long," Mei Ling said, and dismissed all queries by snuggling up most invitingly.

There was more to it than that, Li Fong told himself before Mei Ling's femaleness blotted out his judgment, but a man who has a wife, a concubine, and an interest in a pot of treasure shouldn't give too much thought to evaded queries.


## CHAPTER XIV


SOON after sunrise, Meilan came in with two wooden pails of bath water, one cold, the other steaming. Setting these down by the alcove which contained a boat-

66

shaped tub, she said, "Master's bath is in the other room. Now I bathe and dress *tai-tai*."

"You forget," Mei Ling said, "that the Venerable Lord is almost a stranger in this dilapidated shack. Show him where things are."

Li Fong followed Meilan to the room which they had shared—a lifetime ago, it now seemed. Warm vapor from the alcove welcomed him. A pot of tea sat on the table, and also his garments.

"While you slept, I washed all but the robe you wear. All are dry now."

"Thank you. Chopper in one hand while you worked? Please tell the mistress I want you to sit with us at breakfast. I've something to tell you." As Meilan turned to leave, he detained her. "Last night you forgot an important detail."

"Please tell me?"

"The girlhood fringe of hair should have been cut before she came to me. You'll remember when you dress her?"

"I am so stupid!" Meilan eyed him speculatively. "Was I a good marriage broker?"

"Twice now you have brought new beauty into my life. I will always be grateful. There will be a present for you when I have earnings of my own. Two presents, in fact."

As he stretched out in the tub, he felt almost as divided as he had been while full of that strange wine. Carefully, he tried to count the hours since he had left Mr. Sang's shop, and could not believe the tally. The total was mystery blended with menace.

He stayed in the tub until the water was lukewarm. He dried himself, oiled his hair, and bound it into a neat little hank. He put on the meticulously ironed garments. They had the lingering odor of wood smoke. He pictured Meilan at work, chopper ever at hand.

Having dawdled as long as he could, to give Meilan time to dress the mistress, Li Fong went into the sitting room. Time-killing and curiosity combined to attract him to the book he had noted and dismissed that first evening—the *I Ching*, the *Book of Change*, with its cryptic hexagrams and the names of each, the name of each trigram, the Judgment, and the Commentaries—a book two thousand years old or older, when the Lord Buddha first gave his message to the world.

This was more than a book. In a sense, it was a *person*. Before consulting it, one set out incense; one kowtowed; only then did one respectfully address the Book as one would a teacher, or an Elder Brother, or one's Father.

His wife was evidently an unusual woman in more ways than several.

He spread the accordion folds of the strip, regarding the calligraphy as art, rather than as something to read.

He turned another pleat. The text blazed at him, held him fixed.

Mei Ling's voice broke into his concentration. Her brocaded jacket twinkled as she raised hands to stroke her gleaming hair and run fingertips across her forehead.

"Bangs are now gone. I look married, very much Old Matron?"

"Beautiful, and perfect." He took her in his arms, kissed her, then held her at arm's length, to look for some moments. "Also perfectly beautiful, Number One Lady of Separate Household."

"I kept you waiting too long?"

"Any time is too long."

They took seats at the table. Meilan came in with a small, covered wooden pail of rice, a tray with dishes of bean curd, a sauté of mushrooms and bamboo shoots, and slices of "hundred-year-old" eggs in a pungent sauce. There was also a plate of loquats and peaches.

Glancing at the tray, Li Fong said to Meilan, "Get your bowl. You will eat with us, remember?"

"I was so busy making *tai-tai* beautiful, I forgot."

Meilan had devoted no time at all to beautifying herself. He wondered whether this was from tact, or simply because of haste. When she left the room, Li Fong said, "If she'd taken any longer, the suspense would have been too much."

"Never tell such shameful lies to this homely old lady! You were patiently reading a book." Mei Ling sighed. "You scholar!"

"Wait for Younger Sister, and I'll tell you some things."

When Meilan returned, she spooned rice into each bowl and into a small cup which she set at the shrine, for the Gods and the Ancestors. This courtesy observed, they plied their chopsticks and drank their tea. Finally, Mei Ling said, "You were going to tell us something? And don't forget what the Book told you."

"I'd been doing a lot of pondering. I was still at it as I thumbed the *Book of Change.* I wasn't looking at what I saw and I wasn't seeing what I looked at. Then a page jumped at me."

"You even forgot you were waiting for your new wife, impatiently?"

"Yes, until you spoke."

"Tell us," Meilan demanded.

*"Six at the top—the wall falls back into the moat. Use no army."*

"For you, this means?"

"Do not fight. Get away. We leave, here and now. No porters, no carts. We take only what we can carry. We will walk. The wall has fallen into the moat. Time to run."

*"Walk?* What is this?"

His face and his voice had so shocked the women that they glanced about as if expecting intruders. Li Fong continued, "When two men lose memory suddenly, there is wondering, too much remembering things they said, too much thinking. To get away alive, we must leave right now.

"Meilan, go to the flea-bazaar and buy old clothes, coolie clothes, ragged and dirty, and big hats to hide half the face. We will leave town in the crowd of market people going home." He regarded his wife fixedly. "What do you say?"

"Old Master, you are right."

Li Fong detained Meilan. "Wait, I have to write a prescription. Do not touch the stuff. It would burn your skin off."

When she left, Mei Ling said, "You're all too right about leaving in a hurry. What is the stuff she's to get this time?"

"Get a pot of water heated for mixing a potion."

When she had the pot on the kitchen fire, Mei Ling said, "You are so mysterious at times!"

"Sometimes I perplex myself, being so cryptic."

"So you forget what is plain. You've skipped your Sister Moutan."

"I've been thinking of her, and what to tell her, and what not to mention. Number One Lady, what is your thought?"

"Let's give her a present."

"The clothes you and Meilan can't wear, can't carry with you?"

"Do that, too. My idea was to give Moutan a hundred *taels* so that she and her husband and little son, Chen, can join us. What will you say about me?"

"That you are beautiful, talented, elegant. If the Son of Heaven ever sees you, he'll make you his Number One Wife."

"Silly! Talk like a marriage broker, or like the first lines of a drum-song, and she'll not believe a word."

"Very well! I'll say you are plain, serious-minded, a farm girl, not too homely, not bright enough to make problems for me."

"She'll want to know who I am—who my family are—where we are from—all about brothers and sisters—and whether I was a virgin."

He regarded her with dismay. "What can I say, facing female curiosity? She's bound to think of something to make me give a stupid answer!"

"My clothes, and Meilan's, and a hundred *taels*," she said, "will leave her blinking. Get out immediately, before you talk yourself into something she'll simply *have* to discuss with her neighbors."

"I'll tell her not to say anything to anyone!"

Mei Ling sighed, shook her head. "You are innocent! That will make it all so important she'll be bound to tell someone. You don't know much about women, Old Master."

"You mean I can't trust even you?"

"I'm different," Mei Ling said brightly. "Anyway, I don't know anyone to talk to."

This left Li Fong depressed beyond measure as they set to work making a bundle for Sister Moutan. Mei Ling picked up the lightest cooking utensils, the few they would need on the trip. Next, they went into the room where they would never again sleep and took care of the trinkets on the dressing table.

Mei Ling said, "Let's leave some trifles and a lot of ordinary clothes. The next prowler won't realize, right away, that we've gone for keeps."

# CHAPTER XV

WHEN Meilan returned, Li Fong and his bride were still sorting goods for their pack-march. She was beyond recognition, in grimy rags and mushroom-shaped coolie hat. Over her shoulder she had a carrying pole, with basket aft, balanced by one which hung in front.

"Mistress, this is how you're going to look. I traded my clothes and got all this stuff and some silver to boot. Yes, and I got the medicines the Master ordered." She lowered the baskets and twisted clear. "This won't be fun, all day."

Mei Ling shuddered. "I'll have to look like *that*?"

"*Tai-tai*," Li Fong said, grinning, "you won't bait anyone into attempting any detestable crime."

"And *you* won't want me, either!"

He slapped her hip. The sound was ripe and mellow. His palm had been perfectly cupped for a perfect fit. "I didn't take any memory-killing potion. Now listen—if anyone suspects we're bent double from all that gold we'll be carrying under our rags, we'll never get to Soochow. Now, where's the medicine?"

Meilan handed him several packets. He took two from the lot and handed them to Mei Ling, saying, "Keep these for emergencies, such as putting gate guards to sleep. I'll use the rest right away."

He dissolved the powders and crystals in the pot of hot water, then said to Meilan, "Get some of the old silver *sycees*." While waiting, he dipped enough solution from the pot to fill a glazed bowl.

She came back with the entire hoard. Li Fong picked a silver slug from the lot and dropped it into the liquid. "Keep your fingers out!" he warned. With chopsticks, he caught the silver, waggled it about.

The dove-gray tarnish dissolved.

"Put in quite a few pieces and swirl the bowl, like this, but don't slop any on your hands. When the stuff works slowly, dump it and get more from the pot." He eyed the pattern stamped on the *sycee*. "Nobody but a coin collector would know this is ancient."

"Will it work with gold?"

"Gold is conspicuous whether old or new. *Tai-tai*, do you still have the new silver you got when you changed some gold?"

"Yes, lots."

"Then I'll go right away to give some to my sister. On my way back, I'll buy three small daggers, a short sword, and a few bowstrings."

"Archery, Old Master?"

"Bowstrings can be useful, even when not fixed to a bow. Now give me the stuff for Sister Moutan."

Digging into the loathsome heap which Meilan had bought, he put on jacket and pants. Grimacing, he added his clean clothes to the perfumed garments the women contributed. Into the center of the collection he put the silver, toilet accessories, some bits of jewelry, the cosmetics, and the perfumery.

Li Fong lashed the bundle with a cord and balanced it on his head. He left by the emergency exit and thence made for the city.

As he approached the wall and the West Gate, he felt conspicuous and uneasy. His burden did not match his appearance. Instead of going forward he turned his back on the city and plodded until a turn of the road got him well out of sight of the sentries at the gate.

Those fellows had a nose for extortion. They exacted a reasonable bit of *cumshaw* from everyone entering the city with any cargo, unless that person had a pass stamped with the "chop" of one who paid tribute to the commander of the guard or who was too important to pay anyone.

Squatting beside the road, he watched fishermen carrying their catch and farmers with ducks hung by the legs from carrying poles. Two peasants, shouldering a bamboo stalk, had a good-sized pig between them. Finally came a porter bent nearly double under an enormous bundle of fuel-grass. He responded to Li Fong's hail and disengaged himself from the cords which secured the cargo.

"Hiyah! How much grass you got there, that bundle?"

"Hundred *catty*."

"You can't carry that much. Maybe sixty *catty*. How you sell grass?"

"How much you buy? Five *tael*, take all, I carry any place in town."

Li Fong frowned and pretended to calculate on his fingers, although he already knew that this was at the rate of eighty *cash* for a *catty*. Not a bad price, but he said, "That's only grass—how charge me for sandalwood? And I don't need so much."

"Sell what you can't use." The porter showed all his teeth in a grin and wagged his head. "Stealing clothes, better business? Whose you got?"

Going with the jest, Li Fong leaned forward and confided, "Did not get the name. Nobody at home."

The peddler chuckled. This exchange of humor told Li Fong how the sentries at the gate might have reacted on seeing his bundle. He brushed aside the sweat from his forehead and hefted the grass.

"Huh! Sixty *catty*."

"Hundred."

"Maybe eighty."

The peddler hefted, grunted, dropped the lot. "Ninety *catty*."

They ended by untying the cords and dividing the lot into two equal parcels, then halving one of those. Not quite twenty-five pounds of grass—and since it was released from its bonds, the bulk expanded.

Li Fong divided the quarter lot into halves. "Ten *catties*? Eight strings. I'll help you tie up your bundle. Easy walking to town."

"You stole clothes, now you steal grass. Yes, help me," the porter said, as he took the *tael* and gave Li Fong two strings of *cash* in change.

Once the fellow was on his way, Li Fong scooped up the grass and laid it out under a willow clump near the road. Sheltered from observation, he reconstructed his bundle. When he had finished, there was an imposing parcel of grass, with nothing to show the nature of its core. Shouldering his burden, he followed another porter toward the gate.

He had a string of *cash* in hand, just in case.

The ruffians on guard—that is, the magistrate's soldiers—had settled down to routine. Half a string, and this time Li Fong paid off without bargaining.

"*Na-mo-o-mi-to-fu,*" he sighed as he cleared the gate and put danger behind him. "Easier than I figured, but sweaty for a second . . ."

Presently he turned from the main street and went down the narrow way to his sister's little house. He found her in the tiny court, with Chen, her four-year-old son.

Moutan, a slender young person with fine eyes, and teeth a shade too prominent, looked up at the intruding lout. All in all, she was quite good-looking, and in her feminine way she resembled Li Fong markedly. At the moment, her face tightened into grim lines.

"I don't want any grass! Get out, now!" Then she realized the horrible, the incredible truth. "*Aiieeyah!* Brother, what is this! Mr. Sang sent an apprentice to find out where you are. He's mad—he's—"

"Sister, don't raise the voice. You know more than Mr. Sang."

He dumped the bundle. Moutan demanded, "But what's this? You look like a coolie. The dirtiest, the filthiest!"

Little Chen grinned happily at his uncle. "Got a present for me?"

"Better get this stuff indoors. Yes, very fine nephew, lots of things. Sister, do shut up and listen. I will tell you everything."

Moutan was glad to get her disreputable visitor out of the sight of her neighbors. Chen trailed after and was happy about it all, seeing Number One Uncle in such funny clothes.

"Are you in trouble?"

"More than I have time to talk about. Silence, while I speak! Do not scream when I have done talking. *Shut up!*"

He untied the bundle, scattering grass from wall to wall.

"All over the floor!" Moutan wailed. "What——"

"If I emptied a honey-bucket, there should not be such screeching! The Ancestors would not be proud of you. Silence, while I speak!"

Li Fong snatched a sea-green silken gown from the tangle and unfurled it like a battle flag. The perfume filled the room and masked the odors of cooking. He whipped out a brocaded jacket.

"These are presents. My wife and my concubine send these, with respect and love. They knock their foreheads on the floor."

Moutan's eyes went wide and dark. She stood there gaping. Li Fong thrust garments into her hands. She licked her lips and blinked.

"Feel them, Sister. Smell them."

She held the garments. He raised her hands to her face.

Moutan screeched. "You robbed some rich woman!"

"Yes, I did. She married me."

He plucked out another garment, and another, flipping one this way, one that, until the room looked like a flower bed.

"Wife *and* concubine! Look at yourself!"

"This is a disguise. My wife is an important lady. Her father is a high official. Enemies murdered him. They are hunting her. We are in much danger. So I look like a beggar, a boatman, a clodhopper."

Between the malodorous rags her brother wore, and the costly scents, the toilet articles, and the garments he had flung about, Moutan could make no sense of anything, much less all of this. Little Chen was dipping into the confusion of treasures. Li Fong patted his nephew's head and went on with his fable-and-fact blend.

"We leave town ahead of enemies, at once, right now."

Thanks to the Immortals, she hadn't got around to asking about his wife's siblings, parents, ancestors, talents, or culinary skills.

"Where do you go?"

"I must not tell you. Please say to Mr. Sang that I

am sorry to be such a poor apprentice. Give him the amount you paid for my apprenticeship fee. And give him a present."

"A present—a refund! *Aiieeyah!* How can I? All these lovely things, but no money."

Li Fong handed her a heavy pouch. "Some of this is for Mr. Sang. Also, a hundred *taels* for you and your husband. When my dull-witted wife and my cow-clumsy concubine and I get to our destination, you can join us. My wife is stupid, homely, but wealthy. We will make things better for you than you could do in Kwangchow."

"Your wife," Moutan echoed, incredulously, "*and* your concubine—where are they—"

"I do not tell you. You can swear oaths with blood that you do not know where we are—blood, devils, every kind of swearing. Please do be calm."

"I'll do as you say—oh, this is silver, lots of it. several hundred *taels* anyway—" She hefted the bag, jingled the contents.

"Please, I beg of you, lower the voice, and do not talk to the neighbors. Don't talk to anyone, especially not to money changers. Most of all, do not talk to any Taoist priest. Don't even look at one. Turn your head and get away quickly if one looks at you. Do not go to any fortune tellers. The less you have to do with anyone, the better for us all."

"Brother, tell me the truth, what *have* you done?"

"Don't try to find out. Don't ask anyone to consult the *Book of Change*. Don't ask monks of any kind. And when your husband comes home, tell him not to let you ask questions, not to say things to anyone."

"But *what*—"

"When all is safe, I will write. Now I have to hurry, hurry quickly, to my wife and my concubine. *To face more questions! O-mi-to-fu!*"

# CHAPTER XVI

Li Fong's herb shop in Soochow was so much to his taste that he no longer felt like a demoted scholar. As he sat at his tea table, watching the flow of porters, wheelbarrow men, fishers, and farm women who crowded the steep and narrow streets, he wondered if all this was fact or simply a vivid dream.

At the rear of the open-front shop, joss sticks fumed in the little shrine of the God of Medicine. Along the walls were neatly labeled drawers and shelves with jars and canisters, pewter and porcelain, each with its stock of herbs, roots, animal and mineral substances, concerning which, it became ever more apparent, his wife knew far more than did he.

Ordinarily, it would have been difficult, almost impossible, for strangers to find apprentices. Mei Ling, however, had lost no time in finding two young men, Ah Sam and Ah Lo, as useful about the house as in the shop. They might have been twins, taciturn and speaking an odd dialect which Li Fong at times found difficult. This was offset by their aptitude, their understanding, and their willingness to work. Li Fong was delighted by Mei Ling's ready solution of a problem.

Ah Sam sat in the farther front corner, rocking back and forth as, with bare feet, he moved the wheel-and-axle-shaped roller fore and aft in a boat-shaped mortar, pulverizing herbs.

The customer's corner was vacant.

Although he never shared this thought with his wife, Li Fong at times would speculate as to how effectively they had covered their trail; and whether Reverend Chang Lu's evil memory had been permanently obliterated. Permanence was relative. While these thoughts did not shadow his honeymoon happiness, Li Fong's contentment did not keep him from cogitating on the future.

If ever there were another encounter with Chang Lu,

Li Fong would need more than potions to settle the enemy. The book near his teapot did not treat of herbs. One of its chapters was devoted to the use of a bowstring of hard twisted silk. While the women were asleep, he practiced whipping a loop of cord about a bamboo stump in the corner of the garden. There were gymnastic exercises in which a sword was important. Finally, he practiced "stick fighting" with the quarterstaff—a cool and skillful fighter, armed only with a staff of dried and sharpened bamboo, could kill a tiger.

Pondering all this, Li Fong permitted himself a whimsical smile.

"This balances exquisitely," he mused. "Herbal healer, making customers for surgeons and coffin builders."

Two bearers emerged from the crowd. They carried between them a bamboo litter. They were middle-aged, deeply lined. They wore coarse blue jackets and knee-length pants. The foremost had come to the shop several times for herbs prescribed by Dr. Pao.

The one at the rear appeared to be the man's brother.

The old woman in the homemade litter must be the patient for whom Li Fong had compounded the tonics.

"Good morning, Mr. Wu. This is good, carrying your mother out for air and sun. I hope she is so well she needs no medicines."

"Dr. Pao says treatment doesn't help. Nothing can help."

"What have you paid Dr. Pao?"

"He won't accept any more money."

This was sad and simple. The doctor wanted to get rid of his patient before she died and tarnished his reputation.

She still breathed. Her emaciated face was dry, despite the day's warmth. Her lips were parted. When she blinked and fumbled the coverlet, Li Fong saw that her eyes were blank.

"Maybe you know some other doctor? We have money."

Li Fong gestured. "Up that way. See Dr. Sun."

And then Mei Ling stepped in and took a hand. "First come in and rest. You are tired. Drink some tea."

"That makes too much trouble for you," the first Wu protested.

The second added, "Thank you, we are not tired. This is easier than work."

"Come through the shop. You need not go through the gate."

They eyed Li Fong. He said, "Do as *tai-tai* says."

He followed them through the stock room and into the court between the rear of the shop and the front of the house. Columns supported a tile-roofed canopy which skirted the wall and continued to the house.

Mei Ling called, "Ah Lo, bring a quilt!" Then to the brothers, "Rest in the shade." When the apprentice answered, she added, "And bring tea."

Ah Lo spread the quilt on the paving. The Wu brothers lowered the litter. They squatted on the floor, sleeve-mopped their foreheads.

"Have you come far?" Mei Ling asked.

"Only eight *li*."

"Where is your father?"

"With the Ancestors. Sometimes when she speaks, she says that in her dreams Father tells her he is sending a boat for her to join him."

"Please rest while I speak to the Master."

Li Fong, who had resumed his place at the tea table, stopped plying his fan and regarded his wife. "*Tai-tai*, you're very nice to those poor fellows. But there's more to it than that. You don't like Dr. Sun? You have someone else in mind?"

"Maybe I can do something for the old woman."

"You do something to make herbs work better than their ordinary nature, that I've noticed, and I've often wondered. But you shouldn't treat this one. Let them rest and go their way. You'll gain merit for your kindness."

Mei Ling stepped to the wall and opened a drawer. From it she took a pinch of leaves, sniffed the bits, shook her head. She dipped into another drawer and appraised the contents.

"Don't mix medicine," Li Fong said. "She's too far gone. If she dies here, it will give us a bad name. Even if she dies soon at home, it would be bad for us."

"She won't die here, Old Master, and not soon at home."

"You don't even know what ails her!"

"Of course I don't."

"Then how can you pick out the herbs?"

Mei Ling smiled cryptically. "If the shop loses prestige, we'll buy another business somewhere else."

"Do what seems good," he agreed uneasily.

From the storeroom door he watched Mei Ling put a pinch of herbs into a cup of tea and take a sip, after a moment. Raising the patient almost upright, she said to the sons, "I drank some myself."

"Yes, we saw. It is harmless."

Mei Ling nodded. "Sit in the corner. You mustn't be too near."

They obeyed. Mei Ling lowered the old woman to the cushions. She seated herself at the foot of the litter and poured enough tea to fill the cup. This she held in one hand. With the other, she made gestures, *mudras* harmonious with her purpose and problem.

A customer at the counter demanded and got Li Fong's attention. The aphrodisiac business was picking up.

When Li Fong had an idle moment, he turned to look at the drawer which Mei Ling had not firmly shut.

"Doesn't make sense at all!" he muttered, and stepped into the storeroom.

Cup in one hand, a sprig of foliage in the other, Mei Ling was pacing along the litter, sprinkling tea on the patient. Turning at the head, she paced the length of the other side, flicking the sprinkler.

As Mei Ling completed the third circuit, the old woman spoke. Though her voice was feeble and shaky, it had authority. "Number One Son, take me home. It's a long walk."

She sat up. The sons got to their feet and stood there, staring.

Number One Son fished a few *cash* from his belt. "She looks lots better. Let us have more medicine for tonight and for tomorrow. Give us what's left in the cup."

"You forget your manners!" the old woman said. "I

was dead. Now I'm alive. Kowtow to this lady. Knock your heads on the floor. Give thanks."

"Please!" Me Ling cut in. "Don't let them kowtow. Bad joss for me!"

This made sense. The old woman compromised. "What do they owe you?"

Mei Ling said to the sons, "When Mother walks about the house, buy two red candles for Kwan Yin. Do that, and I am paid." She beckoned to the elder. "Come, I'll give you some herbs."

Once in the shop, the coolie took the packet of medicine, raised it to his forehead, stuffed it into his sash. He eyed Mei Ling intently.

"What is your thought?" she asked. "I did nothing. Thank the Gods."

"She will be on her feet, you told us. With dreams of Father sending a boat for her, how can this be?"

"Your mother is not mistaken. She knows what is to be. She is old, almost expended, worn out. For some while she will be clear and bright and happy with her good sons, and their wives, and their children. This will be to the very end, until she steps easily and quickly and happily to the spirit-boat, to go to your father."

Wu considered this. "How long has she?"

"Long enough for you and your brother to sit with her and to speak of long-ago days, when your father lived. Since you have no more doctors to pay, you have time to save enough for a good funeral."

He put his palms together and bowed three times.

"You may leave now," Mei Ling said, "and with our good wishes."

Meilan, who rarely missed anything, had joined the group. She opened the main gate for exit easier than through the shop. Li Fong and his wife leaned over the counter, waiting for the brothers to carry their mother home. As they passed, Mei Ling raised her hand, waving goodbye.

"What did you put into the tea?" Li Fong demanded.

"Something to give it a spicy taste."

For a long moment he studied his uncanny wife. Smiling, she face the probing scrutiny. "You're going to ask me what I did. Well, you saw me making *mudras* and sprinkling her with cold tea."

"What else?"

"Nothing else."

"What did you say?"

"A silent *mantram*. Don't ask me anything else. I can't explain how or why." Then she told him what she had said to the Number One Son.

Li Fong was content. "That was great wisdom. I admire, but I'm not amazed." After a pause, he added, "If I keep this up, I'll be asking as many questions as Number Two Lady, and then I couldn't give her short answers any more."

## CHAPTER XVII

MEI Ling's miraculous healing of old Mrs. Wu upset the bias against female doctors. The word spread. Patients began to crowd the courtyard. Li Fong was not surprised when profits from prescriptions fell off.

Mei Ling said reassuringly, "We're not actually losing money, and there's a lot in reserve, remember. The buried pot. Meanwhile, you become famous."

"Famous for what?"

"For having taught your wife so much about herbs."

"That's what you tell them?"

"Of course. I always use some sort of herb. I mustn't let them think I practice magic."

"Which is what you are doing."

"Well . . . not exactly, but sort of. Anyway, I give your herbs credit, and those who don't need my methods will want to buy medicines."

"Becoming famous," he conceded, "is nice enough. Meanwhile, every monk and every abbot is expecting bigger donations. Those robes you gave Kwan Yin started off a swarm of them from all the other temples—yellow robes, gray robes, black robes."

Mei Ling frowned. "Black?"

"Yes. Black. It gives me a twitchy feeling, every

time one of them comes near the place. I know most Taoist priests are awfully good men, and wise, and helpful, but after what we went through—"

Mei Ling's eyes twinkled. "Give them a potion to blot out their memories. And one of these days you'll cure an official, or a wealthy merchant, and you'll get a present equal to a year of regular profit."

Now that the Fourth Moon had brought beauty and spring to the land, Mei Ling and Meilan and Li Fong began to have breakfast in the gallery under the eaves of the high, front portion of the house. From there, they overlooked the court and the tiled roof of the shop.

Sautéed mushrooms and rice and bamboo shoots with ginger-flavored sauce steamed in the serving dishes. Vapor rose as Meilan poured tea. Mists wavered and thinned, revealing the river and the network of canals. Beyond the city wall, mists girdled the lower stages of tall pagodas.

Mei Ling sighed contentedly. For a moment, her loveliness and the golden morning became one. Forgetting the many dark hours along the way, she relished the wonder of being human and was grateful for the opportunity to become permanently so. Each time she shared the griefs of humanity, her position became more assured.

Chopsticks poised, she glanced at Li Fong. "Beautiful Soochow! I'm so glad we came here."

When Li Fong set his bowl aside, he said, "*Tai-tai,* this is the fourteenth day. I don't care for it at all."

"For an herb master, your thought is strange. What's wrong with the festival of Father Lu Tang Ping, and Hua Tao?"

"I don't want to go to that Taoist temple. But if I don't go, customers will figure that my herbs won't work."

"You feel that you just might meet some Taoist who would pass the gossip along, so that news of us would get to Reverend Chang Lu or his friends."

"A good way of saying it, though I was just uneasy, not for any special reason."

"Not going would be bad joss," Mei Ling admitted. "Why not go early, pay your respects, and get out?"

"You don't like this a bit better than I do."

"No, I don't," she agreed. "But if we go, we'll learn more about them than they'll find out about us."

"You're right. I'll go openly. You go in a sedan chair, to look and not be seen. You'll hear the unspoken and read the thinking."

Meilan cut in. "Elder Sister, your peachwood sword would be good to take along, just in case."

"Good idea," Li Fong seconded.

For some while, he had suspected that his wife's weapon was more than a good-luck symbol. One day she might tell him why he was never to enter the small room where she spent many an hour, sometimes in silence, sometimes chanting *sutras*.

When he set out afoot for the Taoist temple and the festival, Mei Ling followed in a fully curtained sedan chair. She had paid and dismissed the bearers, and had Ah Sam and Ah Lo take their places.

Presently Li Fong edged into the crowd that jammed the court of the temple. There were devotees, herb sellers, each with his own stand or mat for displaying his wares, which included amulets and good-luck charms. Each cried his own praises. Each struck a gong or bell to win attention. Glancing about, Li Fong saw that Mei Ling's bearers had found pavement space in an angle not far from the entrance and rather near a doctor who had a paper banner fastened to the wall behind him. He was neatly fitted in between two buttresses.

The banner announced: "I AM HERE TO HELP ALL WHO HAVE PROBLEMS. FOR SERIOUS AILMENT, CONSULT ME. I DRIVE AWAY DEVILS AND SPIRITS. I HAVE OCCULT POWER. I AM TAI CHING, DISCIPLE OF FATHER LU AND MASTER HUNG."

Li Fong went into the temple and wedged his way among the men and women at the shrine. Some were kneeling. Others kowtowed. Many were putting fruit, rice wine, cakes, roast duck, roast pork on the altar.

Foremost, and kneeling on cushions, were three priests wearing black robes and tent-shaped Taoist hats. The ridge-pole, as it were, of the tent—a wall tent—was crosswise to the wearer's head.

Li Fong put three parcels of sandalwood on a tray, which he handed to the nearest priest. That one raised the offering to forehead level, lowered it, and passed it to the one at his left. The second repeated the raising and passing; the third repeated the ceremonial move, and an acolyte carried the offering to the rear. Another struck a gong and intoned, "Dr. Li Fong, Master of Herbs, has presented three *catties* of sandalwood." This was purely a formality. Before leaving, Li Fong donated ten *taels* of silver.

Returning to the court, Li Fong edged his way through the crowd, moving crabwise toward Mei Ling's sedan chair. Slow progress gave him a chance to study Tai Ching, the conspicuous Taoist.

Black robe, embroidered hat, a circle of eight trigrams on his tunic—and, near the staff of the seven-starred flag set on the table, a straight-bladed sword. The bare steel brought unpleasant memories to Li Fong. He glanced in Mei Ling's direction. The chair curtains were still drawn, but not so snugly. Her fingers were visible. Ah Sam and Ah Lo squatted on the pavement, apparently asleep.

The big-mouthed priest's thick brows bristled. His glance shifted from eye to eye. He banged the table with the pommel of the sword. His fierce glance fixed on Li Fong. The chatter of the crowd subsided.

"I feel devil-influence!" Tai Ching declaimed. He pointed at Li Fong. "Evil spirit! What do you want in this temple? Go away!"

The crowd laughed and hooted. "Crazy priest! Turtle-child! This is a good doctor. Husband of the lady who saved many lives. Shut up!"

Li Fong stepped toward the priest. "I came with gifts. Put down your sword."

"Is that all you can say?"

Looking about, Tai Ching did not like what he saw, and laid the blade on the table. "I came to save you from evil."

"How save what is not in danger?" Li Fong challenged.

Tai Ching's face became stern as he mustered his forces to resist the hostility of the crowd. A trickle of sweat ran from his shaggy brows and into his eyes, making him blink. Nevertheless, he persisted, as if obsessed—or prompted by someone behind him.

"Your wife is a spirit in human form. She does good to trick all these people. She is a devil."

Li Fong laid five *taels* of silver on the table. "This pays for all your herbs. Give them to the poor, and go home, and gain merit."

Bystanders laughed and cackled, relishing the retort.

And then Mei Ling stepped from the sedan chair. Ah Lo and Ah Sam followed her. Facing the priest, she announced, "I am the doctor's wife. Have you something to say to me?"

The challenge prodded Tai Ching. "I will write a *mantram* to prove you're a devil-spirit."

"Please do so," she said, and gestured to Ah Sam.

As though in response to previous orders, the bearer made his way back to the sedan.

The priest snatched his brush. He wrote two columns of characters on a strip of very thin yellow paper. Meanwhile, Ah Sam came back, bringing something long and straight, all muffled in folds of silk. He stood beside Mei Ling, awaiting her next wish.

With an impressive gesture, most dramatic, Tai Ching flourished the yellow paper with its ideograms in a special red ink.

"Nice calligraphy," Mei Ling remarked. "I decline your malice. It returns to the sender, as does any unaccepted gift. Your own curse, and you will eat it when it returns."

"This you can't decline!" He dipped the paper into a cup of water, rinsing the ink from it. He thrust out the cup. "Drink, and you will become a fox. Refuse, and we know you are a devil-spirit."

Mei Ling smiled, glanced about, for the now silent crowd to enjoy her radiance. "Yes, if I refuse, they will believe you. You are smart, Dr. Tai Ching. Instead of burning the paper and letting ash and char fall into the water, you offer me this—and if I drink that filth and the prints of your dirty fingers on the cup, I'll be poisoned."

The crowd muttered, surly and menacing. "*Tai-tai*," one said, "don't touch it!" And another, "If he harms you, we'll kill him."

She raised her hand. "No matter what happens, you must not harm him."

Mei Ling took the parcel from Ah Sam and gave it to Li Fong.

"Keep the folds of silk about your hands," she whispered. "Touch nothing but double folds of silk."

"What—"

"I don't know yet. I'll tell you in time. We'll settle this fellow!"

"Don't drink that mess! I know it's poison. It must be!"

"We have antidotes." She raised her voice. "Tai Ching, you have occult power, you tell us. Recite *mantrams* while I drink. You do not need your sword. My friends, dozens of them, have promised you your life if any harm comes to me—they have promised not to kill you. They would tear you to pieces this moment if I asked them to. But I spare you."

"Get out of my sight! Get out of here!"

"Easier for you if I did. Start reciting; make good or get out!"

But for that which drove him, Tai Ching would have quit. He glanced over his shoulder. He gulped. He licked his lips. Overcoming his qualms, he began to chant sonorously, with only a few quavers.

Mei Ling drained the cup. She flipped it to the tiles and grimaced. Then, as elegantly as a dancer, she turned slowly, feet scarcely moving as she pivoted. She joined Tai Ching in his chanting, until he ran out of words and out of breath.

"You see? He must be a good man—I spoke the same words he did, and he didn't turn into a fox. And I didn't."

Tai Ching yelled in fury. Teeth bared, he snarled. His hand twitched. Li Fong tried to thrust his wife aside. "He's crazy—dangerous—get away, you've won—"

"He's not beaten yet." She nudged Li Fong toward the priest's table. "You finish him."

This was the final prod. Tai Ching snatched his blade. He knocked a spectator off balance in his haste to get clear of the table.

Mei Ling cried, "*Silken hands!*"

Li Fong swished aside the folds which muffled the peachwood sword. Silk rippled like the flowing sleeves of an opera costume. He endured an endless instant of utter helplessness and fear as he tried to recall his practice and study of weapons, of attack and of defense.

Tai Ching's gleaming steel reached out as he stamped and yelled.

Even in the brightness of the court, the flash which passed from the peachwood to the twinkling blade was blinding-blue. There was a hissing, a whispering sound, the voice of serpent-menace; an acrid odor and the smell of scorching hair and skin. Steel clanged to the tiles as the sword dropped from Tai Ching's hand. He fell across his weapon and lay motionless, not even twitching.

"He'll live," Mei Ling said to the crowd.

From wide-eyed amazement, their expressions shifted to disappointment. This was like hearing a drum-song with a pallid ending!

"Don't hurt him," she said, and turned to the sedan chair. "He's only a fool, the servant of a scoundrel."


# CHAPTER XVIII


THAT evening, after they had set their rice bowls, aside, Mei Ling smiled wearily. "Beating Tai Ching isn't the end of the business—it's only the beginning. Chang Lu has got his memory back again."

"*Chang Lu!*"

"Chang Lu himself," she repeated. "He was in an angle of the wall, coaching Tai Ching. You wouldn't have seen from where you stood. I saw him before I got out of my sedan. Trying to use that loudmouth to turn people against us."

"What good would that do Chang Lu?" Meilan demanded.

Mei Ling shook her head. "He may try to make so much trouble that we'll offer to buy him off."

Li Fong shook his head. "That's not enough, simply making a pest of himself. He couldn't be planning another burglary. He knows we'd have our valuables scattered in too many places for him to collect them. There's only one way—" He checked himself abruptly, then went on, "No, I got off on another tangent—I still don't see it."

"You do see it!" Mei Ling declared. "Why not tell me?"

He regarded her and Meilan, until he finally said, "All we need is some bad luck. A patient dying, and in a way which can be twisted out of shape to make it seem like our fault. Or if there's an epidemic, starting the story going that we created the pestilence to build up business for the herb shop."

"People couldn't be crazy enough to believe anything like that!" Meilan protested. "You and Elder Sister have done nothing but good."

Li Fong gave her a long, dark look. "It's been done before. You're innocent, you don't know much about people out here. They may be different in the mountains where you come from."

"Oh, all right! We aren't used to the folks along the coast. But what could he gain, starting a riot?"

"If he stirred up a crazy mob against us, to break in and murder us, we'd have to pack up our valuables and escape—if we were lucky! Chang Lu would be all prepared to rob us. *Tai-tai*, your thoughts?"

"That came to me when I saw Chang Lu. So I gave you the spirit-sword, to show that you use things stronger than potions."

"I still think a chopper is the answer," Meilan declared.

Mei Ling had a better thought. "Let's have wine, Younger Sister."

As Meilan was leaving the gallery, Li Fong said to his wife, "That was desperate business, handing me a wooden sword to face a maniac with a steel blade. I've been stumbling around in a half-stupor all day. I hope I didn't poison any customer by mistake! I've heard about spirit-swords. What really did happen?"

"You were there, Old Master. What can I tell you?"

"You could tell me plenty! Tai Ching called you a devil-spirit."

"Which makes me one?" she countered, sweetly mocking.

"You have powers. For each of your impossible curses, you have an explanation just a bit too neat. You can't talk that sword away. I felt a blast of force—like striking with a heavy hammer and feeling the shock through the handle."

"So you have to know why?"

"Yes."

"You're as bad as Younger Sister. Always questions! Even if I could explain, what would you do with the answer?"

Li Fong sighed. "Beautiful and exasperating wife, you have made me a great magician in the eyes of a couple hundred witnesses."

"Thousands of people would love to have that reputation."

"But what will I do when someone expects me to work some magic? If I didn't love you so dearly, I'd beat you, I'd choke you. You did something to that piece of prettily carved wood!"

"If I didn't love you so dearly, I'd—I'd—I'd just keep on loving you. All right! I did something to that peachwood. It isn't anything that can be explained in words. It can't be understood with the mind. It is known through a *becoming*, a *being something*."

"So, I am too stupid to understand."

"Respected Husband, you have so much more brain than I have, so much more intellect. But this is not an understanding of that kind."

"Then show me!"

She put her palms together and bowed. "Compassionate Kwan Yin, give me patience! Your questioning presence, Old Master, would rob me of what you call the power."

Meilan returned, bringing the ancient bronze wine jar that Mei Ling had found in the shop of a dealer too dull-witted to realize what he was offering for sale. She filled the cups. The sun was now below the horizon. The very air had a redness which tinged the vapor rising from the wine.

Li Fong and Meilan emptied their cups. Mei Ling set hers down, after barely moistening her lips.

"Drink up, *tai-tai*! After that hard day, you need a few more."

"*Taijen*, this day is not ended. For me, it is beginning."

"You're worn out! What is this business, *beginning*?"

In the court a drum was muttering, muted, so that it was no intrusion.

Mei Ling explained, "I told Ah Sam and Ah Lo to take turns drumming, as soon as darkness fell."

"For a wine-game?" Li Fong demanded perplexedly.

"No, though you and Meilan might try something of the sort. The point is, I don't want the house to seem all asleep. Silence might tempt Chang Lu." She rose, stood for a moment, smooth and sleek. "I have to speak to the spirit-sword. And there are other things to do. So I beg leave to quit your presence. Younger Sister will sleep with you and give back the life and force this day has taken from you."

She did not wait for an answer. They watched her leave the gallery, a shimmering silken length in the dusk.

Meilan refilled the cups.

Li Fong plucked a cassia twig from the flower arrangement and waggled it. "With that drumming we could have a wine-game, but two is hardly enough." He replaced the twig and sighed. "Devils owned this whole day!"

Meilan got up. "Elder Sister told me all about the day." She took the jug and scooped up the cups. Her brows rose. "Or would you like to sit here for a while?"

He regarded Meilan for a moment. She read his unspoken answer and stepped to the stairs which led to the lower level. Nothing else could be as restoring as her body and its femaleness.

They descended into half-gloom. Meilan became a vibrant and luminous shape which he followed into the fragrance, the welcoming darkness of her rooms, just off an inner court. Li Fong wondered whether, as victor in the morning's strange duel, he had not been more depleted, beaten, and battered than the loser. He entered Meilan's darkness and was enveloped and wholly enclosed by it . . . and by her . . .

He sat beside the broad bed in the curtained alcove and refilled the cups as Meilan undressed. Arms and hands made stately *mudras*. Li Fong wondered whether there was magic in every woman . . . but there couldn't really be . . . he was peculiarly favored . . . though he'd never known any other kind . . .

More and more, Meilan was becoming like the mistress, although he had not realized this until now, seeing her undress in dimness unbroken by lamp or candlelight.

In the darkness of the alcove, they found each other on the broad expanse of layered quilts. She smelled like Mei Ling, and her eager mouth had the taste of Mei Ling. But her breast filled his hand in a way that the Number one Lady's did not, and the curve of hip and thigh were not the same . . .

She was not burning greedy, as she always had been. Instead, Meilan was cool, inviting, refreshing, entirely *yin*. He forgot the battle of magic and that moment of facing a bared sword . . . no more worry now about burglary . . . nor about the mob that might storm the Home of Benevolence . . . in the darkness, he began to catch the glow of her eyes . . .

Meilan whispered, finally, "You're relaxed now, like a bow unstrung."

Only now did he realize how perilously near he had come to the breaking point. Strength and life were flowing out of *yin* and into him, leaving him revived, renewed, and enlightened—he had new knowledge, *yang* and *yin*.

"We've never been so close before," she murmured. "While we're this way, I can tell you things."

"Tell me, lovely Meilan, First Woman."

"Elder Sister knows ancient magic. In a way I can't understand, she is making a spirit-servant to guard and help us. I used to sleep with you when the moon was wrong for her. Now her power has to be used for magic. Never think she's quit loving you or quit wanting you."

Her arms closed about him, as demanding as her lips.

The Shang Dynasty wine jug was cool and far from full. So, when Meilan at last slipped out of bed, she had no fear of awakening him. She lost no time picking her way through corridors, which Li Fong had not bothered to explore. She knew her way.

Cheek against the forbidden door, she crouched,

breathless. Even to think too intently might interrupt Mei Ling's mind-power.

"Don't grasp with curiosity," she told herself. "Just attend, only don't fall asleep like the Old Master . . . *aiieeyah!* I needed to be worn out, too . . ."

Poised between consciousness and its opposite, she lost all sense of time, all awareness of cricket-voices, foliage stirrings in the court, and the mutter of the drum. Her hand moved as if without her volition, until the door opened a little.

Mei Ling sat facing a half-circle of joss sticks. A candle in each farther corner picked out the rising fumes and gilded her hands as she made *mudras*. In the crescent of incense sticks, a silvery wavering spindle was taking form. Though still transparent, it became ever more solid, moment by moment. The grayishness became ruddy here, black there. Metallic bits twinkled against a neutral robe.

A stately figure, a stern face, like a mountain crag; neither good nor evil, neither malignant nor benevolent—the face of pure force, impersonal and inexorable, looked through the smoke. Over the apparition's shoulder peeped the hilt of a sword.

Mei Ling recited a *mantram* which Meilan scarcely heard. She was now balanced between awe and terror. Comprehension shocked her.

"She didn't call that spirit. *She created him.*"

Although the apparition spoke, Meilan heard nothing.

Mei Ling demanded, "You are ready to test your force?"

A sign of assent.

"Can you take form without my help?"

The mouth shaped, "No."

"How long can you move with strength?"

Meilan could not read the silent reply.

Mei Ling resumed. "Get one pink lotus bud from the pool of the court of Father Lu Tang Ping's temple. Set it—" She pointed to her shrine. "In front of Kwan Yin."

The apparition turned and stalked toward the farther wall. Stride unbroken, it merged with the paneling and was gone.

93

Presently Mei Ling rose and faced about. She regarded Meilan.

"So much curiosity that you even had to leave the Master?"

Meilan endured the voice and the eyes. "Elder Sister, this is the only time when I can talk to you."

Mei Ling's face softened. She gestured to cushions in a corner.

"Sit down, then, and tell me."

"Did I do any harm?"

"No. And that interests me. Your presence didn't reach out."

"Maybe I am remembering things," Meilan said. "How to be not-noticed. And you could teach me more."

"I'll risk it. But let me warn you. Each time you think of reaching for a chopper, you'll be blocking your own way and undoing some of what you've learned. What did you see during your peeping?"

Meilan told her. She concluded, "He looked like the God of War, only not as fierce. Whatever he had to do, he'd do it without anger or pity."

"You saw clearly. What else was there?"

"He's not like Ah Sam and Ah Lo, not one of the serpent-folk."

"That's right. They are like us. They've always existed. *He* never was, until recently. He becomes more and more. I'm far from done making him complete."

"You really made him? Out of mist and smoke? Like—in the way a woman gives birth?"

Mei Ling laughed softly. "Delivering mists would be a lot easier than what human women put up with. But no! The *tulku* you saw is made entirely of thought, mind, which can't possibly come from that zone of the body! Thought that was projected, solidified, shaped, until it has a life of its own—that's a *tulku*, but its life is never entirely its own."

"You could teach me?"

"Any *tulku* you made would be a homicidal maniac. Sometime I'll give you the basics. But you're at your best in the non-thought department."

"The Master seems to be . . . well, pretty much pleased with that. But he wishes I were you."

"Nonsense! In the dark, he couldn't tell the difference!"

Meilan, making the most of Elder Sister's mood and the occasion, reached for more. "We're in more trouble than you've let on. How bad is it going to be? How will it turn out?"

"I can't read the future. I simply get sensings and feel my way along. That's why I put Ah Sam and Ah Lo to work. I recognized them as serpent-folk, with no special powers, but different from ordinary humans. Mainly because I can trust them. Meanwhile, with the *tulku* and other things, I'll have my hands full."

"I know. And it's a wonder you're not even more absent-minded."

"Absent-minded? Now what?"

"The way you've been telling the Master that I'd be sleeping with him because the moon is wrong for you simply doesn't add up. Why don't you tell him you're pregnant? I know he'd be thrilled."

"He's got too much to think about as it is. I've not even begun to show, and I won't, not for a while. By then, all this devil-fighting may be settled."

"Oh, all right! I'll keep the story straight for you. Tonight you were tired. It was *not* the moon. Let's carry on from the last time you told him that story. From the last imaginary moon. I remember, if you don't."

"Younger Sister, sometimes I really love you! Appreciate you, too. Being human is so complicated that every so often, I'm homesick for our quiet cave in the Mountain of the Gods."

Meilan sighed. "It's lucky I can't get that way, or our lives would be crazy-complicated. Probably I'm not human enough yet."

"Who says you're not human enough?"

"If I were as human as you are, I'd have to be pregnant by now!"

"That's got nothing to do with it, no matter how busy you've been. Any astrologer worth a string of *cash* could tell you that it simply can't happen until your stars and the Old Master's are just right. There's more to it than what I've said; that's only the general principle of it."

"Mmmm . . ." Meilan digested that. "But what would I tell an astrologer—when was I born? A thousand years ago, or five or ten thousand, or that night we became human?"

Mei Ling sternly maintained her calmness. "One of the first things in magic is to learn without asking questions. Now I've got to get some rest, and you'd better be back in bed."

Meilan stepped back, eyed her critically. "Not a trace of showing. But speaking of magic, you always shy away from talking about fire-magic—that's the one I'd love to learn. Is it awfully difficult?"

"No more than the other kinds, such as the Mirror Magic of Master Ko Hung. But it's dreadful, deadly. It could destroy far more than you intended to, including yourself. And even if you didn't blast yourself out of existence from using it, it would be your final incantation, your last spell.

"You'd lose all your other powers, and you'd be just another human being. To make it worse, you'd be loaded with the heavy karma of any mistakes you made in using fire. It isn't fuel-burning flame—it's the cosmic principle, the essence, the source of all fire.

"That's what the Great Dragons impose on whoever shares their power. See why it mustn't be used until there's no other way or help?"

Meilan pondered. "Well, I'd get a lot of merit if I made such a great sacrifice. And I'd be an ordinary human, you said."

"If you managed to live! Now, pay your respects."

They faced the shrine. Meilan put her palms together but did not kowtow to Kwan Yin. She gasped, made a jerky gesture. "Look! *O-mi-to-fu!* A fresh lotus bud—with water drops on it—he did it—"

"The *tulku*," Mei Ling said contentedly, "is a good servant. And *a silent one!* No questions!"

Meilan sidestepped, turned her back to the shrine, and kowtowed to the mistress.

"Don't do that, you little idiot!"

But Meilan touched her forehead to the floor a second time, before Mei Ling could snatch her to her feet. Then she hurried down the corridor to see whether Li Fong had missed her.

# CHAPTER XIX

THE Temple of Father Lu Tang Ping had recovered from the festival. Peanut shells, exploded firecrackers, orange skins, and the stubs of joss sticks had been swept from the court. The priests were in their cubicles, getting a good night's rest. In a cell just off the inner court, Chang Lu and Tai Ching were considering their problems. A peanut-oil lamp lighted their troubled faces.

"Your idea," Tai Ching complained bitterly, "on how to make a fool of that woman and her husband came near to killing me."

Chang Lu's lean face relaxed in a guarded smile. "You shouldn't have lost your head. If it hadn't been for that, the abbot wouldn't have ordered us to get out of here by sunrise."

"You might have found out more before you told me how easy it would be. My head is still muddled up."

"You lived through it. That foxy devil tricked me with a cup of drugged wine, and for a couple of months I didn't even know my own name. What possessed you, calling her a *fox*-spirit? I told you she was a *snake*-spirit."

"I had the feeling that she was a fox-demon. First time I've ever been wrong. I've a notion to dump the whole business. Go somewhere else and start all over."

"Far better," Chang Lu counseled earnestly, "is to stay and win. With the Buddhists undermining us at the Emperor's court, we can't afford to back down." Then, sarcastically, "Or haven't you noticed that they've turned the Son of Heaven against us?"

"You were telling me about some money. Have you forgotten?"

"That was an afterthought. No doubt Li Fong and his wife have been doing nicely enough."

"I don't see how. Not with all the free treatments

and curses. That's what's been spoiling it for the rest of us."

"I still say they're doing well," Chang Lu insisted. "Li Fong sent for his sister and her husband. They were barely making expenses in Hangchow. Now look at the lady! She really dresses, and she's bought some very fine jade, and she has a servant. Her husband isn't earning it. He's only a clerk."

"*Aiieeyah!*" Tai Ching's eyes glowed as his imagination fired up. "We could do with some money. If we could only persuade a few officials and eunuchs at court to favor Taoists again! You'd get back to your soft spot. But how to get at that money? You can bet it's not hidden all in one spot. And the servants never sleep. Music or drumming, all night long. You search the house. I want no more of those devils!"

"That's where you're wrong!" Chang Lu protested. "Those women are serpent-spirits. When they're exposed for what they are, there'll be a panic—a riot—a mob—the place will be wrecked—and when things cool down, the mob will be scared to death to go near the ruins. Then we'll search it with no problem. Simple. Without his wife and concubine," Chang added, "Li's easy to handle!"

"If you had been at the business end of that spirit-sword, you wouldn't be so optimistic."

"I tell you, Madame Mei Ling was responsible for that. Yes, he is clever, but he's no magician. He's just a schoolboy led around by two man-hungry snake-women."

Tai Ching brightened perceptibly. "If the mob does a good job, we might have a chance."

Chang Lu bounded to his feet. "While you were recovering, I was doing some thinking. Between now and the Dragon Boat Festival, we'll get someone to help us. A man with almost the occult powers I have."

"Who?"

"The Number One Buddhist Abbot—Venerable Shen Hui."

"*Shen Hui?* Even for a newcomer, you're crazy! He's a bigoted chunk of turtle-dung. A fanatic. Looting a house is not his way. He is so full of peace-to-all-living-creatures that—that—you just don't know Shen Hui! He's practically a saint, a Boddhisattva."

"And that," declared Chang Lu, squinting shrewdly at his stupid ally, "makes him the man we're looking for. All you have to do is get your story straight, and then we'll see him. As soon as he's back from making his alms route. Sure, we have to be out of here by sunrise, so I'll tell you on the way—"

It was nearly sunrise when they set out.

The White Cloud Monastery was several *li* beyond the wall of Soochow. Pines and cypress surrounded the gray-walled enclosure. Chang Lu and Tai Ching sat in a small pavilion not far from the road which led into the city. From this shelter, they could look out over the parkway to the temple entrance and the adjacent monastery.

As they listened to the chanting of the monks and the *tock-tock-tock* of the "fish head" that marked the cadence, the conspirators ate the rice and meat dumplings they had bought from a peddler.

*"Na mo kwan shih yin po sa . . . na mo kwan shih yin po sa . . ."*

Presently Tai Ching cocked his head. He noted the change of the beat and the reiterated *"Kwan Yin po sa, Kwan Yin po sa,"* which indicated the final phase of the morning service.

After some moments, the yellow-robed monks filed into view. Each wore straw sandals and a straw hat with a brim that reached low enough to conceal the upper half of the face. This insured the downcast gaze which humility required. Bowl in one hand, staff in the other, they set out across the green.

Tai Ching tugged his companion's sleeve. "See that tall one, the one who came out first? The one who walks as if he's proud of how humble he is?"

"The one with the not-lacquered bowl?"

"Yes. Shen Hui."

"You mean that the Abbot goes begging with the others?"

"I told you, he's so holy it hurts him. What can you do with *him*?"

"Please listen carefully—I'll go over it again."

They devoted two hours to planning and to a siesta.

At last Chang Lu nudged his ally. "Wake up!"

Tai Ching sat up and watched the monks returning.

"Their bowls are a long way from full," he observed, and wistfully regarded the little basket of oranges, kumquats, and *lichis*.

"That fruit is for the Abbot. Better get used to the idea of fasting."

"There he is!" Tai Ching exclaimed, pointing.

No mistaking that stately humility.

"In this monastery," Tai Ching continued, "alms are eaten by monks. Not fed to birds and animals or to beggar humans."

They crossed the green and entered the temple. There they made their incense offerings. The monk who struck the gong informed them presently that the Venerable Abbot would see them in the library. They followed him to a passageway which skirted the wall and led to the building at the farther edge of the court.

"Two distinguished and learned Taoist scholars come to knock their foreheads at the feet of Your Reverence. They bring gifts," the monk announced. Then, "You may pay respects."

They kowtowed. The monk presented the basket of fruit.

Shen Hui said graciously, "Please be seated." He indicated kneeling cushions. "You are strangers, newcomers?"

Chang Lu regarded the deeply lined features and intense eyes of the Abbot, the massive, squarish head and face. "I am from Hangchow, Your Reverence. I came to Soochow to consult my colleague, Tai Ching. When he realized that his skill and learning were not equal to our problem, he said that Your Reverence could advise us."

The Abbot fingered the jade beads of his long rosary. "Tai Ching? The talented herb doctor, the disciple of Master Ko Hung?"

"Neither talented nor learned," Tai Ching protested. "Fumbling, stupid."

The after effects of encountering spirit-fire had left him twitching and haggard—entirely convincing.

It was impossible that the Abbot had not heard the entire story of the duel of magic, yet he prompted,

"Please tell me. Except for our begging rounds, we have no contact with the outer world."

"My colleague," Chang Lu elaborated, "barely survived a battle with a spirit-serpent. I was unable to help him. We need your advice."

"Please continue."

"This involves a benevolent and earnest young man, Li Fong, the herb doctor. He gives medicine to the poor and refuses pay. He is well known. Many bless him. No doubt grateful patients have come to this temple to leave gifts for the Buddhas and the monks."

"Yes, I know of him. On festival days, Li Fong sends cooked meals."

"Your Reverence could help him."

"He is in trouble?"

"Most dangerous and deadly," Chang Lu answered. "His wife is a snake-woman. His concubine is a snake-woman."

"It would be better," the Abbot observed, "if Li Fong left home and became a monk. On the other hand, his wife is a very good woman, a gifted healer, a miracle worker. Is it not possible that other healers are ... ah ... unhappy because Mei Ling accepts no pay from the poor?"

"Yes, Your Reverence," Chang admitted. "We are greedy, envious."

The Abbot addressed the monk who stood by. "Fa Ming, you were telling me of a Taoist doctor who quarreled with Li Fong and his wife at the Temple of Father Lu Tang Ping?"

"Yes, Venerable Abbot. The Taoist flew into a high rage. He reached for a sword. Li Fong took a peach-wood sword from his wife and blasted the *tao shih* with spirit-fire."

"Yes, now I remember."

Tai Ching bowed. "I am that *tao shih*. The woman warned me. She told me that my wrath would turn back and go against me, hurt me."

The Abbot fixed Tai Ching with a penetrating look. "You, a Taoist Master, beaten in a contest of magic, and by a woman?"

"I was beaten and humiliated." He touched his forehead to the floor. "I place my head beneath your golden feet. I come to beg your help."

The severity of Abbot Shen Hui's face softened. "There is a simple way of defeating your competitor," he said, smiling benevolently.

"Be pleased to enlighten this stupid person."

"Follow the Noble Eightfold Path. There is room here for you. Put on the yellow robe, take up the alms bowl, devote your days to healing."

This was not going according to plan. Tai Ching flashed a distress glance at his accomplice. Chang Lu said, "Venerable Sir, we must ponder on this. We have the *dharma* of dealing with devils and spirits. This is our nature, this is our Way. Only by sustained and gradual effort can we become worthy of a new Way.

"That is why we come to you. We are envious, greedy, wrathful. We renounce our chance to gain merit. We offer the opportunity to Your Reverence to win merit for White Cloud Monastery."

"It is far from clear," the Abbot objected, "that you had, that you *have*, any chance of gaining merit—so how to convey it to this monastery?"

"Venerable Abbot!" Chang Lu's voice rang with self-assurance. "Every evil has its offsetting good. Each good has its counterbalance of evil! For you as well as for us, enlightenment is that One-ness which goes beyond both good and evil, knowing those opposites to be illusion. With our malice, our envy, our wrath, there was also good. We did not intend good, *but we could not prevent it*. That is the Great Law!"

"Sound doctrine," Shen Hui conceded. "Please tell me more."

"This young man, Li Fong," Chang Lu continued, with assurance that now verged on majesty, "makes many offerings at Buddhist temples and monasteries. He has been generous with his sister and her husband. Two snake-women, Mei Ling and Meilan, tempted him from his work as an apprentice in Hangchow. Since Tai Ching and I have not yet the science to save him from the devil-women, we ask you to save him.

"We offer you this chance. You now have the karma of accepting, or the karma of rejecting.

"Once this serpent-spirit is pregnant, once she has

given birth, she will turn back to her original form and destroy her husband and her child also, drinking their blood to win a further span of youth, beauty, and immortality. This is well known from ancient times.

"Let Li Fong quit his devil-wife and his devil-concubine and become a monk, walking the Eightfold Path."

Abbot Shen Hui's eyes had narrowed. His glance shifted back to Chang Lu, as if for a moment he had had a vision, had seen something beyond the two who knelt at his feet. He was poised on the brink of assent. He was about to speak when Chang Lu resumed his appeal.

"The serpent-woman is becoming a saint. If she leaves now, while she has so much merit, she can become truly human in her next life. Save her."

The Abbot clapped his hands. "Bring tea," he said to his attendant. Then, to Tai Ching, "We must wait until the Dragon Boat Festival to find out what she really is. Then I will decide this matter."

They drank their tea and quit the Abbot's presence.

As they crossed the park, Tai Ching sighed. "That was ticklish business, right to the very end!"

"I told you he couldn't ignore the bait! Converting us, having us put on the yellow robe—well, he'd have his reservations about that, and about us. But saving Li Fong and Mei Ling, he just has to!"

Tai Ching frowned. "We may be sidetracked in this. I still don't think he's sold on us."

"I tell you, it can't miss!" Chang Lu declared. "He's going to need our help, and lots of it, before he's through. Do you suppose Mei Ling's going to be easier to handle *then* than she was when you tried to deal with her?

"Now let's pick a good spot for setting up your herb stand. Between now and the Dragon Boat Festival, we'll have to eat. Especially you."

"And we'll have to do a lot of thinking. Especially you," Tai Ching said somberly. "Did that peddler, over yonder, have any sausages?"

# CHAPTER XX

Mei Ling stepped into the herb shop. "For a wonder," she said, as she set out a pot of tea and a small basket of early peaches, "they've all gone home, and you don't have any customers."

The scales on the counter swayed idly in the warm breeze. Ah Sam was not at the foot-powered mortar. Like Ah Lo, he was busy with chores about the grounds. Li Fong closed his book and selected a peach.

"Old Master, several times, these past couple of days, you've mentioned Abbot Shen Hui whenever we talked about Taoist troubles. Why should he be interested in us? What could he do for us?"

Li Fong flipped the peach pit into the rubbish hopper and managed to get a good bite of the fruit without dripping juice on his tunic. His fingers were not so lucky. He grimaced. Mei Ling handed him a napkin.

"It is something like this," he began. "Some of our customers have been telling me that the Emperor, the Son of Heaven, has turned against the Taoists. There are different stories. For instance, he set the alchemists to work for him. Maybe he expected them to make gold out of cinnabar, or maybe that was a symbolic way of saying that they were to make him immortal, give him divine health, vigor. And something went wrong.

"Or they promised him supernatural powers, just as if being the Son of Heaven isn't enough already! Then there was talk of their overstepping themselves, playing politics and getting too bold about it."

"Politics?" Mei Ling frowned. "Like the Yellow Turbans and that awful revolt?"

Li Fong nodded, eyed the basket, reached, drew back. He was very fond of peaches, but he hated sticky fingers.

"There are too many stories. The Son of Heaven ordered them out of his court. No one was sliced or beheaded." He wagged his head and grinned contentedly. "Which is another way of saying that there are a lot of things ahead for them if the Emperor gets really annoyed.

"And the Buddhists are in again. The Patriarch is in the palace."

Mei Ling poured tea. "If our Taoist enemies become too troublesome, influential Buddhists could settle Chang Lu in a hurry?"

"Something like that. And Abbot Shen Hui is as influential as the Patriarch. Impressive and saintly." He leaned over the counter, glancing up the street and down. "This is a lucky day. Too beautiful for anyone to be sick. While you're resting, you watch the shop. I'll be seeing Abbot Shen Hui, but I'll probably see Sister Moutan first."

He headed for the river, stopping short of the network of canals which served as streets in the lower levels of Soochow. Presently he was picking his way up a series of steep alleys, a few of which were stepped. Reaching a still higher level, he saw the White Cloud Monastery; far beyond it was an ancient pagoda, rising in nine stages, the first few of which were hidden by trees and a vast stand of bamboo.

Li Fong found his sister in the tiny courtyard of the compact house which nestled in the shade of magnolias. Chen, her four-year-old son, knelt at the edge of the pool. He was poking at the goldfish with a stalk of fuel-grass.

Li Fong paused at the entrance and sleeve-mopped his forehead.

"Sister," he gasped, "that slope is almost too much!"

"Brother," she retorted merrily, "if you came to see us oftener, you'd be used to it." Then, as she accepted the small, heavy parcel he handed her: "You're too good to us! It's so nice, bringing this yourself, instead of sending Ah Sam."

"The shop keeps me tied down. And Father Lu Tang Ping's festival didn't help a great deal."

"It made your wife famous—of course I heard all about *that!*" She clapped her hands. "Ying, bring tea."

The *amah* answered, "Yes, *tai-tai.* Immediately."

Moutan resumed. "Someday, I'd like to meet your

wife. I hear so much about her. You'll never know how I felt that morning, when you came racing in and told me about having to leave town in an hour."

"You thought I was crazy, didn't you, speaking of wife and concubine?"

"The things you brought were real enough. Brother, you look worried! You look awfully tired. What's wrong?"

The *amah* stepped into the court to set out cups and a pot of tea. Ying wore a blue jacket and blue trousers. She was small and trim and quick of motion, a sharp-eyed, middle-aged wench.

"Ying, how famous is Brother today?"

"More so than yesterday," she answered, and left the court.

Li Fong said, "The truth is, she has plenty to tell you, later. There is something that Ying has not heard—let me tell you—A *tao shih*, Chang Lu, broke into my wife's house in Hangchow. I caught him at it, digging up some money she had buried. I gave him medicine that blotted out his memory. Just for a while, that is. I thought that would be better than killing him. I was wrong. Chang Lu followed us, and started the trouble at the temple."

Moutan exclaimed in dismay, "*Aiieeyah!* So you really did have a reason for leaving in such a hurry. And now he's trying again to rob you? But you can stop him, can't you?"

"There is more to it than that. After he got his memory back, he must have watched you. And he saw those dresses Mei Ling and Meilan couldn't take along. We went afoot as coolies."

"I just had to show them off; I was so proud of the nice present! And I shouldn't—I should have waited—"

"I was too dumb to warn you. I didn't think of it."

Moutan frowned perplexedly. "But how could he know about me in the first place?" She shivered. "Could he have used magic or talked to spirits?"

Li Fong grimaced sourly. "Once he got his memory back, all he had to do was make the rounds of every herb shop. The things I made him and his friend drink were unusual. When he got to Mr. Sang's place, he would learn that an apprentice was missing. From then on, it would be simple, learning about you. And following you to Soochow.

"What I really want to find out is how many are with him, working against us."

"You mean, this Chang Lu is using Tai Ching—you're pretty sure of that—but you don't know who else?"

"That's the general idea."

Now that Moutan was becoming concerned on his account, instead of being interested only in his recent notoriety, it was time to learn what else she had heard. Whenever two or more *amahs* met, there was an exchange of gossip. This pyramided.

"Sister, how famous is my wife?" He regarded her intently. "Many grateful patients, but how many jealous doctors?"

"Like Tai Ching?"

"Like Tai Ching. If I knew what people are saying, I might not be happy, but we'd know better how to protect ourselves."

"People say nothing but good."

"You're not helping me a bit, not until you tell me all the bad. I can talk with nobody but you. Who else could tell me what *is*? You must say what *is*! Everyone else will say only nice things, nice lies."

"Brother, there's nothing—not really—" Her face twitched. She gulped, choked, raised her hands to her averted face. Her shoulders shook from sobbing. "I can't—it's awful—they say she's a devil-serpent—that she's pregnant—that she'll give birth to little snakes—that she'll kill you—drink your blood—she does so much good till the devil-nature makes her go bad—no warning—"

He laid a hand on Moutan's shoulder, but his hand shook so violently that he withdrew it before she could realize how shocked he was. Steadying his voice, he said, "I asked you to tell me, and you did. No harm, no fault."

She straightened and regarded him through tears.

"You don't hate me for saying this?" She studied his drawn face and watched his color slowly return. "She's really human, really good? But what can you do? Everyone believes such awful things—"

"Even if I killed Chang and his friend, it wouldn't help. The story—just as you said—is everybody's now. Has there been any fear about the harm a snake-woman can do, might do? Do they think she's dangerous to humans?"

Moutan brightened. "No, nothing like that. Just woman talk—such as, is a snake-woman's body like a human woman's—is she cold inside, or is she exciting—or is she just different? Do devil-spirits a thousand years old know things about lovemaking that human women don't? Something fascinating, like magic—so a man wouldn't ever give her up?" She regarded him intently, demandingly. "Is she different from others?"

He was not about to admit having no basis of comparison.

"Mei Ling is a loving wife. All that I know, I learned from her. Otherwise, I'd be an apprentice for years." He sniffed and smiled appreciatively. "You still have some of the perfume she sent the day we left Hangchow. The smell makes me hurry home to Mei Ling." But he paused to add. "If you hear something new, something I should know, come and tell me right away. Particularly if it's really bad."

She regarded him dubiously. "I'm worried—I might go silly and give you false alarms, and she would be worried and—"

"That would be better than being dead or having a mob wreck the house. Promise me," he demanded. "No matter how silly you think it is, you let me know."

She promised.

As he picked his way down from the heights, Li Fong wondered whether cunning and malice could incite superstitious people to mob violence; whether the death of a patient would give Chang Lu his chance; whether Chang Lu would make sure that some patient did die . . .

Li Fong did not like these thoughts which would not stay off the mental scene. A mob, once aroused, would break in, devastate, kill, and after its orgasm of insanity, scatter as a flock of individuals, each appalled by what the others had done.

No doubt at all, Li Fong needed advice and assistance from Abbot Shen Hui.

## CHAPTER XXI

IMPOSING and stately, Abbot Shen Hui kept Li Fong from kowtowing. "Please sit here," he invited, indicating chairs. "Where we can look out across the park." He dismissed the novice who had taken charge of the ceremonial gift and the monastery offerings. "I am happy to see you. We appreciate all that you have done for us."

The squarish face and deep-set eyes glowed as if from an inner light.

"Your Reverence makes too much of trifles," Li Fong protested.

"Enlightenment is the sum of millions of trifles. Your good work at the Hall of Benevolence brings you great merit."

"Venerable Sir, my wife does all this. My part is insignificant."

"Nothing is so small but what it is great in comparison with something smaller. Nothing is so great but what it is tiny in relation to something greater. There is neither great nor small in the vast entirety."

"Nevertheless, Your Reverence, for a race of a thousand *li*, one needs a fast horse. To catch mice, a cat is better. I prepare the herbs. My wife does the healing."

"Possibly you wish to learn how to gain greater merit?"

This was edging out of Li Fong's grasp and control. "My Lord Abbot, your words are jade. Our problem is not to advance, but to remain where we are. We are hampered by people who wish to discredit us."

Monks on their alms routes gathered news at least as handily as did the *amahs*. Shen Hui's pretense of ignorance was not convincing. With elegance, total politeness, he disposed of Li Fong and his problem by saying, "There were even those who mocked the Lord Buddha Gautama. Son, endure these things patiently."

"Venerable Sir, hear me out!" Li Fong's assertiveness grazed the limits of propriety. "A *tao shih*, Tai Ching, has been turning people against us. He's jealous. He hates us because we don't touch the silver of the poor." For a moment he regarded the Abbot eye to eye. "The Son of Heaven set a celestial example when he drove those scoundrels from the palace."

"The Dragon Throne is the seat of wisdom," Shen Hui agreed.

"A word from one as influential as Your Reverence would remind the Son of Heaven that the leading Taoists are not controlling the lower members of their order. That the evils which led to their being expelled from the palace are troubling ordinary people. Venerable Abbot, for you to take action against this Tai Ching and his accomplices would be paying respect to the Son of Heaven. The Patriarch would surely help you."

"I have heard of Tai Ching," the Abbot admitted. "But there is a better way for you to win. You have only to put on the yellow robe, shave your head, and become one of us. You will be permitted to operate an herb dispensary at this monastery."

"Put on the yellow robe? Venerable Sir, I am married."

"Shakayamuni quit wife and son to win nirvana and help all mankind. And he forsook a throne also."

"I'm no Boddhisattva! I'm only Li Fong!"

"A million of million years ago, Gautama the Buddha of this cycle, the revered Shakayamuni of our age, was not even as yet a man. Life after life, eon after eon, he persisted in seeking enlightenment, to win liberation for all creatures from the woes of *samsarra*, the endless Wheel of Life and Death.

"Li Fong, you know all this. Forsake the world, meditate, and do good, in a finer, higher way."

"With so little merit behind me, I have to strive gradually."

"Li Fong, I must tell you why you have no time for gradual action. Your wife is a serpent-spirit."

Li Fong jerked to his feet. "That is nonsense! Slander!"

Shen Hui disposed of unpardonable rudeness by gesturing. "Please sit down. She is beautiful. She is benevolent. But in some hour of carnal desire, she will turn back to a serpent and destroy you."

"I can't believe that! She doesn't eat meat or fish. If it weren't for her, I'd still be an apprentice in a small shop."

"She is everything you say. She is also a skillful magician. Your concubine is a serpent-woman. Two of your servants are serpent-folk. Do as I say, and you will save her from a grievous fate."

"Save *her*? From what?"

"If you live with her until she turns back, all the good karma she has won will be lost. She will have to start all over again. Leave her at once! In some future life, perhaps in her next life, she will be born fully human."

Li Fong had to fight the persuasiveness of Shen Hui's voice, the hypnotic power, the command of those burning eyes. He clenched his teeth and hardened his face. Fists tightened, nails digging into his palms, he wavered between obedience and futile resistance.

"Not true! I won't! I won't!" he shouted.

His cry broke the intolerable power. From head to foot he was quaking, twitching. Growing awareness of what had so nearly overwhelmed him left Li Fong sickened and on the verge of retching.

Sadly, Shen Hui said, "I feared you wouldn't believe. But once you get proof, you'll return to take refuge with the Lord, the Law, and the Assembly."

"If I had proof!" Fire and life returned to Li Fong, and defiance took charge. "Tai Ching tried that and didn't like it."

"I have a better test." Shen Hui clapped his hands. The novice stepped into the room, got his instructions, and went out. The Abbot resumed. "The time for proving will be the day of the Dragon Boat Festival. Many serpent-folk go into hiding because they are in danger of losing human form during the hour or two around noon."

"I've heard *that* one! If she doesn't change, I'll know you're wrong."

"It isn't so simple. There are some of them who have become so well established that they change back only under great emotion. Some regain human form not long afterward, others are unable to."

"Venerable Sir, I'll wait for the Dragon Boat Festival."

The novice returned. He handed the Abbot an onion-shaped jug made of glazed earthenware. It was stoppered and sealed.

Shen Hui resumed his talk. "Finally, there are those who don't change at the Festival, nor under stress. Those are the ones who change at the ripeness of their destiny and destroy lover, husband, child."

"I'm not afraid of her. I'm not worried about myself."

Shen Hui handed him the jug. "Please take this wine."

"Venerable Abbot, some monks do drink wine. But keeping it in the White Cloud Monastery—I do not understand."

"This is Golden Wine. As a medicine, it's not forbidden. No more than is *ng ka pay*. At noon of the Festival, offer your wife a cup. If she drinks and doesn't then and there turn back to a serpent, come back and hear me confess error and humbly beg your pardon, and hers also."

Li Fong hefted the jug. "Venerable Sir, I mean no disrespect. But it is somewhat too much, asking a man to pour from a strange bottle and offer a drink of it to his wife."

The novice was setting out cups. Shen Hui unstoppered the jug, and filled two cups to the brim. "You are a Doctor of Herbs. Drink either, and I'll drink the other."

"Reverend Abbot, be pleased to drain both. Then I'll pour two for myself."

Shen Hui smiled amiably and drank both. "The second," he said in a whimsical tone, as Li Fong refilled the pair, "exceeded the medicinal. But it is lawful, as I propose healing a soul."

Li Fong regarded the jug and noted the characters

112

molded into the shoulder. "No doubt Your Reverence is well stocked for healing?" He drank slowly, savoring each sip. "Nothing harmful. Please accept my apologies. If served warm, this would be even more delightful!"

They appraised each other. Neither wavered. Shen Hui poured tea.

Li Fong took his cup. "I may drink all the wine myself."

They set their teacups on the table finally, and only then did Shen Hui refer to the whimsy of his guest.

"What you give or do not give your wife is your responsibility, not mine. If she drinks and there is the deadly shock which I fear there will be, come back, find peace, do good, with compassion for all creatures."

Li Fong bowed.

The Abbot said, "You have permission to leave, and with my good wishes and the blessing of all the Buddhas. *Gate, gate, paragate, parasamgate, Bodhi, Svaha!*"


# CHAPTER XXII


As the fourth day of the Fifth Moon approached and the city got ready for the Dragon Boat Festival, Li Fong's thoughts centered more and more on his evil hour with Abbot Shen Hui. He found reassurance by saying to himself, "No matter what happens to me, it will be of no account whatever." But this crumbled under the impact of the countering thought, "She has so much good karma, it would be terrible if she lost it."

Memories of those first nights in Hangchow came to life. Those shadow patterns under the skin might have been illusion. Chang Lu's attempt to scare him into dividing the treasure and absconding—simply the wild words of a desperate burglar. The silver serpent's intervention had been too impressive to require any explanation.

"No wonder Chang has snakes on the brain . . .

very well, Li Fong, how about yourself . . . not until Shen Hui put them there . . ."

Time and again he resolved to smash the jug of Golden Wine, yet always wavered. He was aware that a compulsion which had become part of him was staying his hand. This knowledge did not help!

The thing was closing in on Li Fong. His every effort to resist made him ever more the captive of the Abbot. He sensed that in the end, Mei Ling would become aware of his mental disturbance. Before growing unease became obvious to her, he had to obliterate it. There was only one way: drink the wine with his wife and prove the Abbot to be a superstitious old fool, a sun-dizzied zealot. This final clear-seeing, this solidified resolution, strengthened him.

Carnival spirit took charge of Soochow. Boats were readied for the traditional races. Crews practiced. Everyone, from coolie to wealthy merchant, watched the tryouts, estimated the odds, and prepared to bet to the limit. Refreshment stands were set up along the river. Vendors flocked to the city with their portable stoves, their pots, their skewers, their grills. Storytellers, jugglers, and musicians gathered in readiness. Astrologers, *feng shui* men, and Taoist magicians plied their trades—and the whores and sing-song girls were waiting.

For as little as five *cash*, a soothsayer would give infallible information as to the winner of the race.

"The Dragon Boat Festival cures all ailments," said Li Fong, glancing toward the courtyard. "They won't remember to be sick till after the races."

Ah Sam and Ah Lo had been waiting for this pause. The former looked up from the mortar and said, "Old Master, we beg permission to leave tomorrow in the forenoon, for a few hours."

Mei Ling called from the court, "We might as well give them the day off. Right now, they can't tell the difference between ginseng and bean curd. And Meilan asked me, last night, about taking three or four hours off tomorrow, from forenoon till after the races."

"Everyone will take the day off," he declared, precisely as they had anticipated. "*Tai-tai*, let's close shop.

You and I will watch the spectacle. You've been looking tired."

"Old Master also looks tired."

"Yes. Weary of mixing tonics to give the rowers more endurance. Simple, stupid people forget to buy restoratives for heart failure after losing a big bet."

That evening, eating became a laborious exercise for Li Fong. His mouth was dry, his throat was tense. He chewed long and swallowed little. Flute and *samyin*, moon fiddle and the popping of firecrackers, kept him all atwitch.

He said finally to Mei Ling, "Sometimes silence is better than even the sweetest voice."

"Incense, and your library, and golden silence," she suggested.

He went to the Great Book Room to look at a bulb-shaped jug.

He sat, dozing. He awakened every hour, picked up the book which had dropped from his grasp. He would trim the tapers, light another stick of incense, and stare at fine calligraphy again, until his eyes glazed. He nodded, neither awake nor asleep, and less and less able to know the difference between the two.

Breakfast was no easier than had been the previous meal. Mei Ling minced and picked, eating with appetite no better than his own.

"Old Master still tired?" There was no sparkle in her eyes or voice. "Books were dull company?"

"We're both out of sorts!" He thrust aside his bowl of dumplings. "I'm sure you didn't sleep well, either."

"The other night we were just too happy." For a moment, reminiscence glowed in her eyes. "Why don't you go to the races?"

"Let's both go."

"No, you go. I'm not equal to all the noise and the crowd."

She got to her feet, seemingly laboriously. "My stomach is playing tricks." Mei Ling grimaced. "No, it's not *that*! I'll be a lazy bitch and rest awhile, until I feel better."

"And I'll drink wine and sing the Dragon Boat song, and when I'm happy-drunk, you'll get up and sing with me."

He watched his wife skirting the inner court. There was weariness in her gait until, after a moment, she became herself again, straight and beautifully poised.

He got the bronze wine jar, filled it, took it to the kitchen to heat. Presently he carried it to the study and set out cups.

"One for me, one for her," he said to the emptiness, then filled both cups and drained them.

Voices and music reached in from the street and mocked him. Resolutely, grimly, Li Fong kept the cups busy. "*Aiieeyah!*" he grumbled finally. "Forget the whole business and especially the Abbot."

He plucked the strings of a lute and mumbled a few lines about Chu Yuan, the hero in whose honor the Dragon Boats raced. He thrust the instrument aside. As the morning dragged along, his attempted forgetting failed completely.

He stalked out and across the front court and through the shop. Sulfurous fumes of firecrackers stung his nostrils. The rumble of drums and the whang of gongs jarred him. The street was a torrent of screeching, laughing, chattering maniacs. He bought a basket of loquats and early apricots from a peddler, and some oranges. He fled back to the silence of the house.

Mei Ling came to meet him.

"The way you stumbled to the front, I was afraid you were sick."

"I was in a hurry." He thrust the basket toward her. "These look good. They will give us an appetite." He nudged her elbow. "It's quiet in the library. I'm glad I didn't go to the river."

"You *are* twitchy, skipping the races!"

"My music made that pretty clear!"

"It wasn't that bad!"

He grimaced. "Bad enough."

She seated herself at the table, laid a hand on his wrist.

"Old Master, something's worrying you. Always, when we have one of our happy nights, you float with feet off the ground all next day."

"I taste trouble. It's in the air." He gave her a long, dark look. "So do you. And when you send Meilan to sleep with me because you're tired, I wake up and hear you chanting."

"When I'm too tired to sleep, a *mantram* brings rest."

He swished the wine jar, thrust it aside, and snatched the earthenware jug. "Let's drink up and relax!" He filled both cups, without spilling more than a few drops.

She raised a hand. "Old Master, I don't feel quite right. Drink up!"

"I've been at it all morning. Each cup is darkness. Take a few with me. Maybe we'll tell each other what's beating us both down."

"But I shouldn't," she protested, and patted her stomach.

"Long time yet. There's many a drinking ahead of us."

"I'm all squeamish today. Take both and pretend I took one with you."

"That's what I've done all morning. It's like all the rivers running into the sea, and the level never rises."

"Is it Festival wine?"

"I didn't get it for the Festival. It's been sitting around here." He drained his cup. "Anything today is Dragon Boat wine." He poured himself another. "One more, and I'll fall on the floor. Take one and fall with me!"

"Old Master, you wouldn't want all our loving, all our happy nights, to end in a miscarriage!"

Devils prodded him. He grinned across his raised cup. "You're a miscarriage. I'm an abortion. Drink up, *tai-tai*!"

Mei Ling raised her cup. "May you live long enough to know how much I've always loved you. Ten thousand years, Old Master!"

He drained his drink. He dropped the cup when he saw his wife empty hers. He had almost snatched her wrist to check her. Then the devils drove him again. He grabbed the jug for a refill, spilling as much as he served. He swayed a little, then recovered.

Mei Ling dropped her cup. Porcelain shattered. She was now on her feet, clutching her stomach and doubling as if from cramps. She gagged, retched, choked.

Li Fong shoved the table from him, steadied himself. He reached for her arm. She thrust his hand aside.

"I'm awfully sick!" She swayed. "I'll be all right—no, *don't*." Her voice rose, shrill, screaming. "I can't—I won't have you see me puking and spewing—*don't*—"

Mei Ling raced from the room. Li Fong stood, blinking, gaping stupidly as he watched her cross the court, clutching her belly, weaving, stumbling, but recovering each time.

After a moment, he ran to the front, making for the shop. The previous day he had compounded potions for several pregnant women who vomited so violently every morning that they couldn't guess which would first empty itself, stomach or womb.

Nothing to infuse, nothing to steep. He grabbed the jar of medicine and ran back to overtake his wife. "I'm a stupid turtle-child, playing in this way—if I ever see that old bastard again, I'll tear off his leg and shove it down his throat—*o-mi-to-fu!*"

He stumbled and fell but did not break the jar. He lurched across the threshold of Mei Ling's bedroom, tripped, and recovered. No amount of wine could entirely destroy his innate balance, but he had come somewhat too near the border. He was relieved when he did not hear that horrible choking and retching. He was glad that there was no trail of vomit from threshold to sleeping alcove. Her sea-green gown and her slippers lay in a tangle on the floor.

He snatched the curtains, flung them apart.

Li Fong saw, but could not understand the seeing. Time sense and vision were tricking him. Space and dimension were all awry. There was Mei Ling, stripped bare and staring sightlessly. There was also a silver-gleaming snake, terrible in its beauty. Though he saw them as things separate, they were also in the same space. He snatched a chair, to strike the monster which enveloped Mei Ling. He dropped the chair. He could not tell which was woman, which was serpent. The body he had so often caressed was merging into the scaly coils . . . human flesh became ever more misty as the monster became dense in that blending, a transfusion—yet for an instant, it was at once Mei Ling and a python.

The last clear awareness Li Fong had was his own yell, an inhuman sound, as shocking as all that he had seen.

There was no longer any remnant, however nebulous, of Mei Ling. The gleaming serpent in her bed was entirely alone.

## CHAPTER XXIII

MEILAN returned from the Festival before Ah Sam and Ah Lo. Silence welcomed her after those tense hours of hiding in a hillside grotto, wondering whether mid-day magic, the curse of the serpent-folk, would dissolve her human frame. It had been worse, the first time, but this had been grim enough.

There was plenty of silence.

Meilan wagged her head and smiled wisely. "Nothing else to do, and all day to do it in. Now they're having a siesta."

She entered the inner court. The odor of wine drew her glance toward the library. Fragments of a cup lay in a half-dried pool. They hadn't been wasting their time. She hefted the bronze jar. Just about empty.

She moved on, not pausing until she saw the little jar in the doorway of Mei Ling's apartment. She picked it up and sniffed. "Smells like medicine . . . prescription jar . . . doesn't look like fun at all!"

She stepped into the room.

Li Fong lay on the floor. His eyes were closed. His color alarmed her—grayish-bluish. She cried out, knelt beside him. His breathing was barely perceptible. There was hardly any pulse.

"Sister, where are you?" she called.

There came an echo-distorted answer, a thump, as of one falling, and a cry. Meilan sprang to her feet. "Here—in your room—hurry!"

Eyes wide and unfocused, Mei Ling raced in. She

was bare to the skin. Her hair streamed. She stood there, blinking and panting.

"What—what—" The eyes focused. "Where—".

She saw Li Fong and began to understand. "Scared to death. Like that holy monk," she wailed, and knelt beside him.

Meilan snatched a robe. Mei Ling observed his breathing and pulse. Finally she got up and slipped into the garment Meilan held.

Meilan took her by the shoulders. "Sister—is he—will he live? What happened? He saw you changing?"

"I was frightened half to death myself. Be back in a moment!"

She hurried from the room. Meilan put a cushion under Li Fong's head and spread a quilt over him. She chafed his hands and fancied—hoped—that color was returning.

"Old Master," she moaned, "we're bad joss."

Mei Ling returned with a small jade vial and a porcelain spoon.

"That's right, raise his shoulder a bit higher."

She poured half a spoonful of the aromatic, ruddy-orange spirit and trickled it, bit by bit, onto his tongue. He did not swallow, but neither did he choke.

"The elixir is helping," Mei Ling whispered finally, and handed Meilan the spoon. "Pulse is a shade better. Give me a hand. See if we can put him on the bed. We can't wait till Ah Sam and Ah Lo come home."

Dragon Boat festivity mocked them as they made Li Fong comfortable, if indeed the idea of comfort could have any meaning for one so lifeless.

"Shall I get a doctor? You're too worried."

"This is beyond doctors. I've got to think." Abruptly, Mei Ling leaped from her chair. "I'm going to the sanctuary room. If there's any change, tell me right away. If Ah Sam or Ah Lo or anyone else asks for the Master, say that he is sick and must not be disturbed."

At the door, Mei Ling paused. "Don't give him any more elixir. But a few drops would help you."

"You're going to speak to the gods?"

Mei Ling sighed. "If they've not forgotten us!"

Meilan took a scanty quarter spoonful of the elixir.

It was bitter, spicy, sweet, and sour all at once. The contradiction of tastes was complicated by aromatic herbs—hot, savory, fragrant. She puckered her mouth, licked her lips.

"Good joss," she decided. "Even the smell gives life."

She knelt beside the bed and slowly wafted the sticky spoon past Li Fong's nostrils. She saw no trace of animation . . .

"How could she turn back when I didn't, this devil-day?" Meilan recalled the reek of wine in the Great Book Room. "What did she drink?"

She poured three drops of elixir and bird-pecked them with her lips and tip of tongue, coming away with a spot of pungent syrup. She bent over Li Fong, daintily lowered her puckered lips to his mouth, and made a quick tongue-flick along her lips and his.

"Mistress didn't say not to kiss him. That stuff sinks in."

The veins of his hands, entirely too bluish, gave a hint as to why his face had such a greenish tinge. There was hardly any circulation, hardly any breathing; and so all was bluish beneath his tawny-golden skin.

When Mei Ling returned, she had two books, the *Book of Change* and another. She also had a bulb-shaped, glazed earthenware jug. She was quite pale. Her face was fixed in planes and angles which made Meilan regard her in dismay and wonder.

She laid the *Book of Change* on the table and opened the other at a place she had marked. "This tells us what is, and how to cure him." Her eyes were deadly fierce. "Our trouble goes back to *who* and *when*."

"You mean, what and how?" Meilan suggested perplexedly.

"Shock," Mei Ling went on, "scared two of the souls away. Only the animal soul, the Number Three Soul, stays at home, or he'd be dead. The other two, the higher-spirit souls, can be coaxed back. Remember, I've spoken sometimes of the Mountain of the Gods—I mean that special pinnacle where the Dragon Lords live?"

"Yes. Men like gods. Or gods like men."

"The Master of Dragons has an herb garden. There are a few, very few . . . well, you might call them mushrooms, but of a peculiar sort. A fungus with a smell to bait the soul back. Even if all three had left, this Fungus of Immortality would call them back, unless the body had been damaged. So that's what I have to get, beg, steal."

"Mountain of the Gods? *Aiieeyah!* Three, four months of travel, horse travel and camel travel, then afoot a long way."

Mei Ling nodded.

Meilan continued, "Two of the souls would be wandering far, and the one still left would be lonesome and go to join them finally."

"It's not quite that simple, but you're right enough."

"Three or four months each way—he can't live so long."

"Ordinary doctors would give him three or four days."

Meilan jerked bolt upright. "Your *tulku*—he—it—brought you the flower—rode the wind to go and return."

"He did as I ordered because he is part of my mind. I knew where the garden was and what was in it. I've never been at the home of the Master of Dragons, and the Great Lord. I'll have to sneak in, and search, and outwit the guardians."

"But the *tulku* could carry you."

"Not in the way you imagine. It's part of my mind-will, but it lacks my personal sense, it can't figure things out. I'd have to quit my body." She gestured toward Li Fong. "And become as he is, while you're guarding our partly alive forms."

Meilan began to understand. "The *tulku* would really be you, just in a different form. And if anything happened here to your body, you'd have nothing to come back to. I'd be fidgeting day and night until I fell apart. What could I do, in case of fire or earthquake!"

"There's nothing you could do. After all, the greatest danger is going into the garden of the Lord of Dragons."

"He—they—the Great Dragons—they're really men beyond mankind—they're compassionate—they'd help."

"They—the Great Dragons—they're bound by the Law of the Universe, the Law of Heaven and Earth, of all Buddhas, of all Gods. It isn't law passed by a king or set up by Old Custom. It is that which IS; it's what keeps the All-That-IS going the way it goes, always has gone, always will go.

"The Great Dragons couldn't keep the Law from operating. Their land isn't for humans, nor for our kind. They couldn't wish to break that law, even if they were able to break it."

"That's not compassion!" Meilan flared fiercely.

"If ever you meet a Buddha, he might explain this. Though you probably wouldn't understand, unless you were a Buddha yourself."

Meilan's eyes became dark and wide. "So—all you've done may be destroyed. We'll have to start over, through the centuries, if you try and fail."

"There's no help for that. If I can't come back, and if he dies, you'll carry on. You've learned a lot, the past few months."

"You leave me to face something almost as bad as what you go to face."

"I leave you to something worse, Little Sister." Mei Ling cocked her head. "I think that's Ah Sam and Ah Lo coming back. Go and see, and remember what I told you."


# CHAPTER XXIV


MEILAN returned before Mei Ling had completed her divination with the *Book of Change.* "Elder Sister, this is important. Ah Sam and Ah Lo had hardly come into the court when that Abbot, Shen Hui, was at the door. He must have been waiting for someone to come back from the Festival and let him in. He's awfully anxious to see the Old Master."

"What did you say?"

"I said I'd ask the Master. I had a feeling that he's bad joss. He gives me the creeps. You deal with him."

"You didn't say the Master was very sick?"

"No. I had a feeling that you ought to handle him."

Mei Ling fingered the bulb-shaped jug. "That was good sensing." She got up, took the jug. "I'll wait in the Great Book Room. Let that devil in the yellow robe think he is going to see the Master."

Once in the library, she opened a book and held it as though squinting in the dim light. Presently Meilan came in to announce: "Old Master, the Venerable Abbot, Shen Hui, honors you with his presence."

Staff in hand, stately in his robe, Shen Hui entered. In his eagerness, he so far forgot himself as to speak before the figure in the shadows got up to pay respects.

"Master Li Fong, what happened? Did you give her—"

The sitting figure rose into better light. The folds of the open book were lowered, exposing Mei Ling's deadly face, her biting eyes. The Abbot's mouth gaped. He chewed air, making sound without words. Finally he contrived to speak.

"I came—the maid told me—" He glanced over his shoulder. "Where is Master Li Fong?"

"Please be seated, Reverend Sir. Master Li Fong's cow-clumsy wife has the honor of welcoming you. My uncouth husband is ill, and should not trouble your Venerable Presence with his sickness."

Shen Hui seated himself. He leaned back, grasping his staff. When he remembered the proprieties, he straightened up and placed his hands fittingly. "Madame Mei Ling, your distinguished and learned husband's illness distresses this humble servant of the Buddhas most deeply."

"Thank you for your profound concern." She took the bulb-shaped jug. "This tonic-wine has the seal of the White Cloud Monastery. It is the cause of my husband's illness."

"How can that be? It would—ah—effect a serpent-woman, such as yourself. Not a human being."

She clapped her hands, and called, "Younger Sister, please get lights. For the Master's room, and for this one. And tea for the Lord Abbot, here." She addressed her visitor: "Venerable Sir, you are known for wisdom, great devotion, great benevolence. Your sincerity is beyond question."

Shen Hui bowed. "To deserve such words has been my life's aim."

Despite her fury, she knew that this was honestly spoken.

"Venerable Abbot, this medicinal wine has done great harm. I fear that my husband will not live."

"You didn't kill him?" He raised a hand. "I know your kind. No evil intent, but your inner nature, the law of your being."

She said not a word until Meilan came to set out lights.

"Please follow and see for yourself." She led the way along the verandah skirting the inner court and into the taper-lighted bedroom. "Look closely! Yes, he still lives. You understand medicine and magic. Shock. Coma. Two souls frightened away, and the animal soul is too lonesome to linger very long. This is your work."

"I did not intend this. " His eyes leveled, his voice steadied. "I told him what you are. He would not believe. I gave him the Golden Wine for you to drink. You changed, as I told him you would. Naturally, he was seriously shocked."

"His death is your karma."

"Please consider a correction. This is, will be, *his* karma for living with one of your kind. He rejected spiritual advice and then was not able to face the terrible facts. He gave you the wine. I did not."

"You have won great merit," she said with low-voiced bitterness. "Be happy!"

"I pointed out the way to enlightenment."

"You didn't suspect that seeing me change would kill him!"

"I knew only that seeing you as a serpent would make him quit you and devote all his great talent to serving humanity. I knew that if he quit you before you did him harm, you would keep all the merit you have won so nobly these many months."

She was thinking, *This pious old fool, this yellow-robed devotee, actually believes from the bottom of his heart what he says!* She sank to her knees, kowtowing. "Three times I bow to the Boddhisattva!"

"You must not kowtow," he protested earnestly; he reached out to raise her to her feet, but drew back his hand, as if afraid to touch her.

"Living among spirits and devils for a thousand years, maybe ten thousand," she cried, "I have never met one who killed, caused to be killed, and believed he had won merit."

He raised his hand, calling Heaven and Earth to witness. And then: "I can revive him. He will be unharmed. His wits will be normal."

"Lord Abbot, in your mercy, do so! And forgive my words of anger!"

"Madame Mei Ling, there was no offense. I will revive him. Swear and promise that you will quit him, cut your hair, and become a nun, devoting yourself to good work."

"Compassion for sale!" she flared fiercely. "Keep it! You're a spiritual whore! I'll seek the mercy of the Dragons of Wisdom. I'll go to the Mountain of the Gods."

"*You?* Under the Great Law, you'd be destroyed."

"Under that same law, I'd be destroyed by your terms. If you had ever slept with a woman, even a serpent-woman, your mercy would not be so deadly. Out of love, I'll face the Master of Dragons and get either the Mushroom of Life as his gift—or death, not from him, but through the Law. That is better than what you offer."

"I'll ride the wind and warn the Dragon Lord that you're coming to steal the Fungus of Immortality. Neither humans nor devils nor spirits are allowed to take it, not from *that* garden."

"I bow again to Supreme Compassion. Tea is in the library."

He followed her.

She filled the cups. "Please drink, Lord Abbot."

"Please think before it is too late."

He drank the ceremonial cup.

"I beg Your Reverence to think." Then, haughty as an empress: "You have my permission to depart. Meilan, please guide the Lord Abbot."

Once Shen Hui was out of hearing, her imperial

poise fell apart. She crumpled, sprawled across the table.

"*O-mi-to-fu!* I didn't have the sense of a serpent, nor the sense of a human! One or the other, I should have known better than to drink—all wrong, all wrong, all wrong!"

The convulsion of sobbing wore itself out. Emptied of a parcel of misery, Mei Ling straightened and grasped the arms of her chair. Presently she opened the book of Master Ko Hung—doctor of medicine, of magic, of alchemy. Nothing in the ancient volume was new to her. The best she could hope for from reviewing it would be the revelation of some hidden hint, some indirection which in her extremity she might perceive.

Presently Meilan returned. They went into the room where Li Fong lay, inert and unchanged.

"Elder Sister, can that turtle-child help the Master?"

"He believes he can. He doesn't doubt that I can ride the wind and go to the Mountain of the Gods. He is sure I can't deal with the Dragon Lords or sneak into the garden and loot it."

"Could you?"

"It's as dangerous as he says. If I didn't come back, he'd be in a position to command Li Fong. That fanatic is dangerous. In his own way, in his own terms, he is working for the good. He has power, never think he doesn't."

Meilan regarded her intently. "I said, a long time ago, that you really loved the Old Master. Let Shen Hui revive him. Then change your mind about becoming a nun. Instead, pay an indemnity, or have some girl go in your place. After all, a man sentenced to death can get a substitute, if he bids enough. The law is content."

"Younger Sister, we aren't dealing with human law. Karma is not outwitted or settled by offering a substitute. There's more to it than breaking or keeping a promise."

Meilan snatched her arm. "Don't be so spiritual! Or you'll be a female Shen Hui, right now, in this life!"

Mei Ling halted the debate by checking Li Fong's

pulse in seven critical spots. Finally she said, "No change."

"Let me stay here and watch," Meilan proposed, "while you go to your sanctuary room to speak to the gods."

## CHAPTER XXV

MEI LING was gathering up her two books when Ah Sam came in to announce, "Mistress, a Taoist priest is anxious to see you. The spirit-sword didn't kill him. Maybe next time, better luck?"

"Tai Ching wants to see *me*? He didn't ask for the Old Master?"

"He did not ask to see the Old Master. He wants to see *tai-tai*."

"Take him to the Great Book Room." Then, to Meilan: "What's your guess? These visitors—it's all just too neat."

"Maybe this tells us something, Elder Sister. First, one comes to see The Master; next, one comes asking to see you. If they were working together, the second one would not be so stupid, coming so soon. If they are working against each other, this is good joss."

"Tai Ching must know as much about this as the Abbot. You stay out of sight, but listen and look."

Mei Ling went to the library. Her waiting was short.

The *tao shih* came in, bowing. His eyes were alive and eager, under his shaggy brows. "This time, you and I meet in peace. You proved your power. Now let me prove mine—for doing you some good."

"Who says I need any good from you or anyone else?"

"The spirits of earth and water tell me that Master Li Fong is in a deep trance. He is dying."

"Bad news and grief ride the wind."

"Good news and joy come quickly after," Tai Ching countered. "With medicines, you are supreme. I deal with spirits. Yes, I was jealous, and I learned that this was evil for me. Now I will help."

"Your friend, Venerable Chang Lu, will also help and share your merit?"

"He is my comrade in penitence, but in this I am alone. It is better he does not know that I am helping you." The *tao shih* grimaced sourly. "His advice made too much trouble for me."

"What can you do—how can you help me?"

"I can revive Master Li Fong. The Venerable Abbot is a saintly man, but his terms are too harsh. Why should your husband leave the Red Earth and go into a monastery?"

"The Abbot has taken you into his confidence?"

"Sure he has! He had to, otherwise he couldn't have consulted me. He wanted to learn more about serpent-folk and spirits. I didn't know what he had in mind or what he planned, not till he explained. Being so zealous, he apparently went further than he intended. He's much upset!"

"So he wants you to help him undo the damage?"

Tai Ching regarded her with smiling frankness. "No, *tai-tai*. He doesn't know I'm helping you. He wants to do that himself, without sharing merit with me. Do not tell him about me. Don't mention me at all. I'll set things right. I'll get Master Li Fong back to full health, his mind and wits all as they used to be. Pay me one hundred thousand *taels* of silver, after he's cured."

"Bargaining with grief!" Mei Ling cried. "If I had a hundred thousand ounces, you'd haul the silver away in a cart, and I'd be waiting here for nothing at all! Grief hasn't left me silly."

"I said, pay when your husband is cured. Deposit the silver with any banker. Give him a written order not to pay me until Master Li Fong is clear-witted, all-one, looking natural, acting natural."

She closed her eyes and pondered. "You're still at the temple, the one where we met?"

"Yes, *tai-tai*. My Venerable Superior ordered me out, but because I pleaded and promised to do no more rude things, he let me return."

"I need time to borrow here and there, giving the Hall of Benevolence as security. To sell jewelry. By then, it may be too late, even if I could find so much money."

Mei Ling choked, raised her hands to her face. "You with your smiling greed! If I deal with you, and you don't cure him, it may be too late to take the Abbot's offer. I'd better see what he can do. If there's nothing accomplished, I could still try your magic."

"*Tai-tai!*" he exclaimed, clearly disturbed by the prospect of competition. "Don't waste time with Shen Hui! He doesn't have my power. I have the Way, the knowledge."

"If I could only believe you! Can't you see I'm at my wits' end—I'm ready to scream till I go crazy!" Her voice rose to a pitch which proved her words. "I'd go wild, trying to haggle, bargain, speed things up. Everyone would take advantage of my trying to raise quick money—they would be as greedy as you, and I'd never get a hundred thousand *taels!*"

"But you haven't spent all that wealth you had back there."

"That's Chang Lu speaking, that devil! What he saw, that burglar, wasn't as much as he thought, and it went into the Hall of Benevolence! It takes a pot of treasure to buy a house this big! And it cost a lot to move my sister-in-law and her husband to Soochow and buy him a job. And I had to hand out presents to the prefect and to all the monasteries and Taoist temples so that I could go into business without too much local objection. And now the Buddhas have forgotten me. I'll go to the Abbot, I'll be a nun! I've had nothing but grief, being a woman! *Aiieeyah!* Grief! Misery!"

The rising pitch of her voice made the *tao shih* grimace and shudder.

"*Tai-tai!* Don't deal with the Abbot, that fanatic! Imagine, cutting your hair! I knock my head against the floor. Forget what I said about a hundred thousand *taels*. Listen to a new idea—"

Hysteria subsided. "Yes?"

"Sign a contract giving yourself and your maid to me, as wife and concubine. I'm not afraid of you. I understand serpent-folk, and they can't hurt me.

"Ten thousand *taels*, and a half interest in the Hall

130

of Benevolence. Your husband will keep half. He'll be grateful for the noble sacrifice that saved his life. You'll be revered as the supremely dutiful wife. They'll make up drum-songs about your nobility."

Mei Ling appraised the *tao shih* from head to foot. "If you returned to the Red Earth and got some decent clothes, you wouldn't be at all bad," she admitted. Relenting a bit more, she added amiably, "In spite of a violent disposition, you do seem to have a nice personality, and I see now that you can be reasonable and a man of good will."

"Distinguished and talented lady, we met as enemies, which was our great misfortune. You're so right! Already I'm improving with acquaintance. We could have a very good life."

"I really do have to think a bit more."

Tai Ching beamed. "Haste would be improper."

"Since you're still at the temple, I'll send word this very night. Perhaps in a few hours . . . yes, sit and wait in the court for my servant." She clapped her hands. "Meilan, go with Venerable Tai Ching to the gate."

As he turned to follow Meilan, the *tao shih* paused to say, "Not a word to Chang Lu. It would be dangerous if he knew."

"Don't worry! I'll send a stupid coolie who speaks a barbarous dialect. Even if he tried to talk out of turn, nobody would understand."

When Meilan returned, the mistress asked, "How does this look now?"

"That turtle-dung believes what he says. What do you think?"

"It looks very much as if the Abbot has one of the Sacred Mushrooms and Tai Ching knows about it."

"How could that be? I'd always heard—"

"Master Ko Hung—" Mei Ling patted the book. "He tells that the fungi are awfully rare, yes. But the Mountain of the Gods is not the only place where they grow. Some have been discovered in Taiwan. That's an island of wild men, cannibals. Maybe every century or so, someone finds a fungus and brings it to the Emperor. For longevity, and for keeping the concubines happier."

"Taiwan sounds as dangerous as the Mountain of the Gods."

Mei Ling continued, "Shen Hui may have got one intended for the Son of Heaven. In that case, he is keeping it as a supreme present, in case the Buddhists lose favor at court. You sit with the Old Master." She picked up the *Book of Change.* "Now I have some thinking to do."

Once in the shrine room, Mei Ling bathed ceremonially. She fired up incense. She laid the Book of Divination on a silken scarf in front of the altar and kowtowed to it three times, as to a superior person.

Mei Ling recalled the words of the Great Treatise: *When it is required to act, consult the* Book of Change. *Do so in words spoken as to a person.*

Once seated on a cushion, in front of the Book, Mei Ling began to realize the difficulty of putting her question into words. The Book was the representative of Heaven, of Man, of Earth, and of the Law of the Cosmos. The Book was more than paper and ink. In its peculiar mode, it was a living presence which would make a statement as to the manner of change operating at the moment the question was posed.

The answer of the Tao, *that* out of which all things came, and *that* into which all returned, would come as an echo; whether relating to the near or the far, there would be a reply, but it would be only as the question itself was—wise if spoken by the wise; folly in response to a fool.

*"How can I revive Li Fong?"* That would be emotional bubbling over, the fluttering of an idiot without a clear thought. The Book would answer in the same way.

*"What will I do—"*

Muddle-witted as before. Don't talk gibberish. Don't even mention, don't even think of, Tai Ching.

*"Can Li Fong be revived—"* Stupid again. Whether yes or no, what could she do with the answer?

*"The Sacred Fungus—seek it near at hand or far away?"* Sober, level; no fluttering, no twitching. She spoke the question aloud, addressing the Book.

This completed Mei Ling's conscious preparation. The act of picking up the coins and tossing them was in the realm of the unconscious, that shadow-land linked to the changing-ness of all that existed.

She noted the three coins. "Each is *yang*. First line is nine."

Thus, throw by throw, she built the hexagram of solid and of broken lines, the former *yang*, the latter *yin*. The resulting pattern was called "*Chan, Thunder, the Arousing.*"

She read the Judgment, the Image, the Commentary.

"*Shock brings success . . . In fear and trembling the superior person prepares for whatever may occur. He looks within himself to see whether in his heart he is harmonious with the Tao or whether he asks what goes against the nature of things.*"

This gave Mei Ling a cruel moment. She read on: "*Six in the third place, shock makes one muddle-headed. But if shock drives one to action there comes no harm.*" And then: "*Six in the fifth, shock strikes here, there, everywhere. There is danger. Still, nothing is lost.*"

She clenched her teeth and glared at the Book. "As if I didn't know a thing or two about shock!" Her exasperation subsided. "Looking within—to see whether I reach for more than the Great Law allows. Shock has been striking *here*, yes. Now some shock *there*, just for a change. And where is *there*? Let's see, now . . . shocking the Dragon Lords in their home, in the Mountain of the Gods—quite too much to attempt! That leaves nobody but those turtle-children who came to deal with me. So a shock for the Abbot, and one for Tai Ching."

She got up and kowtowed to the Book. She wrapped it in the silken scarf. Having taken her portion of shock, she was moving now to distribute some to the enemy.

# CHAPTER XXVI

WHEN Mei Ling came out of the innermost room, a misty, grayish figure followed her. Though of human shape, the *tulku* seemed to glide rather than pace. Although it appeared to wear jacket, trousers, and coolie hat, the apparition and its garments were of the same, ever-varying substance, now dense and dark, now fragile and translucent. Instead of changing direction to follow its creator as she skirted the court, it merged with a column, flowing through the lacquered wood as well as around and about it, and resumed its original shape.

Meilan jumped to her feet and cried out in alarm when she saw what followed Elder Sister into the room where Li Fong lay.

"You've seen it before," Mei Ling said reassuringly.

She carried the peachwood sword, wrapped in folds of silk. The spirit-weapon was in a scabbard fitted with cords, for suspension from the shoulder.

"Is he—is it—going to watch with me?"

"No. I'll need it where I'm going."

"How about Ah Sam and Ah Lo?"

"You might need them here. We may hear from Chang Lu. Odd if he didn't figure this to be a good time for troublemaking. Now get me some of Ah Sam's clothes, and some of that stain we put on when we sneaked out of Hangchow. But first, the writing kit."

As soon as she had set out ink slab, brushes, and paper, Meilan went to borrow a suit of coolie clothes.

Mei Ling brushed three columns of ideograms.

She checked Li Fong's pulse at each of the critical areas. She dripped three drops of elixir on his tongue. "Old Master," she murmured "if this doesn't work, I'll go to the Lord of Dragons. If I don't come back—" She choked, then went on, "After many lives, we'll meet again—we'll both be human—don't try to find me in the serpent-spirit world. I'll find you in this world."

The *tulku* was thinning, wavering. Through it she could read the verses of the wall-scroll. She composed herself, drawing deep, slow breaths. The figure solidified, the face became sharply defined. Her ally, her other self, was never stronger than she was.

Meilan came in with a bowl and a sponge. She had garments draped over her arm. Mei Ling slipped out of her tunic. She sponged her body with the brownish fluid and stained her face and arms and hands. The tincture dried quickly. She put on the trousers, slung the spirit-sword from her shoulder, and got into the jacket.

"*Tai-tai*, you look all humpbacked," Meilan objected as the mistress twisted and wriggled about until she could button the garment. "Why not wear it outside?"

As she folded the letter she had brushed, Mei Ling answered, "I've written Tai Ching, just in case he forgets what I told him, that my messenger is a stupid hunchbacked slave who speaks a barbarous gibberish hardly anyone can understand. All Tai Ching has to do to win himself a wife, a concubine, and a load of silver is to get the Sacred Fungus. Once he reads the letter, he'll get busy."

Meilan began to see the outline of things. She rearranged Mei Ling's hair, set the coolie hat in place, and nodded. "He'll never recognize you. Not in that outfit and all hunched over. *Aiieeyah!* This will be good! As soon as he gets the fungus, you'll—"

"Younger Sister, I don't know anything. Neither do they. Just watch out for Chang Lu. He's our Number One Enemy."

She left by the secret wicket at the rear. Mei Ling and the *tulku* merged in the darkness of the alley. Leaning on her staff, she stumbled along, dragging her straw sandals. She avoided the wine shops and the stands where cooks still offered dumplings and sausages.

No need to glance back to see if the *tulku* followed. Its perceptions came to her through the psychic link which bound them. She and it were never wholly out of touch, yet Mei Ling was far from certain of the bond between her and her part-self, her mind-without-soul self. There had been practice enough, but that had been like the drill of soldiers, whereas this was deployment for battle.

A patrol of the night watch wasted not a glance on the hunchback.

Torch bearers lit the way for a gilded sedan chair.

"Make way! Make way!"

Mei Ling shrank against a door. Nevertheless, she got a whip slash on general principles. She caught the sweetness of jasmine and sandalwood: a high-grade sing-song girl on her way to entertain a merchant or an official. The whip did not speak again. Apparently the footman had not noticed the *tulku*.

Mei Ling got a reflection of strength from her companion. She had fed it, and it was feeding back to her.

Bit by bit, she strengthened the contact, leveled her mind. Although walking, she was as if sitting and facing the wall in her sanctuary, in a state of attention. Quit picturing Tai Ching! Attention, instead; attention to everything and to nothing, and thus be ready for everything, anything.

By the time she reached the Temple of Father Lu Tang Ping, she was inwardly balanced. She moved harmoniously, and she was one with everything. From the *tulku* she got a sensing from far behind her . . . a wine-sodden fellow lying in an alley mouth . . . two men stumbling across the street . . . inconsequentials . . . nothing was important and nothing was unimportant . . .

Mei Ling shuffled into the court. In a far corner, a burning wick floated in oil, making a blob of wavering light. She could just discern the shape of someone sitting on the tiles, his back against the wall.

"You look for someone?"

She stood there, stupid and silent.

"What you want?"

She answered, "Tai Ching."

The man got up. "You want Tai Ching? What for?"

She didn't answer.

"Turtle-child, what for?"

No answer.

The flickering flame, at tile level, made nose and jaw and cheekbones cast shadows which gave eerie motion to his fixed face. His eyes were luminous, terrifying in that floor-level lighting.

"Dung-eater, speak up!"

Mei Ling waggled the message. He snatched it and squatted by the lamp. He squinted at the writing. He looked up, shaggy brows rising. He lowered his glance, and read another column.

"Tell *tai-tai*: will do."

Mei Ling stood like a stump.

"All right, go! Get out, blockhead!"

She didn't move.

Tai Ching reread the message, some of it aloud. ". . . stupid slave does not speak civilized language . . ." He got up and thrust the paper into Mei Ling's hand. "Tell *tai-tai*: yes, can do. Now go!"

He repeated the last in several dialects. Finally, the stupid slave turned and shuffled toward the street. Tai Ching pinched the wick.

Without looking back, Mei Ling knew that her *tulku*, a shadow among shadows, remained to watch. Poised and at attention, she dragged her feet. She had no need to look or listen. She was getting sight and sound and undefined sensings.

This was no time for exultation. No time for anxiety. She was fully aware in a way she had never before been. Aware of what? Simply *aware*. Mei Ling could not even give thanks. There was no one and nothing to thank. She had become everything and nothing. Delicately poised on the razor-edge bridge dividing heaven and earth, seen and unseen, she moved away from the temple. Tai Ching had snapped at the bait. Whichever way he went, she would know.


# CHAPTER XXVII


AND now Mei Ling followed her advance guard, the gray shape which could cover a *li* in the fraction of an eye-flicker. She no longer shuffled. Poised like an acrobat, she kept herself in accord with the sensings of the *tulku*.

Apparently Tai Ching was inspired. Anticipation of his prize gave him the smoothness and swiftness of a tiger closing in. He was well ahead when Mei Ling cleared the Western Gate and entered the shadow patterns and moon glamour of the park.

Tai Ching knew what he was doing, where he was going.

Ahead was the White Cloud Monastery . . . Abbot Shen Hui . . . *O-mi-to-fu!* Steady, woman, don't start fluttering!

She lurked for moments in the shadow of an enormous cedar to hitch up her drooping garments. She discarded the straw sandals and dug her toes into the turf to get strength from the naked earth. She reached over her shoulder and shifted the spirit-sword. Then came the sensing. She stretched her legs in long, fluent bounds—

Mei Ling was in the monastery court. The odor of burned-out joss sticks . . . the far-off glow of an altar lamp . . . brooding sanctity, something more conspicuous than anything which the five senses perceived . . . the very presence of Buddhas and Boddhisattvas . . .

The Sacred Fungus should not be plucked until it was to be used. That eliminated the cells of the monks, the storerooms, the Abbot's quarters, and many another area of concealment.

Mei Ling skirted a wall. In its shadow, she entered a farther court. Presently she picked out something dark that moved in the gloom, avoiding moon patches. This was Tai Ching, soundless as herself. In her eagerness she lost contact with her guide. Alone, she picked her way into the court. There she scented jasmine and magnolia, and heard the gurgle of water. A small stone bridge spanned a pool. A miniature pavilion's gilded eaves glinted in a blade of moonlight reaching through foliage. A bird made querulous twitterings. Crickets chirped.

Mei Ling tasted the many sweetnesses of the garden. She caught the scent of hair oil, the smell of garments not too recently washed . . . stale incense exhaled by robes . . . she could almost see him in the shadows. He was pausing and, like her, savoring the air . . .

Mei Ling closed her eyes so that she could hear more clearly and more readily separate the blended odors. She caught a scent foreign to Soochow—

Her heart pounded, came up and choked her. The link between her and the *tulku* snapped. She paused and regained control of her breathing. The invisible bond formed again. Opening her eyes, she now saw, in a far corner, a faint phosphorescence.

As she moved, the alien odor became stronger. It was pungent, a confusion, a contradiction—neither sweetness nor spiciness, neither of sea nor of land. It combined the scent of plant and animal, yet went beyond either. Perfumers had told her that the most elusive fragrance they could blend had to contain a trace of muskiness and of putrefaction, to bring out and to fix the ethereal overtones of sweetness. Now she understood what had been a meaningless explanation.

In the shadows, Taoist lore guided Tai Ching. Master Ko Hung had written of all this seven centuries ago. When Tai Ching finally perceived Mei Ling, each was no more than a long stride from the fungus. It glowed, bluish-white, in a sheltered corner near the trunk of a magnolia. The scent was now dizzying. The aroma stung Mei Ling's nostrils. She could hardly keep from sneezing.

Tai Ching started. His teeth gleamed in a snarl. He gathered himself to lunge. He reached out—

A blur of motion. Two figures blended.

Mei Ling fell with the attack. Off balance, Tai Ching lurched. Her hand flashed in a cutting stroke. The edge of her hand had the impact of a chopper. Tai Ching crumpled, rolled as limp as a bag of rice. Unfortunately, he splashed into the pool—a loud splash. Bungling as usual, he'd forgotten that some women had mastered *kung fu*, weaponless defense.

In the passages of the monastery, voices echoed. One was all too familiar; Abbot Shen Hui was in charge. Something had gone awry, well before Mei Ling ran afoul of Tai Ching.

Light reached into the court. A torch flared. The phosphorescence of the fungus dimmed. It shimmered, instead, like a peacock's vesture. Mei Ling flung herself toward it, uprooted it.

Monks followed Shen Hui. With him was that thin-faced Chang Lu. His head was shaved. He wore Buddhist dress.

"As I told you," the former *tao shih* was saying, "this was to be expected." He pointed toward his accomplice, still floundering in the pool. "He expected it, but didn't have sense enough to warn us. The stupid fellow must have wanted the merit of stopping Madame Mei Ling himself."

Shen Hui halted. "Serpent-spirit, you do not belong here!"

Majestically, he gestured. The monks fanned out, forming a half-circle behind him. They were bewildered, blinking and squinting.

On her feet now, Mei Ling counted the odds. The Book had told her of shock. Here it was, and more than enough.

Shen Hui spoke to a monk. The man hurried away. The Abbot commanded, "Return what you have stolen. I will revive Li Fong, and you will be bound by your acceptance of his life. You will cut your hair."

Fury and tears choked her. The power had left. She whipped out the spirit-sword. The Abbot advanced without hesitation and without haste.

"Avoid the karma of violence," he said gently, and then he chanted: "*Peace to all living creatures. Peace to those that fly and those that crawl, those that walk and those that swim. Peace to the great, to the medium, and to the small—to those visible and to those not visible.*"

"You *sutra*-mumbling devil!" she screamed—and lunged.

Blue fire flashed. Shen Hui did not flinch. "You have no power against me. Accept that which is and go in peace."

The monk who had hurried away at the Abbot's command now came back with a porcelain bowl in which was a sprig of foliage. This he handed to Shen Hui. The Abbot recited a *dharani* intended to drive devils away. Advancing, he made ceremonial gestures, *mudras* formal and stately, sprinkling water to right and to left with the leaves.

"Back, devil-spirit, back to your true form."

The drops which splashed Mei Ling's cheek burned like acid. Her skin crawled and twitched. Instead of changing her to serpent form, the corrosive water stirred innermost depths. In desperation, she reached for and regained the power which had quit her because of her emotional whirl at having the Sacred Fungus within her grasp.

"The sword failed me, and you failed yourself," she declared, her voice cold and level and deadly. "Now we are even. Try again and finish this! Kill me, or I'll destroy you."

"You are stronger than I reckoned, but must you contend with me? Must you reject salvation? Must I destroy you before you commit an evil that will condemn you to the realm of hungry devils for a thousand-million years? To start all over again the long way of becoming what you now are?"

"Destroy me! You're my destiny—I stand here."

Her presence and her voice made the half-circle of monks draw back. Shen Hui retreated a foot-shuffle and recovered. Once more Mei Ling had contact, though she could not see her *tulku.*

"Most benevolent, most compassionate, you come to save all living creatures!"

"Yes. I renounce nirvana until every sentient being has attained enlightenment. I have taken the great vow."

"Destroy me!" Mei Ling challenged. "Join me in the land of devils and spirits. I'll be the second one that you've killed."

"The second?" he echoed, puzzled beyond expression. "The *second*?"

"Finish me before I finish you!"

He flung aside the sprig of herbage and the bowl of enchanted water. He snatched the staff which his acolyte held. He gestured and flung the staff to the ground. It became a dragon which filled the space between them. The creature tossed its head, snorted, and looked back, as if awaiting command. Shen Hui folded his arms.

"I am a Master of Dragons."

The monks fled, Chang Lu with them.

Mei Ling cried, "Kill me as you killed my child! That deadly wine!" She flung open her jacket. "See how flat I am now!" She raised her arms. "He could not live when my body changed from human to snake. Killer in the robe of the Buddha! Spare nothing, spare no one!"

The Abbot recoiled. Out of the shadows, a tremendous grayish form glided between Mei Ling and the glittering dragon. It enveloped the several yards of scaly body. It became ever more dense. Its shape was now neither human nor animal, except for the head, the stern, implacable face. Its form was serpentine, like hawsers of rattan, coiling and constricting.

"First your dragon, then you, you killer of my child!"

The grayish mist became a spindle, upright and in its former shape. A carved staff lay on the ground.

"Master of Dragons, where's your dragon? Fraud and killer!" Her voice followed the Abbot as he fled. "I'm one of the Nagas, the Divine serpents."

Spirit-sword in one hand, Sacred Fungus in the other, Mei Ling walked from the inner garden and through the outer courts, into open space. She moved with magnificent grace until she came within sight of the Western Gate. There she stumbled, falling across the sword, and buried her face in the grass. Sobbing threatened to tear her apart, until she went limp and lay there, inert.

The smell of the fungus recalled her to the here and now.

Mei Ling got to her feet, hung the sword from her shoulder, and went her barefooted way, hatless and hair streaming.

Of a sudden, she flung back her hair and laughed. There would be a thing or two to tell Meilan, about the power centering somewhat below the hips. Being a woman did at times have advantages.

"Learning that he was an abortionist gave that sanctimonious old bastard the king of all shocks! No male magician could have played that one!" She sighed. "Blessed *I Ching*, blessed *Book of Change*, you told me of shocks . . ."

# CHAPTER XXVIII

SITTING in the room where Li Fong lay inanimate, Mei Ling and Meilan regarded the precious fungus. A pot of water steamed on the brazier. Meilan moved as if to touch the iridescent mushroom, which was shaped somewhat like a miniature pagoda, with nine stages of eaves. She drew back her hand.

"Tiny home of the gods," she whispered. "A ladder to heaven. Elder Sister, I'm almost afraid—what if it doesn't work—?"

Mei Ling reached for the fungus. Her hand shook as she held it to Li Fong's nostrils. She murmured a *mantram*. Her voice was like the stirring of air among leaves.

In the silence which followed, she heard Meilan's breathing for a little while, and then there was not even that sound. Moments passed. As if from the warmth of her touch, the exhalation of the fungus became stronger. The rising sun reached into the room. A long, wavering shadow crept toward the edge of the bed.

Mei Ling gestured. Meilan turned away, seated herself on a cushion, and began caressing with her fingertips the head of a small drum. First there was a whispering, a rustling, then a faint ripple as her fingers paced a stately rhythm and evoked small, flat sounds. The cadence changed. The notes became as the echo of far-off footfalls, the dance of Shiva, Lord of Names and Forms.

Mei Ling's lips moved soundlessly.

The greenish-bluish tinge of Li Fong's face changed. Bit by bit, his color became tawny-golden.

"*O-mi-to-fu!*" she murmured.

Li Fong sneezed.

"*Aieeyah!*" Meilan screamed. "Compassionate Kwan Yin!"

His eyelids fluttered. He sneezed, he choked, he gasped, a hard fight for breath.

"The knife!" Mei Ling demanded. "The knife!"

Meilan handed her the blade. Mei Ling made a steady cut, dividing the fungus lengthwise. She put half into a bowl and added hot water.

Li Fong stared without seeing anything. Meilan, seeing his eyes wide open, cried out. Mei Ling made a peremptory gesture. "Don't be afraid—Number Two Soul is coming back—Number One Soul soon will be here."

Daintily, she moved the other half of the fungus about his nostrils. The bared inner substance gave off a tingling fragrance. Each shallow breath drew the exhalation deeper into her body, spreading like fire creeping through tinder. Tears flooded her eyes. Fires of life invaded her brain. With each breath, she knew that Li Fong was absorbing the pungent fumes, responding to their power.

He moved as if to sit up, but slumped. He came near to shaping a word, but stopped short and licked his lips. He made a fumbling reach for something he could not see. Mei Ling caught him up in the crook of her arm.

"Lover, you're back again— Meilan! The bowl!"

Meilan knelt. Shaking, she spilled a few drops of the infusion.

"The Guest Tea!" Mei Ling cried as Meilan held the bowl to his mouth. "Old Master, drink—drink the Guest Tea—the Lord of Shadows gives you leave to depart from his house—make your bow, quit his home!"

He gulped, choked, spewed back some of the hot liquid. He swallowed some. The Shadow Lords had given him leave to depart, but he was not yet sure that he had passed the gatekeeper.

Another gulp. Mei Ling set aside the fungus.

Although his eyes were not yet in focus, there was a sensing and a perception in them. "*Aiieeyah!*" He licked his lips and reached until he touched Mei Ling's cheek and throat. Uncertainly, he fumbled a strand of hair. His nostrils flared, as if seeking to separate her perfume from the overwhelming aroma of the fungus. As Meilan took the bowl out of the way, he caught Mei Ling by the shoulders.

"What—coolie clothes—all dark face—how back in

Hangchow——" Gaping, all bewildered, he grappled with something fighting to reach the surface of consciousness. "What happened—that big snake—I saw—"

He let go of Mei Ling. He crumpled to the pillow.

She had read his face. She knew what was fighting for shape. It was as if that deadly wine were again tearing her vitals apart. In his returning awareness, he was reliving that moment of transformation. It would haunt him. It could not be dismissed as a nightmare or a hallucination. She had recalled him from the shadow-kingdom, but not for herself.

"Let the Old Master rest. Now that he's come back, he needs alone-ness till he's used to his old home."

They paused in the far corner of the court.

Meilan said, "That memory will die. He won't be afraid of you." And after a moment, "Of us."

"Little Sister, I'm awfully, deadly afraid for you and me."

Meilan caught her arm. "Come into the room next to his; we can hear if he gets up. Tell me how you got the best of that dog-fornicating Tai Ching and that old fool of an Abbot! You settled them. You can handle this, too."

Mei Ling let herself be persuaded. She followed Meilan. They seated themselves on cushions against the wall, so that any stirring in the adjoining room would alert them.

Listlessly, wholly without heart, Mei Ling told her story.

"What wonders you did!" Meilan cut in. "That spirit-servant of yours! Imagine, telling you what you couldn't see or hear!" She kept up her chattering interruptions, trying to hearten Mei Ling. "Sister, you're worn out—of course you'd feel low, fallen apart."

Without any feeling of triumph, Mei Ling continued her story.

"*Tulku* couldn't help?" Meilan wondered.

"I was all beaten and scattered. What could I do? I was finished." She choked, recovered from her moment of reliving it. "So I told him to kill me, destroy me."

"Could he—can they—anyone—really kill us? With fire or weapons?"

"I don't know! Destroy our bodies—probably they could."

"So you told him to do his worst," Meilan prompted.

"I wasn't afraid any more. Too desperate to be afraid. What knocked him apart was when I told him what the wine had done. The shock of hearing, knowing, he'd been an abortionist settled the old bastard! The power came back to me, and Shen Hui didn't wait for my next move. But now what can I do? Li Fong doesn't want any snake-woman—I read it in his eyes—it wasn't fright. I'll go back to our old cave in the mountains. You stay with him. He's never seen you changing, you won't be revolting—but *me*! Just imagine anyone making love with a snake!"

"Elder Sister, he can't feel that way!"

"You saw it yourself." She got up. "Make the Old Master a bowl of soup while I get myself cleaned up."

Mei Ling took her time about bathing and dressing. Soaking in the hot tub helped. As she relaxed, she examined her fears and her feelings. Though she could not dismiss her premonition of loss, she was regaining her balance.

With a bitter grimace, she said to the steamy silence, "Sometimes I understand Younger Sister's passion for settling things with a chopper!" She permitted herself one luxurious vision of whittling Shen Hui into bits small enough for broiling on a skewer, but before she got to the actual skewering of the pieces, she rejected the image. The karma of killing a monk was at least as terrible as that of killing a parent.

She got out of the tub and regarded her exquisite body. "This really isn't so revolting . . ."

She had scarcely dressed when Meilan came in.

"The Old Master drank his soup. He's asleep."

"*O-mi-to-fu!* That's good. Now give me a hand with my make-up."

The mirror remained covered. Neither had ventured to look into it. So she set to work with lipstick, and rouge, and greenish-blue eyeshadow, and all the rest. Eventually she'd bait him, coax him back to his earlier memories of her and of their meeting at the lake.

They were almost done when Ah Sam sounded off

from the court: "*Tai-tai!* The Master's sister, Madame Moutan, she wants to see you. She's in a terrible mood—nearly broke in before I could open the gate. This is something bad—I think she's half crazy!"

# CHAPTER XXIX

MOUTAN'S mood had not been exaggerated. Wife and sister-in-law, meeting for the first time, tore protocol to shreds. Each saw and inwardly admitted that Li Fong had done nicely in choice of sister and of wife. There was a blurted-out thanks for the darling-est garments—one of which Moutan wore—and for jewels, some of which Moutan was wearing—and for perfumes, some of which made Moutan smell exactly like Mei Ling and Meilan.

"Old Master's Sister," Mei Ling said, abruptly breaking in, as she knew Moutan wanted her to do, "my husband is sleeping. He had an awfully disturbing experience."

Moutan blinked, gulped, and rearranged her features. "Brother is—ah—*well*? Really all right?"

"He sleeps comfortably, After much worry, much trouble. Something bothers you, Master's Number One Sister?"

Mei Ling nudged Moutan toward the Great Book Room. Meilan was busying herself with refreshments.

"Does something bother me?" Moutan's voice cracked. "My stupid *amah* came from the market, saying Brother is dead."

"My husband is sleeping deeply. Healing the sick wears a doctor out, in about the same measure that it rebuilds the patients."

"That's not the whole story!" Moutan screeched. "It's all over the markets. They say that you're pregnant—going to give birth to snakes—"

"Do I look pregnant?" Mei Ling patted her very sleek belly. "The wise old women who thought they saw that expression on my face ought to look again. You look. What do you see?"

Moutan eyed her intently. "Sister, I'm too worried to see straight."

Mei Ling sat there, serene, immovable—and cryptic.

"Please tell me more," she prompted.

"They say you killed your husband. With magic!" Moutan blurted it out, then sat, gaping, horrified by what she had said.

Mei Ling laughed softly. "They say so much! What else bothers you?"

"There's danger. People are afraid. Scared crazy. There's going to be a mob to tear the house down. To kill you, kill his Number Two Lady."

Mei Ling glanced up; from the shadows in the court, she guessed the height of the sun. "When will this happen? Not before the day's marketing is done?"

"You sit here like Kwan Yin! Calm—calm—*are you a devil?* This is bad, this is not talk—this is crazi-ness—deadly—" She sprang to her feet. "I want to see my brother—*now!*"

Gently, Mei Ling detained her. "Your brother is alive and well. Some hours ago, yes, he was close to death. But there were medicines. An enemy made this thing, and came too near to succeeding."

"Enemy! Brother did only good. Everyone loves him."

"You forget—grateful patients will come to avenge his death. And people who never saw him will kill him by mistake."

"Crazy mob. Fear-crazy!"

"You came in a sedan chair, without your *amah*?"

"She's with my son. I ran, I couldn't walk."

"I wish," said Mei Ling, "that I could talk to your *amah*, to ask her if a man dressed like a Buddhist monk was making the rounds of the markets. A man with a thin, sharp face and biting eyes that look through you. Always smiling-without-a-smile. Thought-ful, benevolent."

"How did you know that?"

"He tried to rob us in Hangchow and came near to killing your brother."

"Let me see my brother," Moutan pleaded.

Leading the way, Mei Ling said, "No talk. Not a word. We mustn't wake him up or he'll get worse, much worse."

They took off their shoes and tiptoed. At the entrance, Mei Ling gestured and checked her. "See? He breathes. He stirs, he's troubled in sleeping."

She guided Moutan by the arm, gently, but ready to throttle her if need be. When they were within a foot of the bed alcove, she detained her sister-in-law. They stood for a moment, listening to his breathing.

Moutan let herself be led from the room and into the court.

"Now you know," Mei Ling said as they made for the reception room.

Ah Sam came in, his face troubled. "*Tai-tai*, too many people are in front of the shop. They're mad about something. Muttering and mumbling. They want to see the Old Master. Maybe I ought to open the shop front and say he will be out soon?"

Mei Ling and Moutan exchanged glances.

"Is there a man dressed like a Buddhist monk? Going around among the people?" Mei Ling asked.

"I saw a shaved head and yellow robe, yes."

"What face does he have?" she demanded sharply.

Ah Sam squinted, closed his eyes. "Thin—sharp—not very dark."

"How does he stand?"

"Like a man of importance."

"When he moves around, what does he say?"

"Cannot hear. Too much other talk-jabber."

"To whom does he talk?"

"To each one, never much to any one, always moves around."

"What kind of eyebrows?"

"Smooth. High points, like this—" Ah Sam finger-tipped his own brows, outlining pointed arches. "Mouth is thin."

"Is bath water heating?"

"Yes, bath water heating. Kettle for laundry boiling-hot."

"Close everything tight. Block the gatekeeper's lodge. Have Ah Lo get pots of water. Heat more water. Get oil and rags and burning coals."

"Number One Lady, the Master has a sword and dagger somewhere, the ones he uses for warlike exercise."

Meilan came running, chopper in hand.

Moutan cried, "Get me one, too. They'll kill us all!"

Mei Ling raised her hand. "This can be stopped before they're near enough to kill or be killed."

She was sure, from Ah Sam's description, that it was Chang Lu who was inciting the crowd. The muttering now reached into the court. The composite voice was gaining volume. Presently someone heaved a roofing tile. It cleared the gate and shattered in the court. Weighing well over twenty pounds, the missile was deadly. Shrill voices pierced the foundation of grumbling, shuffling, and complaining.

Ah Sam announced, "Plenty hot water."

"I'm going to my private room to talk to the Gods. If the mob starts battering the gate, call me right away. Don't wait. I'll come with whatever I have."

Meilan fingered the edge of her chopper. "Bring some coffins. Those idiots won't need bandages."

The muttering swelled to a sullen roar, a sound laced by screeching and screaming. The magistrate's police patrols were by now safe under cover, as they always were when a riot was brewing. The barred gate shuddered. The shop front drummed and groaned and squealed. Another tile smashed against the flagstones.

Then came grunts, gasps, cries of terror from those caught in the surge of the rearmost of the mob and crushed against the barrier. They wanted no more of this, but they couldn't escape the deadly pressure.

Ah Sam pounced upon the tall earthenware jar at the angle of the gatekeeper's lodge and balanced himself. He snatched the pot of boiling water which Ah Lo held. The drenching which the mob front got was an extension of his lithe move. Howls of pain shrilled above the uproar.

Another pot, this one heaved as a monstrous grenade, turned at the peak of its arc, to shower a boiling rain. Peeping through a crack, Ah Lo said, "Trampling each other. More water, quick. *Aiieeyah,* bad!"

"What's wrong?"

"Bringing post, for ramming gate. Get oil, get tongs, quick."

Time was against the defenders. Someone was directing the show.

"*Hu! Hu!*" The grunt was as of boatmen pulling oars in cadence. "*Hu! Hu!*"

With each "*Hu!*" came the thump of the battering ram. A plank bellied in and tore loose at the top, splintering nearly free. Ah Lo leaped from his perch and raced toward the house.

"Ah Sam," he yelled. "No time for fire! Get one axe, one chopper." Still on the run, he banged on Mei Ling's door. "Tell women to run out by the back! This is bad! Go away, get out."

He screeched like a violin bowed by a heavy-handed drunk. Planks, tearing loose, prolonged the sound. Meilan came bounding out with her chopper. The foremost of the mob tumbled through the ragged opening. Splintered wood tore at them. Those who followed stumbled over the stunned first wave.

Mei Ling stepped into the sunlight.

Resplendent in green silk, gleaming with rubies, tinkling with jade, hairpins agleam with gems, she stood there, imperial and immovable. Those who had been screaming "Kill the snake-devil!" had regained their feet: a sorry pack of men and women, market people, coolies, farmers, loafers, beggars. Stupefied, they stood, except for some who still crouched and stared.

A clear, cool voice from the rear prompted them. "She killed the doctor. Go, take her!"

Mei Ling raised her arms. Out of the shadowy entrance behind her, a tremendous grayish figure glided into the sunlight. The slanting rays made the misty shape gleam as if of inner fire. She pointed at the invaders.

The apparition's arms reached out, mimicking her gesture. As she advanced a pace, it advanced, though covering thrice the distance she did. It paused when she paused. It kept exactly in step with her. The only sound in the court was the breathing of the intruders. The yelling and screeching in the street had died out, as if terror in the courtyard had touched those still well away from the broken barrier.

There was the yellow splash of a Buddhist robe,

briefly visible beyond the shattered planks. The clear, cool voice was not heard again.

Mei Ling's gesture indicated him. "Get the monk!"

And then Li Fong came into the court, to stand beside his wife.

The gray apparition thinned, faded. Mei Ling cried out in dismay.

"Who says I am dead? Go, while you still can. Or must she call the Gray God to kill you all?"

They backed away as he advanced, facing them down. Finally, at the battered gateway, he halted. "Breaking into the Hall of Benevolence—hasn't it always been open, to welcome you? What nonsense is this?"

From the outside came the familiar voice of Abbot Shen Hui. "Go, and leave Master Li Fong in peace! Whoever does any harm to him or to this place spends a million years in Number Eight Hell." And in the following moment the Abbott stepped into the court. "You see, I always think of your welfare, Master Li Fong. I am happy to arrive in time to save your wife and your home."

Chopper in hand, Ah Sam manned the breached gate, to menace the curiosity seekers who had heard enough to make them wary.

Ah Lo hustled up a sedan chair for Sister Moutan. Now that she was assured of her brother's well-being, she wanted nothing more than to get far from her uncanny sister-in-law.

Li Fong invited the Abbot into the Great Book Room. He gestured to include wife and concubine. When they were seated, he said, "My Number One Lady's presence and my own appearance are quite enough to settle the mob. I cannot say that Your Reverence had anything to do with the outcome, but we are grateful for your solicitude."

"I live to serve."

"Your service in the matter of the Dragon Boat wine came close to killing me and caused my wife's miscarriage. The solicitous mob came to avenge my death. Somehow, they had the idea that my wife was responsible. Even if they knew your part in all this, they would not dare harm one of *your* holiness, one who wore the yellow robe."

At Mei Ling's gesture, Meilan went to prepare Guest Tea.

The Abbot said, "I am here to beg your forgiveness."

Mei Ling replied, "We commend you to the Lords of Karma, who neither forgive nor condemn. My husband and I may never see their judgment. You will. And now we are eager to hear your thoughts."

Shen Hui was not disturbed. He addressed Li Fong. "You have been telling yourself that your wife's turning into a snake was illusion."

Mei Ling spoke before her husband could answer. "Lord Abbot, Younger Sister and I spent a thousand years as serpent-spirits. We gained human form through eating herbs instead of animal creatures, and because of the devotions of a blessed monk, a true servant of the Lord Buddha. We revere his memory. Through trying to imitate his benevolence, we have the right to live as human women."

Li Fong said, "Whatever good you intended, we accept with thanks. Whatever evil came of your intentions, it will return to the source."

Meilan came in with the jade pot and the tiny jade cups.

"But for my wife," Li Fong continued, "I'd be dead, or would have bought my life on your terms. I seemed dead, yes, but I heard your bargaining with her. My soul wandered, but was near enough to know."

Mei Ling poured the Guest Tea.

The Abbot drank and made his bow. Then he said, "Master Li Fong, will you go with me to the gate, instead of letting a servant guide me?"

"Less than that would be uncourteous, Lord Abbot," said Li Fong, and went with him to the battered gate.

"Venerable Abbot," Li Fong continued, "I respect your robe. If you were not a monk, I would surely kill you. Perhaps the Lords of Karma will assign that task to someone more fitted for it than I am. Meanwhile, I have only love and gratitude for my wife."

Shen Hui smiled. "When you have tried, let me know of your carnal desires for a snake-body like hers, or like your concubine's."

## CHAPTER XXX

As if there were mob penitence, the Hall of Benevolence was crowded with patrons and visitors who brought gifts and testimonial scrolls in recognition of real or fancied benefits. Graciously, Li Fong accepted these offerings.

Within him there was darkness. "Some of these I've never heard of. Others send presents to fool us, to keep my wife from sending devils to curse them." But at times he brightened from recognizing the name of one who had indeed been cured by Mei Ling.

That Chang Lu had incited the superstitious and the ignorant was no consolation. The knowledge that people could be so easily turned against Mei Ling was hard for him to swallow. Worst of all was the awareness that Shen Hui's conviction that all he had done had been for the good was entirely sincere.

Li Fong reflected, "He's worse than Tai Ching and Chang Lu. He's a sincere fanatic, deadlier than any man knowingly devoted to evil and malice. If I were the Son of Heaven, I would have every idealist beheaded. The one-pointed, dedicated scoundrel causes far less trouble than the zealous, the idealistic!"

In reaching this awareness, Li Fong had come a step closer to the wisdom of the Great Men of Old . . .

Li Fong's sojourn in shadow-land had depleted him physically, but this was of little force compared to the psychic wrenchings he had endured. However much the gray apparition had cowed the mob, his own appearance had been the finishing touch. He was still dazed by the response to his advance, after Mei Ling's dismay had made her lose control of her magical power for the moment.

He ignored the evening-meal summons and contented himself with the bowl of soup which Ah Lo, despite rebuffs, finally brought.

"I'm too busy with my accounts," he grumbled, and resumed bookkeeping.

However little he cared about profit or loss, the pretense helped him focus his mind on the here and now. Despite his efforts, he could not expel the memory of that terrible transformation—of his gropings in shadow-land—of his return from the many dimensions of space into the three dimensions of the Red Earth. He could win freedom only by fixing his attention on his accounting.

He sat most of the night. After a few hours of sleep, Li Fong got a pot of tea, a mango, and some rice cakes. He took these to the shop and busied himself with examining the canisters and jars. He realized, presently, that he had been auditing books several months old. No matter . . .

This became Li Fong's regular nightly routine.

Soon he was peaked and sunken-eyed. He needed sleep but sleep was dream-riddled, wearying, disturbing. Indian opium, he knew, would make matters worse.

Shen Hui's parting words wove their way through his thoughts whenever his attention wavered from the abacus, or from brushing letters to vendors, or from preparing prescriptions.

Meilan and Mei Ling sat in the meditation room.

"You invaded a monastery, you knocked Tai Ching silly, you fought the dragon shape, you faced the mob—now look!" Meilan raged. "Now he won't even eat with us."

Mei Ling sighed. "He's obsessed with the notion that the books won't balance."

Meilan spat, with contempt for more than the idea. "I saw the books. Old records. Same lot, night after night. We might as well go back to our cave and be snakes again!"

Mei Ling smiled somberly. "Or cut our hair and be nuns."

Meilan eyed her sharply. "Elder Sister, he hasn't been sleeping with me."

"I'm sure of that. I read his eyes, that moment while

he was coming back to his body—I was revolting—he tried to hide it but he couldn't."

After a long silence, Meilan said, "If you put the right herbs and stuff into his wine, you might not be so revolting." She quoted a highly obscene proverb, to the effect that in an emergency, anything female, even if it were a snake, was acceptable.

Mei Ling shook her head. "For coolies, soldiers, sailors, yes; but the Old Master is sensitive. If he did anything at all after drinking wine with stuff that helps old men with young concubines, he'd find a nice human sing-song girl or flower-girl and keep on with nothing but spiritual love for you and me."

"And end up being a monk!" Meilan cried, half in tears, half in fury. "That dung-eating Abbot will talk him into shaving his head and putting on a yellow robe."

Mei Ling sighed. "I was afraid of something like this. But I was so awfully worried trying to keep him alive that I couldn't keep my mind on anything else."

"And now we've got nothing else to think of, and where does our thinking get us?"

"Let's fight illusion with illusion."

"You mean magic?"

Mei Ling nodded. "It's a tricky business. If I'm to work what I've been thinking of, I'll have to open the doors wide and be awfully sensitive, inviting illusion builders, the shapes and forms of illusion. Inviting things from across the Border is risky. The not-invited can't always be kept away. There might be more than I could cope with—"

"You mean devils?"

Mei Ling sighed and shook her head. "Not really devils, not the way you mean it. Blind forces muddling my mind. Worse yet, deliberate *sendings* I might not be able to keep out or resist."

"*Sendings*," Meilan echoed, and frowned for a moment. "*Aiieeyah!* Now I get it—forces from the dog-fornicating Abbot—to spoil things between us and Li Fong?"

"No better way of putting it," Mei Ling admitted after a moment of pondering. "And that's what's bad—

it's all so vague that it's like trying to scoop mist in a sieve or build fog into shape."

She leaped to her feet, caught Meilan's hand. "The more we talk, the more we get bemuddled. We've beaten the Abbot once. Of course the old fanatic's going to fight us. Don't try to figure so far ahead. When he makes his next move, we'll know what to do—just the way we did this time—are doing now."

Meilan brightened. "Once the Old Master's himself, the three of us will be a sticky package for the Abbot."

Meanwhile, night after night, day after day, Li Fong sat with his book by Master Ko Hung, doctor of medicine, of magic, of alchemy and philosophy, the supreme Taoist. Whenever he looked at his exquisite wife, now that he had begun to sit with her at supper, he burned with desire and he froze with revulsion. The more he fought, the deeper the poison ate into him.

One night when Mei Ling came into the study, she saw him reading the Taoist book. She said, "Master Ko Hung knew what's good for the soul. His wisdom goes beyond the body."

Li Fong thrust the book aside. "Number One Lady—*tai-tai*—there's no cure for a sick soul. I'm crazy—I've always loved you and I'm shackled."

Her smile was a sweetness and a moon glow, and it was silent music. "We three love each other, Old Master. While you were across the Border, in that shadow-land, we were in our own Red Earth darkness. There is a healing for sick souls, lover—you call me a healer using magic—and when this happens, it's the soul that I've cured, with the body following its example. Trust me, I know, and you'll know, too."

She sensed his eagerness and the inner chilling which quenched it. "No, not the way you imagine, not the way you fear. There are many ways."

"*Tai-tai!*" His voice broke. He choked, he groaned, he fell across the table, face buried in his hands. "He sent devils to shackle me."

"*Taijen*," she said, her voice a caress and a promise, "this is only the way of nature, and devils weren't needed. Serpent-folk don't hate humans. The fully human have a horror of us."

"I'm just crazy-sick. I won't quit you, ever."

She went on, "I'll adopt the son of any woman, any human woman you love."

He looked up, eyes burning in his haggard face. "I don't want any other woman. I'm damned, I'm lost, there's no help for me."

His voice cracked, and he blinked, but he couldn't stop the tears. "I'll be a monk!" he yelled. "I'll face the wall! Go back to your mountain cave! I'm a dead loss. I can't kill the Abbot—I can't do anything—the words he spoke to me at the gate—that old bastard! There was poison enough already in me, and he added the final drop. I need ten women and I can't touch even one."

"You can do more than you know, Old Master. Listen. Empty-handed, and with my *tulku* destroyed by my fright when I saw you beside me, when you should have been asleep, you went to meet the mob. You always do more than you can! How many of those people knew that you were really Li Fong?

"Your power beat them down. Your presence, your just being there, was all that we needed. I tell you again, again, and again, you always do more than you think you can. Li Fong, you're going to win again. You won against two burglars in the old house."

"With a silver serpent to help me when I was helpless."

"There will be a silver serpent to help you again, Old Master. Being helped takes nothing from you. You have power, willpower."

"Ever hear of any man trying by force of will to make love to a woman?" he challenged.

"Li Fong, First Lover, Respected Husband, eons ago I was a male devil, and my blessing and my punishment was to become female. My punishment—my blessing—and your blessing, too! But I do have rememberings of male handicaps and male advantages, and that's going to be your blessing, too!"

"Tell me!" he demanded.

The challenge in his voice, in his eyes, in the outthrust of chin—these heartened her. He wasn't as beaten as she'd feared.

"The rememberings are dim, lover." She sighed. "So very dim. But I'll reach back, way back, until I recall . . ." Her eyes widened, became a glowing blackness, a dark enchantment, dark and wide, far-seeing, looking beyond Li Fong and through the centuries, or so he thought as their eyes met, and he saw in hers a power and a promise. She said, "Old Master, I'll stay in my shrine room to think and maybe to remember. You mustn't disturb me. You might make my reachings fall apart and fumble—"

"Wait—if it's going to be dangerous—this magic—"

"Dangerous, no. Groping in darkness and haze, yes. Stay away from the shrine room. If you must disturb me, trust Meilan with your words, your message." She saw his glance shift to follow the rhythm of her breathing, the rise of breast against the shimmering silk of the brocade-trimmed tunic—but she resisted the temptation to come nearer. She drew back and said, "You think I'm helping you, but you may finally have to help me out of trouble."

# CHAPTER XXXI

As the days lined up in ranks, Li Fong became accustomed to Mei Ling's absence, and to the barely audible vocalization of *sutras*; or were those *dharanis*, which were more a force than a sound? There was something strange about it all: Meilan's femaleness, always radiant, withdrew from the surface as it had never done during her earlier days as concubine and happy substitute for the mistress, *tai-tai*, the Lady of Ladies.

At times Li Fong speculated so far as to wonder whether this was his wife's exceeding subtlety, exposing him to Meilan. He had never seen her change from woman to serpent; Meilan, indeed, had been his first woman, and there had been nothing revolting about the shadow pattern beneath the skin surface.

Yet he shrank from laying hand on hip or thigh or breast. The fear still gripped him. Meilan's body was mentally acceptable, but more than mind was involved.

And Li Fong's thought remained: "Might as well be a monk . . ."

Then one evening, Meilan had him wondering anew; this was when she sat down and, instead of serving the meal, clapped her hands thrice, smartly, in the mode of Number One Lady.

A slender, long-legged girl stepped into the room. She set out a tray from which she removed a tureen of fungus jelly soup and a dish of black mushrooms with *to fu*, another of mixed vegetables, a plate of steamed buns, and one of rice. And there was fruit of several sorts. What aroused Li Fong's interest were the three bowls, the three sets of ivory chopsticks, the three soup spoons of translucent porcelain.

"Will the mistress be eating with us?" he asked.

"*Tai-tai* regrets that her devotions will deprive her for many more days of your fascinating company," Meilan answered. "She regrets also that she will require my assistance, soon after we have eaten. She asked me to learn whether you would like to have Tien Yuk eat with us, and later sing and pour wine for you during my absence."

Li Fong had a busy moment assimilating the situation. Ignoring all logic, he found Tien Yuk a pleasant distraction. She was neither as solidly built and square-rigged as Meilan nor as excitingly fragile as Mei Ling. If she wore even a trace of cosmetics, she had been most skillfully made up. There was no artifice in the suggestion of apricot-flush in her cheeks. Her tawny-golden color was more opulent than the old-ivory tint of Meilan or Mei Ling. And he liked the sweetness of her mouth, the friendliness of dark eyes which reminded him of those of a slave girl who had been described to him as Syrian—large, luminous, and shaped as no Chinese eyes he'd ever seen.

Aside from ivory hairpins, the girl wore not a single adornment, neither bracelets, ear pendants, nor rings.

"Tien Yuk," he said, "Heavenly Jewel, you wear no jewel either of heaven or earth. But I'll tend to that. Eat, you two, don't wait for me—"

With a gesture, he dismissed food. As he turned from the table, he heard Meilan say, "That's been his way, nibbling a few *dim sum* when the notion strikes him, and never a real meal!"

As Li Fong went to his bedroom-library-sitting-room suite, he was warmed by the urge to respond to Tien Yuk's friendliness, her sweetness. These masked her femaleness, and this was good. That she was somewhat short of outright beauty made him wonder how she'd look when smiling in happy surprise.

He also had a vague feeling of annoyance. This was the lowest ingratitude, yet his wife had been wrong in presenting Tien Yuk without a single adornment. Not intentional belittlement, of that he was certain—yet female thoughtlessness.

Li Fong dislodged a skillfully camouflaged loose brick and dipped into the space exposed. In addition to Indian gold coins, there were trinkets which neither Mei Ling nor Meilan had ever worn. He considered bracelets, ear pendants, a ring—and replaced each.

"These would be decorating her like hanging *mantram*-papers on a festival tree! Reminding her she'd arrived without a trinket, like a household wench . . ."

It did not occur to Li Fong, as he dipped and dug, hefted and eyed and replaced this thing and that bit, that he was taking an unusually long time to pick an ornament for a sing-song girl. Granted that, until that nearly fatal Dragon Boat Festival, he'd been up to the eyebrows in fascinations of wife and of concubine, quite too much so to be aware of other women, Li Fong was nevertheless much more solicitous than the "Heavenly Jewel" warranted. Meanwhile, let them eat and gabble.

He finally took a chain of gold with a pendant of jade, translucent and veined in a paler green—not ostentatiously precious, yet uncommonly good. Nodding contentedly, he retraced his way to the dining room, which opened onto the large court.

He found Meilan sitting alone. The dishes had been taken away. "Old Master," she said, "*tai-tai* hopes that you like the present she offers you, and so do I. Tien Yuk is an awfully sweet girl, and she'd love to please you. I'm sure you'll have no problem with her—she'll make much clear to you, as much as you make clear to her."

An unspoken thought: *If this Tien Yuk and I get along together, she'll show me snake markings and convince me that I've always had a passion for serpent-women* . . . What he said was, sourly, glumly, a sad quip out of his inner corrosion, "No doubt she's a virgin?"

Meilan didn't skip a beat. "I didn't ask the astrologer, who said that you two would please each other. Three virgins in a row would do nothing but give you unhappy memories, or be monotonous. Maybe she can teach you things we couldn't." Meilan put her palms together, got up, and bowed. "Old Master, *tai-tai* and I hope that our gift pleases you. As soon as she's washed up from handling the dishes, I'll bring her to your door."

In a strange house, she would need a guide.

Li Fong did his best to read snatches of the *Pao P'u Tzu*, but couldn't concentrate. He was on his feet before she fairly stepped into the library. With both hands, he presented the pendant.

"Welcome guest gift. I should call you Jade Lady, since jade is a heavenly jewel."

The glow of her face showed how she savored the compliment built into her guest-name. Tien Yuk took the pendant with both hands, raised it to eyebrow level, then lowered and admired until, looking up, she said, "Tien Yuk is too pretentious. I'd rather be your Jade Lady."

"Please me by wearing it?"

Her hands, though a bit squarish and practical, moved gracefully. The jade came to life against the persimmon-red of her tunic. Li Fong said, "It's too bad there's no mirror at hand."

The facts as he knew them were that not in the entire house was there a mirror, except perhaps in the servants' quarters.

"Of course not, *tai jen*! Not in the Lord's library. But I have one among my things." She dropped the pendant inside her tunic. The chain was of just the right length. She bowed. "This will bring me luck. May I get wine and my lute?"

Instead of waiting, Li Fong followed her to a small apartment which opened from an inner, farther court, conveniently near his own suite. Jade Lady had been comfortably installed, with her simple wardrobe, her few cosmetics, and her lute. A bronze wine jar was warming near the coals of a small brazier. A tea service was at hand. An alabaster urn, in whose depths a candle burned, glowed from inner radiance. There was a chair and a settee. Li Fong seated himself on a deep red cushion.

Jade Lady exclaimed in annoyance and stopped fumbling among garments and gear. "*Aiieeyah!* Either I lost it on the way—no, it's just not here! My mirror, *tajen!*"

"Your make-up is perfect."

"Mistress Meilan tended to that. To be sure I looked just right! I couldn't possibly, but she tried her best. To please you."

No mirror. She had only one possession less likely to be forgotten! Or lost. *O-mi-to-fu!* Another snake-woman? During that shocking black instant, he shook his head as if to clear it, and drew a breath of incense-weighted air. He opened his eyes and indicated the censer.

"Indian?"

"Yes, Indian."

Jade Lady's lovely eyes, not quite Chinese, evoked speculation, thoughts of far-off lands—Iran, Turkestan, the Cities of Jade, Khotan and Kashgar . . . Aimless notions and alien incense lured him from his moment of inner coldness and panic.

Jade Lady filled the cups.

He drained his drink and had an apprehensive qualm as she emptied hers. Nothing happened. She wasn't going to turn into a snake. There was only sweetness, friendliness, so often better than seductiveness and female magnetism.

"Warm enough?" she queried, over the fragile porcelain cup, when she noted the qualm which had darkened his face. "Too hot?"

"Only a far-off worry, not quite forgotten."

She refilled the cups. His glance strayed from her hands and lingered on the lute nearby. Jade Lady took up and handed him the *pip'a*. Its four strings were stretched over ivory frets. The body, shaped like half a pear cut lengthwise, was of teak, with a sounding board of *wutun* wood, inlaid with ivory. He plucked the strings, listened to the dying voice of the heaviest one.

"Play, Old Master," she invited. "Music is good for the soul."

He recited at random a few phrases from Po Chu Yi's composition in honor of the *pip'a*, a newcomer to China from Persia. In its short five centuries or so in its new home, it had captivated the land.

"*. . . now loud . . . now frail as the patter of pearls poured on a plate of jade . . . now liquid as the warbling of orioles hidden among flowers . . .*" He stilled the murmuring strings. "You play, while I sit, and drink, and listen, and look at you."

"*. . . loud as the crash of pouring rain,*" she recited, midway between singing and declaiming. "*. . . soft as the whisper of murmured words . . . now sobbing as a brook on its downward course . . .*"

The phrases, all out of sequence and more than half improvised, danced through Li Fong's memory, enchanting him as Jade Lady bewitched the vibrant strings. They pealed like temple bells, in a resonance that promised never to die; they clacked at times like a rattle; they sighed, they whispered, they cooed, they purred; they sobbed all the misery of life and they sang with all the heart's joy. They clashed like swords against armor and they slashed like the rending of silken cloth.

He watched her fingers dance and ripple. He saw her other hand creeping along the neck of the *pip'a*, saw its advance, its retreat; and heard the strings cry and sing, exult and grieve . . .

"*. . . now the music suddenly stilled . . . like a torrent stilled by frost . . . in a passion too deep for voice . . .*"

For a long moment he sat bemused. He blinked, and he swallowed, and he sighed. Almost laboriously, as if not yet in full command of his body, he got up and bowed most formally.

"Jade Lady, how silly I would feel if I had played, then heard you!"

She set aside the lute. "I spent some time making a

soup. Just in case you like a foundation for wine singing. An herb soup."

"I am hungry," he answered, as if announcing a pleasing novelty. "But first the musician must have a cup of wine." His gesture checked her before she could rise. "That I'll get for you."

After filling the cups, he touched light to several more tapers of long-burning insect-wax. Then, kneeling behind her cushion, he plucked the chain and drew the pendant from its warm haven. He let it rest against the persimmon-hued tunic.

"Lovely! When you get a mirror, you'll see why I called you Jade Lady."

"Old Master, how generous, throwing away my name and giving me a heavenly jewel instead."

He laughed at her play on Tien Yuk and Jade Lady. She fingered the low-relief design and offered him the pendant. "Good jade! The fingers feel more than the eye sees; close your eyes and try."

She was quite right. The endless-knot design tricked the eye because of the translucence of the substance, but to sensitive fingertips the pattern became as plain as a magistrate's vermilion "chop."

"This is the best-feelingest jade," she resumed, retrieving the pendant and caressing it with thumb and forefinger. "Most friendly jade."

They drank their wine and spooned the bland, subtle soup of herbs, slices of lotus root, and two dried plums. The fragrance was quite too delicate to note. Only its absence could be sensed.

She cleared away the bowls, the orange peels, the loquat seeds, and brought a steaming small towel for Li Fong's face and hands. When she seated herself beside him again, he said, "Jade Lady, you're as subtle as your herb soup."

She laughed softly. "Old Master, was there ever a poet who compared a woman to a bowl of soup? Explain to my stupidity!"

"That was a most savory soup of no-smell, but if the no-fragrance were left out, then one would notice the absence. Without perfume, without a seasoning of jewels—I understand now what those word-mongering monks mean by *sunyata*, the Emptiness-Which-Is-All."

165

"So! Now I'm a Buddhist *sutra*?" she mocked.

It was good to get lost in this happy-silliness. He couldn't remember when he'd relished feminine playfulness and whimsy, and he did not dare recall the hours he had similarly spent with Mei Ling—he was afraid to recall Meilan. He must not taint this exquisite giddy here and now . . .

He nuzzled her cheek and throat. "The no-fragrance which is all-fragrance. No jewels, no perfume," he said as he plucked the pendant from concealment.

"Jade viewing," she whispered, "is best with touch and eyes closed."

Li Fong twisted about to regard her eye to eye, and burlesqued a ferocious closing of the eyes, as if playing a role in the opera. With equally stylized gestures, he reached, hands cupped, and mimicked the intonation of the villain. "Jade viewing is now commanded! Hear, tremble, and obey!"

"Old Master," she protested, "keep your eyes closed, and please desist from hasty viewing. Hearing, trembling, and obeying."

Going with her play, he drew back. He heard a soft stirring, a rippling whisper. Sternly, he kept his eyes screwed shut. He could almost smell, almost taste, no-fragrance.

After an interminable delay, she said, "Jade Lady may be viewed, but only with eyes closed, like Cha'n Master seeing-without-sight."

He caressed and could almost see the exquisite breasts and the pendant between them. She murmured, "For good luck, jade mustn't be slighted."

Now he "saw" every convolution of the endless knot. He read the characters so cunningly abraded into the pendant.

"Viewing with eyes is now permitted," she announced very formally.

Li Fong blinked his vision into focus. The tunic and its companion garments were fluffed about her hips. Jade Lady sat as straight as a sculptured Boddhisattva. Her eyes, however, were not downcast. They smoldered behind long lashes. The shadow-smile which lurked at the corners of her mouth was entirely Chinese.

"*Taijen*, you don't look at the gift-of-welcome!" she reproached.

He lowered his glance to the pendant.

After endless moments, she closed her eyes and affectionately fondled the jade.

"I see it better now. Please try."

Experiments in jade feeling, however fascinating to the connoisseur, the true *amateur*, began to seem overdone, but Li Fong still had the patience to humor her whimsies. Indeed, he was eager to carry on. And by dint of keeping his mind on jade, he began to realize that he was responding to her femaleness in a way that was long forgotten. Jade Lady, whether by instinct or by artifice, was entirely right.

They regarded each other. "Old Master, please humor, please indulge, this cow-clumsy stupid woman?"

"Yes, *tai-tai*," he promised, without even being aware that this was in fact his Number Three Lady, and not the Number One Supreme who alone rated the honorific he had spoken. "Please tell me?"

"Touching finally is better than eye-looking."

When she rose, he didn't notice that she fell short of the fluent motion of a serpent-woman. Watching her pinch out one taper after another was engrossing; but best of all was her snuffing the tall candle which had made an artificial moon of the alabaster jar.

When he followed her to bed, she wore only a chain from which depended luxurious jade. It would win splendor from her skin. It would bring luck to her and also to him, if only he could be close enough to it and to her, long enough.

# CHAPTER XXXII

AWAKENING, Li Fong found his companion asleep. Recalling the jade viewing, he fondled her smooth body; in the darkness, he could "see" it. He listened to her even breathing, her silent contentment, and was happy and at peace, finally, and liberated from his shackles.

He did not even remember that he'd had any cause for other than serenity.

Nonetheless, something far and deep in the unconscious made him stir and draw away until he could reach the cords which secured the alcove curtains. These he released. They closed. He scarcely realized that he wanted Jade Lady to share the tiny world which excluded all else—that he wanted to shut out healing, and magic, and the occult, and all enemies, and all burglars, all monks. It was so dark behind the curtains that jade viewing would be at its supreme best.

During interludes and breathing spells in their first lovemaking, they had drunk wine, and she had played the *pip'a.* Though her voice was by no means the best, he loved the way she sang Li Po's *Farewell to Comrades.*

She was nicely shaped. She didn't have subtlety, but sweet good humor gave sparkle to whatever she said. She would never, no matter how she tried, be a high-grade sing-song girl for scholars. Jade Lady was, finally, so much the relief from the soul-sickness that had been destroying him that whatever she had or had not, was or was not, was beautifully right.

Just contentedly drunk . . . to feel fine in the morning . . . this was a wonder to relish in advance. Li Fong fingered the jade pendant, and traced the endless knot, and read the characters.

He didn't want to awaken her, neither for music, nor for posing with the pendant, nor for song. Delicately, he grazed her from throat to knee with his fingertips, the barest shadow of a touch. From jade fondling he'd graduated to caressing a jade body, an exquisite experience. He began to recall his wife. He began to remember her goodness, her loyalty, her courage, and the generosity which moved her to give him the Heavenly Jewel, Tien Yuk. And the remembering, though without any tinge of desire, had also not any taint of revulsion.

He didn't dare dwell on this, which seemed to have come from the magic of Jade Lady's body and her presence.

Perhaps it was the earnestness of his thinking and feeling that finally made his companion stir and arouse herself, to stretch and sigh contentedly. He said, "I didn't mean to disturb you. But you're so beautifully beautiful—"

"Only in the dark," she whispered.

"Darkness, daylight, or dawn," he continued, "and maybe viewing in darkness is most rich of all, *tai-tai*."

She tightened as he spoke the final word, then relaxed. "You mustn't call me that, not ever," she murmured.

"All ladies of all numbers . . . become Number One . . . too sleepy?"

She wasn't a bit sleepy. "*Aiieeyah* . . . I've lain here wondering when you'd wake me up."

He couldn't tell then, or later, how little time she lost in following her drowsy whisperings with a greedy embrace.

"Like wine and—"

"Like nothing that keeps us from closeness. I'm starved, lecherous—no elegance—no music—" Her voice was throaty, not the voice of any one woman— simply the tone of passion. "Love me to death, and my ghost will sing—"

For a long while, the survival of either did seem improbable . . .

"Solid, for a ghost," he finally said.

She sighed and said, in her whispering no-voice, "Old Master, can you read my jade now? . . . How it brought me luck? . . ."

"I'm illiterate . . . Well, if I must read . . . yes, I did . . . and I'll tell you a thing or two right now."

"Yes?"

"Let's have more wine."

"Tell me first. A thought lives with you, *taijen*?"

"So you read my thought? Yes. My wife is a wonderful woman and most exquisite. My Number Two Lady is the same. I love them both. How can I be so lucky, that they gave me a Jade Lady for my birthday?"

"Love your Jady Lady?"

"More than ever, but let's get our breath first—"

Then the little apartment blazed into light. The alcove curtains failed by quite a stretch in remaining drawn together. Exposure of the lovers was far from total—still, somewhat more than necessary. The curtain gap was sufficiently wide for Li Fong to blink into the glare of an enormous candelabrum which Meilan was carrying.

The intruding concubine cried out in dismay, "*Aiieeyah!* I didn't know—I thought—"

Maybe Meilan had expected the Heavenly Jewel and the Old Master to be in his apartment, enjoying wine and music. Whatever she might have been thinking, Meilan stood there as if fascinated by the dancing shadows of curtain edges and curtain rail.

Li Fong was having a busy moment—too busy for anything but total confusion. He snatched a handful of quilt and a garment his companion had carelessly flipped aside. Still blinking and gaping, he didn't know which of the exposed areas to cover first. And there were other confusions. He was exclaiming, "Jade Lady—I'm sorry—"

Then he had nothing more to say.

Not when he got his first real seeing-look at his companion, who was now sitting up, entirely in command of the situation. She was not Jade Lady, also known as Tien Yuk, the Heavenly Jewel his wife and his number one concubine had offered him as a gift.

She wore the jade pendant which Li Fong had learned to read by touch, in total darkness.

Even with years of study, Li Fong could not have uttered a remark less appropriate to the occasion: "Where's Jade Lady?"

"Old Master, wasn't I doing well enough during all our jade feelings?"

The lady was Mei Ling, *tai-tai*, the Number One Supreme Lady, his wife. Whether he'd been in bed with Meilan or with Tien Yuk, no harm, no question; his wife and his concubine had not presented a singsong girl qualified only for song and music.

Mei Ling was sweet, smiling whimsically, waiting for his answer.

He couldn't think of a word. He caught her in his arms, buried his face between her breasts.

"I'm Tien Yuk, I'm your Jade Lady, Old Master, and you said the sweetest thing, telling me you'd always love me and Meilan."

He raised his head and eyed his elegant wife, his seductive wife. "All healed, all cured, all well, all new. But—where—"

"Old Master, I've been Jade Lady all the time." She cocked her head, made a teasing grimace. "There never was a Jade Lady, never a Tien Yuk. You had me and an armful of illusion—of course it was magic, illusion that went beyond illusion, but everything else was real, really as real as you thought it was."

The rising sun cast long, slanting rays of ruddy light into the apartment. Seeing Li Fong happy-bewildered, she said, "Tonight, Sister Meilan can explain a lot of all this—she did truly help me rebuild myself."

Meilan, snuffing the lights of the candelabrum, turned at the sound of her name. Mei Ling's gesture checked her. "Before you leave us, Younger Sister, I'll tell you about Chang Wo before she turned from being the most beautiful woman in all the empire to become Moon Goddess.

"A very high official was in love with her. During her husband's absence in a war, he kept after her, day after day, until Chang Wo finally invited him to her home for dinner and music and wine-games.

"Her admirer was so mighty-important that instead of nine or seventeen dishes, she served thirty-four. And each dish was brought in by a different one of her maids—each a strikingly beautiful girl, each differently dressed.

"Each dish, when uncovered in its turn, seemed different from its predecessors. But the guest of honor tasted and learned that each was of chicken—no beef, no lamb, no pork, no fish deep-fried, no fish steamed, no *bêche-de-mer*, no bird's nest or shark fin or shrimp or fish maw. The guest of honor had never heard of such a dinner, and finally he asked his hostess what message she was conveying in her amazing bill of fare.

" 'Distinguished Lord, Friend of the Son of Heaven, this clumsy cow begs leave to point out that these thirty-four elegant girls are for your exalted pleasures —I invite you to take to bed with you any one or all who please you.'

"Courteous and formal, the Great Lord appreciatively regarded each girl and finally said, 'Superlative

Hostess, this crude plowboy would prefer you, yourself, to the entire lot of them.'

"Then Chang Wo, who would one day become a Goddess, said to her distinguished guest, 'Great Lord and Honored Guest, you were puzzled when you tasted thirty-four dishes and found that for all the differences of appearance, you had nothing but chicken from start to finish. I beg leave to say that if you uncovered thirty-four beautiful girls and this withered hag, you could tell no difference. Chicken is chicken, no matter what the dressing or the sauce.'

"So said the almost divine Chang Wo," Mei Ling told her husband and her sworn sister. "So I remembered, and I made magic."

"The Divine Chang Wo," Li Fong said. "I'll burn an armful of joss sticks for her next Moon Festival, and eat a basket of Moon Cakes—"

His glance shifted from wife to concubine.

Meilan, never at a loss, said something about wine-games, and matching for turns . . .


# CHAPTER XXXIII


AFTER a week of enjoying the Hall of Benevolence and again relishing his work, Li Fong set out for the White Cloud Monastery. He was quite too happy to take a sedan chair. Stretching his legs, he walked. Soochow was beautiful again, and so were the green slopes, the stands of rustling bamboo, the tree clusters of the parks beyond the city gate. Each deep breath was a luxury which stirred him like wine—or a hand laid on Mei Ling—or the smoldering darkness in Meilan's eyes.

Presently he slowed his purposeful, triumphant gait and strolled as befitted a gentleman. He savored the impending encounter.

". . . tell Shen Hui some things no one ever told an abbot," he mused. His glance strayed and lingered on the golden bands of early morning light which reached through river mists and made the entire prospect shimmer. ". . . got to give Old Turtle-Dung time to come back from his alms rounds . . . and then, gifts for every temple for miles around . . . thanks offerings . . . even for the White Cloud Monastery . . ."

Li Fong found the Abbot in his study. There had been no delay in receiving him. For a moment he regarded the benevolent face, the yellow-robed figure, the gesture, the smile of welcome. Li Fong presented a red envelope on which good wishes had been brushed in gilt. It contained three *mohurs* of Indian gold. From his sleeve he took three packs of joss sticks and presented them. All this, with his three kowtows, was the form of what he'd planned.

"Lord Abbot, I remember the words you spoke, after assisting in scattering the mob. I offer gifts in remembrance and thanks."

Shen Hui radiated peace and compassion. "You've come to join us? Welcome, most welcome!"

"I'm here to thank you for liberating me. From the very beginning, there were things that gave me disturbing thoughts about my wife. Outright accusations and, worse yet, suggestions and hints often repeated."

"Naturally," the Abbot agreed. "Nevertheless, her beauty and her many good deeds made you ignore instinct, inner wisdom. Now that you have seen the truth, you come to enter the Way?"

"I am here to thank you for the confession that your presence and your menace extorted from my wife. And for the words you spoke to me at my gateway before you left."

Li Fong paused. The Abbot prompted, "Ah . . . you tried?"

"With ease and wonder and ecstasy, Lord Abbot. There's no barrier between me and her or my concubine. We three, we love each other with the bodies of man and woman. You freed me from what was hidden and poisoning my soul, and from what you brought into the open to turn me against her." Li Fong lowered his eyes so as to avoid seeing the shock which he knew was warping that saintly face. He bowed and retreated a pace; a second and a third retreat, each with a bow.

173

"I beg leave to quit your venerable Presence, Lord Abbot."

"You may leave, but without my blessing."

Li Fong was so engrossed in having won far more than he had hoped that he was unaware of the two who sat in a corner, well within earshot of the Lord Abbot's study and reception room. Li Fong had confronted Shen Hui not as a gesture of defiance, nor to mock the venerable fanatic. He had gone to clinch his own liberation, Mei Ling's, and Meilan's. True, his heart had been bursting with triumph and defiance and mockery when he set out; but he had remembered his wife's words, long ago, when she had said, "*Hatred and contempt bind us to those we hate and despise, just as firmly as love binds us to those we love—you're shackled to your enemy just as you're bound to your lover.*" There had been this, and then the Lord Abbot's venerable presence.

So Li Fong was unaware of the two who sat in a corner with their well-washed bowls, not realizing that they had watched him leave. Chang Lu and Tai Ching, the Taoist schemers who had come to the monastery to impersonate Buddhist monks, were concerned with personal problems which related to Li Fong. Their low-voiced and bitter wrangling appeared to have begun somewhere along the morning's alms-begging rounds.

". . . your trickery," Chang Lu declared, "got us to this—Li Fong is free from the Abbot's influence—you and your bungling again!"

"It was my inspiration," Tai Ching protested, "to make a deal with her. I wasn't trying to cut you out of things. Can't you get it through your head that I had to act fast, while she was still shaken? We might not have got a hundred thousand *taels*, but there would have been plenty for us to divide. Suppose we'd fooled around, and she'd made a deal with the Abbot?"

"Dog manure! If it had to be done the way you tried, I could have handled it better."

"Your mob didn't do so well," Tai Ching countered. "Don't tell me I was trying to collect and run out with the loot. You had a partner in Hangchow, the man who got wind of the treasure pot, the one who asked you to figure a lucky night for raiding the place. Lucky, wasn't it?"

"I miscalculated, I bitched it up, but not the way you did!"

"Speaking of what you call *my* trickery, what happened to the fellow who consulted you in Hangchow? You got your memory back, but how about him? Anyone trusting you is an idiot!"

Chang Lu smiled. "I heard he got drunk and couldn't remember he was drunk, so he fell in the river; and he'd forgotten how to swim."

"You got him drunk, I bet."

Chang Lu sighed. "He hadn't forgotten he liked wine. I didn't push him in. Listen——" He commanded and got attention. "Chipping away at each other pays no profit. We can still make it. The Abbot doesn't know you were trying to steal the fungus. I covered up for you. He thinks you were the first to realize that the snake-woman was up to tricks. I won't do you dirt by telling him the facts."

Tai Ching studied him. "Threat, or a gift?"

"Neither. Distrusting each other, we lose. Working together, we win. The Abbot has a lot of occult power, but there are things he doesn't know. We'll teach him."

"Just what?"

"About the Mirror of Master Ko Hung, and serpent-folk."

"Let's get at it, then, and never mind the Abbot."

"Master Tai Ching," he retorted sarcastically, "that *tulku* is dangerous, and it becomes more so. They know we're not Buddhist monks. They wouldn't dare harm a monk, but they would most happily kill us.

"And Li Fong—now that he's at ease about his wife, he's a smiling killer. The way he talked sweetly to the Abbot just now didn't fool me."

"He did fool the Abbot," Tai Ching muttered, frowning. Then he brightened. "I begin to think you're right, and we can do the same."

# CHAPTER XXXIV

IN her new happiness, Mei Ling couldn't recall which had come first, the yellow strips of paper pasted on the door of the Hall of Benevolence or those nagging dreams. Naturally enough, it was not until each had persisted for some while that either set her to worrying, although it was the combination which made her uneasy.

At first, she had been glad to see such testimonials as *"Great gratitude to Mei Ling, the Healing Boddhisattva."* The wordings varied, and the script ranged from elegant calligraphy to "grass" writing. Whereas an especially adorable child might be called "a regular little Boddhisattva," and an indigent patient might hang such an extravagant tag on a benevolent healer, this was laying it on a bit too thick. It could even be mockery to call Mei Ling by a title originally reserved for those exalted and rare persons who decline to become Buddhas and instead renounce nirvana to continue working for the good of all living creatures.

Compassionate Kwan Yin, worshipped in hundreds of temples, was the superlative, the supreme, Boddhisattva.

Mei Ling could not confide in Li Fong; she could, however, and did finally, nudge Meilan into the shrine room for a talk.

"In the first place, it's bad joss, getting so much praise. If nothing else, it will make other doctors jealous. And I don't like it when I'm compared to Yakshih—"

"Calling you the Buddha of Healing is no worse than this Kwan Yin, this Boddhisattva, business," Meilan cut in.

"Wait a second, Sister! In each of those dreams, I'm making a pilgrimage to the Temple of the Yakshih Buddha, the one not such a far stretch from the city. It's bad enough running into every possible obstacle on

176

my way to a spot I've actually visited—simply walking along a road everyone knows, and getting lost, and sometimes the road comes to a dead end; again I ask other pilgrims where I am, and they get all bemuddled and can't understand me, or else they give me wrong directions—but that's not the worst of it. In my dream, I just have to go to the Yakshih Temple and pay respects, make an offering—as if I'm being driven—and I never know why I'm compelled to go there. The first thing when we came to town, I went to that temple and kowtowed, and I've sent gifts every so often."

Meilan nodded. "I remember. I went with you while the Old Master was busy arranging the jars and boxes and stuff in the shop. I don't think we skipped a temple within fifteen-twenty *li*." She caught Mei Ling by the shoulders. "Elder Sister—before you turned yourself into Tien Yuk, the imaginary Jade Lady, you told me of that kind of magic, and that you might have trouble with devils. But you never told me how you made yourself look different and how you changed back. It seems to me that it would have been easier just to find a nice sing-song girl, one he couldn't help liking; once he got good and drowsy from girl and wine, you could have taken her place and worn her jade pendant. In the dark, he would have awakened and the honeymoon would have started up again; and when I brought in the lights, he would have realized he couldn't tell you from Tien Yuk-Jade Lady."

"I thought of that, from knowing the story about the thirty-four different dishes, each of which was nothing but chicken. But I couldn't risk it. He's always told me that you and I are different—in spite of my body disguise, I wasn't really a stranger, so our getting along so cozily was taken for granted. But if I'd been a stranger—anyway, it worked beautifully, and here we are, and we'll—"

"But I still don't know how you became so changed!"

Mei Ling sighed. "So you have to know!"

"Of course!" Meilan grinned impishly. "In case I become too monotonous and he has to have a new concubine, I'll know what to do. But I have learned a few things—like charging the peachwood sword—and I'm halfway to making a *tulku*—" She sighed. "Those weeks of nothing to do, nights, but practice magic."

"I know what you mean. Well, explaining is harder than doing! No matter how plain a girl is, almost always she's lovely as a bride. Children have smooth faces, but a lifetime of thinking and feeling changes the expression. I remember one of our patients, an old fellow almost sixty, who told me of himself and a woman; they'd been lovers in their early days, and they met again, more than thirty years later. He didn't look his age, but she was a battered wreck, looking old enough to be his mother. She invited him to be her guest for several days. For old-time friendship, but not for sleeping together. The strange thing that happened puzzled him so much that he had to ask me, as people do ask healers. When she woke him up for breakfast and kissed him good morning, that falling-apart old hag was beautiful, just for the moment, in a way she'd never been during their lover-days. Her rememberings changed her looks for a little while."

Meilan squinted, shook her head, opened her eyes. "I almost get it, but—"

"We have three souls—animal soul, feeling soul, and permanent soul, the one that comes back each time into a new body. The thinking-feeling one changes the body, makes the face look different, makes the body sick or healthy. That's just a hint—

"Anyway, I went into the thinking-feeling world, borrowing thought-feelings, building a sing-song girl, which changed my looks and my shape, but not my bones. And I stayed myself, but mixed up with my borrowings.

"It took me a couple of weeks to become Tien Yuk, and only an hour or two of the Old Master's sleeping for me to unwind and send the borrowings back to— oh, if you wish, call it the feeling-thinking bank. I had to open the doors, and take what I wanted, and accept some of what I didn't want, and so I'm in a fine muddle. Getting thinking-feelings, it's like inviting a village to a feast—and look at all the tramps and beggars who crowd in.

"But I'll get straightened out. Simply by going on

that dream pilgrimage. Tell the Old Master I've gone to heal an important patient. That's no lie."

"I'll go with you."

"No. You stay here. He may not be as healed as he seems."

"Whoever—whatever," Meilan protested, "sends dreams and thoughts—those *sendings* mean trouble. This isn't fun; it isn't playings!"

"If I get into trouble, the Old Master will get me out. I told him that, before he met Tien Yuk. Now I'm leaving—"

Mei Ling had not hoped for an early start, but when at last she did slip out through the escape gate, it was later than she had calculated. Setting out with staff and wooden bowl, she had difficulty in restraining her gait and laboriously lifting and setting down the straw-sandaled feet supposedly wearied by days of plodding.

Stained face and hands, straw hat with brim well below eye level, gray robe torn, wrinkled, and convincingly soiled—she picked her way, glance downward, toward the nearest city gate. Mei Ling appeared to be just another of the devotees who plodded to distant shrines to offer thanks or to crave blessings.

At last she emerged from the network of canals which girdled Soochow. Farmers still worked in their fields, but they and their buffalos would soon be quitting for the day. The sun was low. Beyond the checkerboard of rice fields were wooded areas, rocky hills, and farming settlements.

Somewhere, well beyond a stand of cypress trees, the bell of a monastery sounded. Presently Mei Ling got glimpses of the Yakshih Temple. Sometimes, as the wagon track wound among rustling bamboo, she lost sight of the tiled roof. This made her uneasy, reminding her of those wearying dream quests.

"I'm awake now," she told herself. "I can't get lost."

That she reassured herself was a disturbing indication of the degree to which someone or something had shaken her.

Presently a landmark encouraged her: the Rainbow Pagoda. From now on, she had only to keep it on her left. This she remembered, and thus the occasional crossroad or fork did not disturb her.

The pagoda had come to ruin because of time and neglect. Some said that the stairs to the ninth and uppermost stage had been so hazardous and difficult that only an acrobat could make the ascent without serious risk. Others asserted that the place had been shunned for so long because a pilgrim had fallen to his death. For a "stairway to Heaven," devotees found other modes of winning merit. Following the example of pilgrims, the monks found other centers where the devout gathered.

Reaching the next low summit, Mei Ling again got a glimpse of the Yakshih Temple. This heartened her. There was more to this quest than compulsion. She sensed that once she found the temple, she would be liberated from the harassing dreams which had been making her nights wearying. No matter what kinks and quirks the wagon track might make, she would reach her goal, and there would be no further shadow quests. Her tired feet were aching, but this was happy assurance that she was wide awake.

The descent was gentle. Deepening shadows did not yet disconcert Mei Ling. Ahead, as overhanging trees became more widely spaced, long, ruddy rays lanced into the local dusk. Eagerly, she stretched her legs. This had been a longer course than she had reckoned. The temple would offer good refuge for the night, as it did for all pilgrims and wayfarers.

The twitter of birds and the chirp of cicadas heightened her eagerness to get back into the open, where daylight still dallied. The memory of oppressive dreams made her uneasy. Only a few yards ahead, a stretch of ruined wall, shoulder-high, skirted the road. There she'd halt, deliberately, to defy growing tension—

This was no longer as simple as it had seemed. "I've brought my pack of devils with me," she told herself, and fingered the jade pendant concealed by her robe. This was to be an offering, the breaker of soul-shackles. "I'll get there. I will. I will!"

She stumbled. Her staff kept her from falling.

Something caressed her ankle and broke the stride of attempted recovery. Something soft, yielding, clinging, impeded her next step. She stooped to liberate her feet.

Silken strands settled about her shoulders. It was too late now to resort to *kung fu* defense, which might have served had she been alert. Her belated attempt at evasion tightened the snare. The net was as clinging as quicksand. Two gray shapes closed in from the sides. A third came from behind the ruined wall.

"Don't fight. We'll carry you."

There was enough light for her to recognize Abbot Shen Hui. He continued, "This concludes the first lesson in magic. Soon there will be a second. You'll be too busy to shape your unpleasant *tulku*."

She now knew the source of her dreams. Shen Hui, catching her off guard during her peak of happiness, had directed them to bait her into a trap. Each dream had been skillfully shaped and sent to take command of her.

# CHAPTER XXXV

THE Abbot's crew thrust a bamboo pole through the mouth of the net and lifted Mei Ling off her feet. They followed a trail which branched leftward. Deepening gloom did not hamper them. Everything moved with the precision of a well-staged ballet.

The final ruddy-sky glow, as they emerged from the thinning grove and entered a weed-clogged clearing, revealed the nine stages of the Rainbow Pagoda. There were no lights in any of the buildings in the court. However, Mei Ling caught the odor of cooking, and of oil lamps, as her captors carried her through a breach in the enclosing wall. They dislodged loose bricks as they scrambled up and over. Roots of trees had lifted flagstones from their beds. A stand of bamboo blocked the entrance.

The high foundation platform of the pagoda appeared to be solid. By the light of tapers, Mei Ling saw that the interior chambers in the foundation had been cleaned up. The porters unshouldered their cargo, withdrew the carrying pole, and quit the room.

Kneeling, Shen Hui unsnarled the net. Once his prisoner was free, he gestured toward the hearth, where water simmered and a pot of rice was steaming on the ledge, near the embers.

He made tea and shoveled rice into bowls with a wooden paddle.

"Eat," he invited. "You're hungry and tired."

She shook her head.

"Don't be afraid." He smiled winningly. "I sent dreams that brought you here. If I'd wished harm, I wouldn't have to do it with food. And I'll eat with you."

She ate and drank her tea.

The brick walls exhaled the odor of incense, which had been burned to purify the crypts and expel the devils unharmonious to the occult.

Shen Hui said, "Now I'll show you a new magic."

He went toward a doorway which opened into a further and larger compartment. In a tall niche, originally designed to contain a large urn, was a tripod on which was a bowl of translucent porcelain. A lotus pad, with a single blossom, floated in the bowl. Tall candles of scented wax lighted the crypt.

From a sandalwood chest the Abbot took what resembled an alms bowl, except that it was larger and of golden-gleaming metal. He raised it with one hand, and with the other made *mudras* as he recited a *mantram*.

From somewhere beyond the crypt came the pulsing of a small drum and the throbbing of a larger one; she heard the deep note of a wind instrument, a solemn sound which had somewhat the quality of a drumbeat. The pitch became ever lower, until Mei Ling felt the impact rather than heard sound. Presently there was nothing which addressed the ear. The silent concussion sent up waves which evoked soundless echoes from all the passages of the labyrinth in the pagoda foundation.

Shen Hui stepped to the center of a circle outlined in chalk. Mei Ling was not surprised when she saw the Taoist symbols which skirted the perimeter of the circle. Somewhere, Chang Lu was playing his part.

The Abbot gestured commandingly, pointing toward the lotus.

He intoned a long *mantram*. Now holding the golden bowl with both hands and at eye level, he caught the many candle flames, blended them in the glittering concavity, and projected them to form a lobed disc of light. With each shift of his hands the lobes moved, gliding along the luminous perimeter. The Mirror Magic of Master Ko Hung was at work.

The lotus petals began to shrink. Bit by bit, they resumed bud-form, retreating in time. The implication shocked Mei Ling, making her aware of the Abbot's ultimate purpose. She, instead of a blossom, was to be secured in that niche, to face Taoist magic. Like the lotus, she would diminish in size and go back through time, from blossom to bud . . .

Bounding sidewise, Mei Ling knocked the Abbot off balance and out of the circle. At the instant of contact, she snatched the mirror-bowl. Outraged, gaping, incredulous in the face of insolence, Shen Hui stood there. Before he could recover sufficiently from astonishment to regain the mirror, Mei Ling had it leveled. She resumed the chant where the Abbot had left off. For a moment—an interminable moment—the lotus remained unchanged.

Shen Hui smiled indulgently, as if dealing with a dull-witted child. "You're impatient. The lesson isn't completed."

She ignored the mockery and shut out his presence. The contraction and the change of color were resumed. Finally, the bud vanished, leaving the pad bare.

"*Svaha!*" she cried, then turned and bowed. "I thank Your Reverence for the second lesson."

He forgot his poise. He snatched the bowl. "So you realize, then, that you'll go like the lotus, into other time and space. And when Li Fong is done mourning his loss, he'll put on the yellow robe and shave his head." He added persuasively, "Accept this gracefully. No other woman will ever take him."

She regarded him with wide-open, luminous eyes. "Your words give me something to think about. It is written and it has been said from old times that whatever one truly loves cannot ever be truly lost."

The Abbot gestured. "Spread your mat in the adjoining room. This pagoda is secured by a barrier of power. The thought-force of the many of us is stronger than any devil-power of yours!"

Bowing, he left her to herself.

Mei Ling stepped into a small room lighted by a single candle. On the floor was a mat. Fresh air came in from a small court. She edged through the narrow slot in the wall and stood at the coping of a pool.

The moon was high enough to reach into the court. Weeds and vines had been pruned and the tiles swept clean. She peeled out of her robe and stepped into the water. For a moment, her serpent image was mirrored faintly, until ripples broke and scattered it as she bathed.

All a-drip and gleaming, she dried herself with the inside of her robe. "A pilgrim without a spare stitch!" She grimaced ruefully. "Undue optimism about my early return."

Stretched out on her mat, she began to wonder whether completing Shen Hui's magic had been a brilliant move. Pondering wearied her to sleep.

Soundless concussion awakened her from troubled rest. Shen Hui, his monks, and his Taoist allies were at work, some no doubt asleep while others carried on with the incessant enchantment which must finally break her resistance.

She got up and went into the court. Kneeling at the coping of the pool, she washed the dusty garments, dipping them, twisting them compactly, thumping them against the masonry. She repeated this until they were clean and fresh.

The final wringing was vigorous. She put on the wet clothes and smoothed them against her body. Seating herself in the lotus posture, she harmonized mind and breath. The warmth which began in the pit of her stomach spread until it permeated her entire body. This was mind-fire, and not forbidden. At times she had memories of the supreme magic, that of the Lords of Fire, and of the flame which consumed brick and stone as readily as wood or flesh. Even thought-shaping the words of evocation was hazardous. She dismissed these before they could form.

Mist from the drying garments enveloped Mei Ling for awhile, then thinned and vanished. She had not lost the power. However, there was the problem of keeping it in the face of day-and-night opposition.

She considered what she had at her command. Short of the dreadful fire-magic, there were other ways of combatting Shen Hui, even ways of destroying him if she had to. The karma of any such act would send her to the realm of Hungry Devils for uncounted thousands of years, but first she would have an ordinary life span with Li Fong—at least a few years.

"And *that* could never be destroyed . . ."

The Abbot, from whose make-up the very idea of man-and-woman love appeared to have been omitted, might unwittingly push her to desperation by assuming that she would not dare to destroy him. Thus he might doom both her and himself.

When Shen Hui stepped into the cell and saw her sitting there, he did not suspect that she had as carefully considered his fate as he had been considering hers.

"Sunrise. Come and get a bowl of *congee*."

"I'm fasting."

"You're still afraid of the food I eat?"

"Wine which didn't hurt you was deadly to me." She got to her feet as quickly as a striking snake, startling him. "That crime will take some of your power when you most need it. When you do not have a pack of adepts working with you, you ought to risk yourself and see how you can deal with me. Right now, if you're not afraid!"

"You'll face the Mirror of Truth?"

He gestured toward the room where the lotus bowl sat in its niche.

Mei Ling cried, "Wait!" When he turned, she continued, "You've prepared that space, prepared a trap. Do you need such an advantage?"

"You said—"

"I said I'd face your mirror. Get it. I will get mine."

She edged through the slot in the wall. Kneeling by the door, she selected a lotus blossom which had seventeen petals. Rising, she fixed her eyes on its golden center, spoke a *dharani*, made a *mudra*.

When Mei Ling stepped back into her cell, the Abbot was waiting. He held the golden bowl by its rim, with the gleaming concavity facing her. She held the lotus against her breast and made a gesture of power with her right hand. Shen Hui shifted to collect as much as he could of the early sunlight reaching into the cell.

"See yourself as you truly are!"

The mirror became a whirlpool of light. In its depth, she saw her serpent form, first the head only, and then the entire body. The radiance was neither hot nor cold. It was a penetrating force which permeated her flesh, liquidating its firmness, its cohesion. Her separateness from the serpent image was wavering; though she stood firmly, there was a drawing, a gentle tugging, as if her essence were quitting her body and moving into the mirror image, solidifying it. Though she remained fixed, she felt that some of her physical substance was leaving her.

Mei Ling raised the lotus until it screened her face. She looked between the flower petals. She advanced a pace, stately and assured. She was now less a shadow-form and somewhat more solid than she had been. The mirror image was no longer as clear as it had been. She was regaining what had flowed out of her.

The Abbot's face became tense. His chanting was labored. His hand trembled as he rotated the mirror-bowl. Presently the lotus began wilting. A petal dropped. Shen Hui's voice steadied and his hands became firm again. The mirror now shaped a lobed circle. The lobes began to glide along the perimeter. Once more, Mei Ling's substance began leaving her, and she was nearing the breaking point. Unseen allies were helping her enemy. The silent vibration, ever stronger, pounded her apart. On the verge of failure, he had called for help and he was getting it.

Mei Ling was beyond the point of caring whether Shen Hui's treachery merited whatever death she could deal him. In this vortex of enchantment, it would be disastrous to revert to a serpent and crush him. She was already on the verge of a transformation which could not be reversed. She knew now why Younger Sister was so devoted to her chopper.

"*. . . be a homicidal maniac . . . or be swallowed*

*up in the mirror . . . kill him with a* kung fu *stroke
. . . accept the penalty . . . and Li Fong . . .*"

A gong clanged. The tremendous brazen peal echoed, re-echoed, piling sound upon sound, like the boom of the sea or the roar of a typhoon, an explosion of power that was felt by the whole being, not merely heard.

The Abbot dropped the Mirror of Truth.

The gong had shattered the rhythm of his hidden allies. After a moment, he sat up. He was twitching, groping, fumbling between incredulity and—whether fear or fury, she could not guess. She tossed the wilted lotus into the mirror-bowl.

"Alms for you, Lord Abbot. Next time we fight, let's exchange weapons."

Mei Ling went into the court to sit in the sun patch, before she fell apart. She knew that she had not won the duel. Someone, something, had intervened to save her from the karma of killing Shen Hui.

"If I ever get out of this, I won't be so virtuous in reading the law to Meilan." An odd, twisted little smile brightened her face. "Younger Sister may just be a lot more really human than I am."

# CHAPTER XXXVI

IN the courtyard and pool, Mei Ling found roots and herbs and seeds. These she ate raw. Her human experience had not been so long as to make such food unacceptable. From time to time, as the day wore on, she heard voices and stirrings about. There was none of the silent-sound. Apparently her encounter with Shen Hui had left him depleted.

Somewhat past noon, a gray-robed monk brought a bowl of *congee* and some steamed vegetables.

"I'm fasting. Give it to pilgrims, to birds or animals."

He obeyed. His apprehensive manner encouraged her. Nonetheless, this gain was only the first step. She had to devise a way of cracking the imponderable barrier which secured the pagoda area.

The tinkle of a bell alerted Mei Ling. It meant the end of meditation. She stretched thrice from the waist, drew a deep breath, and finally looked toward the source of the sound. Two monks stood in the entrance. Each wore the yellow robe. One carried a little bell which was fixed to the end of a handle less than a foot long. This one was sharp-faced Chang Lu. The other, blocky and bushy-browed, was Tai Ching.

"End of meditation," the former said, smiling amiably. "Sometimes talk is better than cogitation."

There was whimsy, good fellowship, merry humor, in Chang Lu, who had brought the bell only as a play of fancy. Chang Lu was multiple treachery, a double-dealer, an adept scoundrel, a serene assassin—yet, in a flash, Mei Ling saw more good in him than in Abbot Shen Hui, the sincere fanatic.

They followed Mei Ling to the pool.

From beneath his robe Tai Ching took a small case of dark wood. The hinged top was secured by a hasp. Mei Ling seated herself in a corner. They set the case between them.

"Your battle was magnificent," Chang Lu began. "I hated to stop it, but I had to."

"*You* struck that gong?"

Chang Lu waggled a hand toward Tai Ching. "We did more than that. We broke the rhythm of soundless sound. We're the Abbot's teachers. He's a good student. He had a good start because of Buddhist studies. So he's learned a bit too well, too much; he's gone too far in mastering Mirror Magic and other things."

"So the fanatic Abbot is a master magician? That fumbling clown!"

Tai Ching's eyes gleamed fiercely. He still hated Mei Ling, having none of his comrade's detachment and humor. "After the way he beat you around, do you call him a clown?"

Mei Ling now understood the entire operation. "You two needed a crew of monks and their chief, so you offered to help Shen Hui blast me into another time and space, another level of existence. But if he succeeded, you'd have wasted all your effort. Unless I remain human, my husband wouldn't pay a ransom, no more than he would if I cut my hair and became a nun."

Chang Lu bowed. "I couldn't express it better. But no matter what you told Shen Hui, he wouldn't believe you, not against me."

"Of course the old fool wouldn't! Now I'll tell you something. The jar of treasure never did amount to a hundred thousand ounces of silver. And my husband and I spent a lot."

"We're not unrealistic," Tai Ching said.

"We're not unreasonable," Chang Lu seconded. He flicked the hasp and raised the cover of the box. It contained an ink slab, brushes, and sticks of ink. "Please write your husband and ask him to put the ransom on deposit with any banker he trusts. The silver will be paid only to one who comes with you to claim it. We will sell the order to any ignorant, innocent, reputable speculator, giving him a fair discount. No crime could be charged against him."

"One hundred thousand—I told you—"

"Always, reasonable negotiation," Chang Lu reminded her.

Tai Ching interposed, "Write and say, *Do not try to follow the messenger who brings letter. He will not return to this place.*"

Mei Ling reached for brush and ink stick. She handed Tai Ching the slab. "Please dip water from the pool?"

He hastened to oblige.

Mei Ling whispered to Chang Lu, "I don't trust that blockhead. He may make a mess of things again."

"He can never exceed his first effort. But he's useful, essential."

Then Tai Ching handed her the slab. Deliberately, she ground the ink stick into the shallow pool of water. She lifted the stick, watched it drip, and resumed her grinding. Presently she dipped a brush. Not quite right. She resumed the grinding.

"Get on with it," Tai Ching urged and brushed sweat from his brow.

Chang Lu remained calm, but he did appraise the height of the sun.

Presently they heard the *slip-slap* shuffle of sandals in the cell adjoining the pool. Chang Lu reached to close the writing case. Mei Ling checked him with hand and glance. She picked a sheet of paper from the case and spread it on the back-turned lid.

Abbot Shen Hui entered the court.

This man was useful to the conspirators as a menace to Mei Ling, yet he was as dangerous to them as to her. Chang Lu and Tai Ching exchanged a biting glance. Mei Ling saw once more the serene expression when Chang Lu considered whether to kill or spare another. One inference, too nearly correct, would be Shen Hui's final deduction! Final awareness. Although of great value, he was no longer indispensable. To suspect his accomplices would doom him.

The Abbot's strained features suggested that his understanding would not be as keen as it normally was, that his wits would lag a little. The two ex-Taoists came to their feet and bowed.

Mei Ling said, "Lord Abbot, I have composed a poem."

"A poem?" he echoed perplexedly.

"These learned persons have told me how hopeless it will be if I meet you in another battle. I've set my mind at rest. I've composed lines of farewell. To my husband and to the Red Earth."

Tai Ching and Chang Lu straightened, and separated their palm-to-palm hands. The latter said, "Our presence makes it difficult for the serpent-devil to shape her verses."

Shen Hui raised his hand. "Let her be alone with her thoughts."

They followed him from the court.

In many a wine-game, Mei Ling, Meilan, and Li Fong had extemporized verses. As she picked up the brush, she wondered whether she had saved the Abbot's life.

Swiftly, she brushed column after column of characters, beginning in the lower third of the sheet and coming very near the left-hand margin. She took a second sheet and repeated, with diverse variation, what she had written on the first one. This brushing was well centered.

The deep voice of a bell sounded. Monks intoned, "*I seek the Buddha . . . I seek the Excellent Law, the Teaching . . . I seek the Assembly . . . the Lord, the dharma, the sangha . . .*"

"And I seek Li Fong, my lover, my husband," the serpent-woman added as she swiftly brushed the ransom request. This was on the sheet which had farewell verses on its bottom portion.

When she was sure that the ink would not smudge, she thrust the ransom request under her mat. She tucked the writing case under her arm and took the farewell poem with her. Following the smell of cooking, she came to the large crypt in which the Abbot and his monks and his ex-Taoists ate their rice gruel, pickled bean curd, and vegetables. She waited respectfully at the entrance until each bowl was empty.

Stepping into the candlelight, Mei Ling knelt before the Abbot. She touched her forehead to the tiles. "Lord Abbot, be pleased to read my farewell to my husband and to the world."

As he regarded the paper, her glance flicked right, flicked left, catching the eye of Tai Ching, the eye of Chang Lu. Their glances answered her, and in entire understanding.

The Abbot read the verses. "I will send them."

She glanced toward the cooking-hearth. "If I send my farewell through the Way of Fire, the knowledge will sink into his heart. If he reads writing, he gets only words in his mind, not real knowledge."

Shen Hui returned the paper. "Permission granted and with blessings."

Mei Ling raised the sheet to her forehead, got up, and went to the hearth. She fed the verses into the coals. As the paper flamed up, she recited a *mantram*. Then she came back to kneel before Shen Hui. "Venerable Abbot, I beg permission to withdraw. I must compose my thoughts and prepare for what is to be. Let it not be painful, if I must go by the Mirror Way. Do what is necessary."

"Go, and again my blessing. There will be bliss and no pain. I am not sure as to which way it should be, but there is this I must remember: hair that has been cut can grow again and nuns are not prisoners."

Head still averted, Mei Ling glanced sidewise, catching the eye of Chang Lu. The flash of perfect understanding told her that he had accepted her as a partner in double-dealing. Sometime during the night Chang Lu would come to get her letter to her husband, the real one.

# CHAPTER XXXVII

LI FONG and Meilan were not surprised when a coolie came to the Hall of Benevolence to present a small parcel. "Someone else will get your answer," he said. "I don't know what this is. Following me is useless. Waste no time trying."

They watched until he merged with the crowd. Meilan gave Li Fong a hand in setting up the heavy shutters to close the shop front. This done, they went to the Great Book Room.

The packet contained Mei Ling's jade pendant. It was wrapped in a letter. Li Fong read, "*Revered Husband! I am in a secret place, a prisoner secured by strong magic. There is one who tries to send me back to the serpent-kingdom. There is another who will release me when you pay one hundred thousand taels. Do not follow any of the messengers who come to you. Each time, a new one. Sell or borrow as you must. Better to be in Hangchow with a single string of cash. If the Mirror Magic of Ko Hung succeeds, no silver can ever bring me back. Those who ask for ransom may not be able to overcome the sorcery working against me. If it is already too late, I have written my farewell poem. Three times, I knock my head against the floor.*"

Meilan cried, "Those dog-fornicating Taoists! They taught Shen Hui too much. He's behind all this, but he couldn't have managed it by himself. That poem, read it!"

He regarded the sheet and shook his head perplexedly.

"Old Master, read it!"

"She's trying to tell us something."

"That's what I want to hear!" she screeched. "Read it to me!"

Li Fong read:

*"A lute player from Omei Mountain*
*With one touch of the strings*
*Brought back memories of meeting in Hangchow*
*By the nine-stage pagoda at the Lion Bridge:*
*Now I sit in the depths of nine-stage sorrow;*
*Ask this river flowing to the east*
*If it goes farther than my love!*
*And do not tell me that robes of Chin*
*Are tattered and soiled with ancient grime."*

Meilan blinked away tears but could not stem the flood. "So sad—" She choked. "And beautiful— *aiieeyah!* Sell everything, borrow, steal, beg, buy her freedom."

Li Fong seized her by the shoulders. "You've missed the whole point! Even when we're up to our eyebrows in a wine-game, she does better than this blob!"

"What's wrong with it? It's beautiful!"

"She lifted several lines from Li Po and, for luck, a bit from a drum-song. And what she didn't steal bodily and bitch up in the borrowing, she butchered all to pieces."

"You're nasty, you haven't any heart!"

"Just listen," he implored. "How could a lute player from Mount Omei bring back memories, when we three met at the ferry slip, in the willows, at West Lake? And there's no pagoda at the Lion Bridge.

"An imaginary nine-stage pagoda; and in the line she didn't crib, she says she's in nine-stage sorrow. Then, in the practically unbutchered line from Li Po—"

Meilan cut in. "Ask the river flowing to the east if it goes farther than my love—that's awfully sweet!"

"That's how the blockhead who checked this letter must have figured. So he didn't catch on. From Soochow or Hangchow, anything flowing east doesn't go so far but what you could swim it easily. The poet was a couple of thousand *li* upstream, saying goodbye to a friend. This thing isn't as addled and chewed up as it sounds."

Meilan's mouth rounded. "She's telling us to come and get her?"

"What else could she mean by that quip about *robes of Chin* being ragged and grimy? *Robes of Chin* is poet talk, meaning a scholar, which is what I started out to be."

"So the robe is not ragged!" She backed away, regarded him. She nodded her approval. "Your First Woman's going to see you do your first killing?"

"If they don't outrun me. And no spirit-sword, not this time!"

"There should be, just in case man-weapons aren't enough. Elder Sister taught me a lot. But to sell out, go away, start all over—might that not really be better? Mightn't it?"

"If that fanatic has become so powerful, he'll catch them off guard and finish her before we can buy her out. Can you put fire into the spirit-sword? Do that and skip the chopper. I'll handle the steel department, if those fellows want to play that way."

"I can bring the peachwood sword to life, but not with the power she can put into it."

"Do what you can."

"How much time?"

"I've got to make a show of trying to sell and borrow, just in case we're being watched. While I'm doing that, I'll be finding out about a nine-stage pagoda in the general direction of her pilgrimage."

He paused, frowning. "Ah Lo's wife—have her put on some of your most conspicuous clothes and make up her face so she'll look quite a bit like you, as far as strangers are concerned. Ah Sam and Ah Lo will watch in the court. They should call to her, using your name, so snoopers will believe you're at home. Tonight you and I are going to look for Mei Ling."

That evening Li Fong sat in the Great Book Room, eyeing Meilan and Ah Lo's wife, who'd gone to work in the kitchen when her husband had been signed up as one of Li Fong's apprentices.

"Not bad at all," Li Fong declared. "Better than Number Two Lady was doing. How did you learn the trick?"

"For a while I put make-up on actors at the opera,"

the serpent-man's wife answered. "Sometimes I'd change faces for fugitives."

Li Fong regarded her for a moment. "You're Ming Ta, is that right?"

"Yes, Old Master. Ming Ta."

Li Fong fingered the sword which lay on the table, with the strangler cord and the well-loaded truncheon. "Ming Ta, staying here may be as dangerous as what Number Two Lady and I are undertaking. *Tai-tai* is in great danger and she is one of your people. If you are here when this is over and any of us don't come back, you'll always be one of those who lived through this."

Ming Ta's eyes widened. She made as if to speak, but did not.

"Second Lady," he said to Meilan, "I have promised a promise. Do you promise with me, swearing by gods and spirits?"

"Ming Ta is my sworn sister, from this minute." Meilan caught the kitchen girl in her arms for a firm embrace. "Before gods, devils, spirits, I swear and I promise."

Dressed as pilgrims, Li Fong and Meilan left the city well after dark.

"Old Master, you're sure this is the right road?"

"There are several ways to Yakshih Temple. The only abandoned nine-story pagoda is on this road—Rainbow Pagoda."

Meilan sighed. "This is bad joss. It's always lived with me. That awful moment when the shock of seeing me turn human killed that good monk. I can't outlive the karma."

"Don't be so dark!" he chided. "When I finish those kidnapers, I'll have a package of karma to keep you company for ages."

Finally they had the farmlands behind them. The wagon track wound into the darkness of the woods.

"Let's rest here till moonlight."

"We can't afford to waste a minute," Meilan protested.

"The first moonlight will show us the pagoda top, and we'll save time."

They rested beneath an enormous tree, their backs against the trunk. After a long silence, Meilan said, "When we get there, I'll know what to do."

"The sky has a different face. The moon rises soon."

They resumed their plodding.

After another long silence, Meilan demanded, "Tell me this thing. Tell me and I promise never to repeat it. This is my night for swearing and promising. Because of Mei Ling, you almost died, and tonight you risk life again. Can you really love a snake-woman?"

He didn't fancy that question at all. He liked things less when she added, "Suppose I couldn't come back from tonight and Elder Sister wanted someone to take my place—would it be a human woman or one of our kind—your choice, I mean?"

"Wait till we get her out of this mess and then ask her! You ask more questions, most of them silly!"

"Why do you and Elder Sister always say my questions make no sense? I just wanted to know if a real human woman is different-nice."

"That's what real human women ask about serpent-women."

"*O-mi-to-fu!* Tell me, I really want to know!"

He smacked her on the rump. His palm had been perfectly cupped to the curvature. "No human woman ever sounded that good! Get your mind on here-and-now problems. No human woman would be competition to you or *tai-tai!*"

Moments passed. In the thinning gloom, Meilan's teeth and eyes gleamed; Li Fong caught the impish grimace, and he was ready for it when she wagged her head and announced, "I'm still thinking of our future. I can't stop."

"All *right!* Now what is it?"

"Whom does the Old Master chop first with that sword? Or slug with the no-killing club full of lead?"

Li Fong felt better. What he'd taken for dark premonitions were only insatiable curiosity and compulsive chattering. If ever he had a second concubine, he'd be sure she was silent!

Moon glow against the sky was beginning to help them. Presently they saw the upper stages of a pagoda, high above the forest. Vestiges of gilt and lacquer mirrored a moon still too low to be seen from ground level.

He squeezed her arm. "Good joss, First Woman."

Meilan turned, pressed against him, snuggled up, and held him in a possessive, almost fierce embrace. "First Lover, I'll always, always remember. *Aiieeyah!* I'm crazy-excited—tonight will make me human-beyond-change-back!"

She led the way. Whenever they came to an open area, a glimpse of the pagoda eaves justified her sensings. He hefted the neat little truncheon with its core of metal. He loosened the sword in its sheath. He fingered the coil of silken cord for silent strangling. Li Fong hoped that this would be another of the nights which Chang Lu considered lucky!

# CHAPTER XXXVIII

MEILAN wormed her way along a trail which Li Fong could barely discern until, from a small clearing, they got first sight of the pagoda's lower levels. They heard the muted sound of drums and chanting. As they pressed on, shafts of brightness reached between the trees, touching the masonry of the pagoda's substructure and the earthquake-riven bricks of the enclosing wall.

They skirted the perimeter. There was more to the drumming than they had at first suspected. A vibration that the ear could not sense suggested wind instruments with voices lower than any drum could have. At times, as they passed a deeper gap in the wall, they felt the rhythmical concussion.

"Dragons mumbling in their sleep," Meilan whispered. "Devil-music, dreaming dragons worried by spirits . . ."

After moments of ever stealthier advance, he caught her arm and pointed. "Light from inside and from below."

They edged in among whispering bamboo. The stalks were half a foot in diameter and towered sixty feet or higher. The advance became ever more difficult. Where the growth was not in clusters, the space between stalks was so narrow that they could only twist their way through.

Finally Li Fong said, "Gateway—over there, to your left."

The barrier thinned as they neared the spot he had pointed out. The drumming and the wind-instrument vibration beat against them in blasts.

"All clear," Li Fong decided, after a long pause to probe the treacherous pattern of light and shadow.

He stepped forward. He recoiled as if thrust back by a blow. Meilan clung to him to regain her balance. Instead of a numbing impact, he felt a strange tingling. He stood for a moment, bemused and disturbed by an obstacle at once yielding and solid.

He nudged Meilan. "You go, you look and listen."

She got no farther than Li Fong. Instead of recoiling, she drew back, since her approach had been more deliberate and tentative.

"A wall of power. This is bad."

"Let's try together."

Clinging to each other, they shouldered the invisible barrier. Insofar as it yielded, its elasticity only served to push them back.

"There must be a way," Li Fong declared. "The messenger went through to bring us the letter."

"Power was chanted down, and he went through."

"Try somewhere else."

They squirmed along, skirting the masonry. Neither was able to touch the bricks. Presently they came to a small wicket. Only a little of its rotting wood remained. Li Fong thrust his companion aside and drew his sword. He slashed, a gesture of despair and fury. The blade bounced, twisting from his grasp. There was no sound.

'*O-mi-to-fu!* Do we have to wait for a messenger, to see how he goes through?"

There would be someone coming to report Li Fong's doings that afternoon. However, they could not keep the entire perimeter under observation or guess the time of the man's arrival. Meilan kicked off her sandals. Effortlessly, she began climbing a bamboo shaft. Incredulous, Li Fong watched the ascent. She moved with a serpent's continuous and flexible contact with the hard, smooth bamboo. The stalk swayed. Up— up—twenty—thirty feet. He wondered whether she would drop from the now bending bamboo and fall into the spreading top of a tree in the courtyard.

"If she makes it, how can I follow?"

At last the shaft came to rest, as if against invisible support. Meilan descended. "Not even a bird can make it," she said despairingly. "The way the stalk felt when it stopped bending—something like the cover of a jar—it curves—I touched what I couldn't see. Not even the *tulku* could get through that. And Elder Sister couldn't ride the wind through that force. If she'd only taught me more!"

"She did teach you."

"What did she teach?"

"The spirit-sword. Let me try it."

"I forgot. But you want it again?"

"I did use it once. I'll risk it again."

"No, let me," Meilan countered.

"And leave me stranded outside? Woman, give me that sword."

She handed him the silk-swathed peachwood and huddled behind him.

"Let go; I've got to move fast."

She clung. He knew she would not let go. He whisked away the silken swathing and presented the blade. Blue-white, blinding flame seared his eyes. An acrid scent stung his nostrils. He lurched headlong, propelled by Meilan. He rolled and for an instant threshed about as if kicking free of an entanglement. He clawed the flagstones. Meilan had gone through with him.

"Not blind—can see—nothing moves," she gasped.

Through spots of red and green, of black and blue-white dancing behind his eyelids, Li Fong's vision returned bit by bit. Meilan was with him, to share all the risks. With her spirit-sword expended, there were only mundane weapons left. Trying to keep her out of trouble by insisting that she not bring her chopper had not been a bright notion.

Huddled in a dark angle of the foundation terrace, they paused to learn whether the momentary breach of the barrier had alerted Shen Hui and his adepts. For moments they listened. The chanting and the vibration had not varied.

"Does the chanting mean anything to you?"

"No—it's something like things Elder Sister taught me, but it's different, too. How long do we squat here, doing nothing?"

"You find a spot, right now, where you'll be out of sight. A cell or room those fellows haven't cleaned up. Then fire up the spirit-sword."

"That will take too long."

"We have more time than anything else. Figuring how to get out may take us the rest of our lives. And finding her is another problem. I'll have to settle whoever is guarding her."

Presently they found a storeroom not too heavily littered with rubbish. There was just enough trash to afford good cover. "Snakes and scorpions won't hurt me, but that human vermin will be afraid of them."

He handed Meilan the loaded truncheon. "This might come in handy. Stay right where you are until you know that I'm in bad trouble and that I haven't liberated Mei Ling."

Groping in darkness, they cleared a corner of the musty room.

"Once I know where she is and what's going on, I'll come and tell you, and you can help with whatever there is. And we'll leave all together, if it's possible. Don't worry!"

She caught him with both arms. "I won't. I feel the power, the way I did that night when the blessed monk was chanting for the lonely ones. We've got good joss tonight. First Lover, our little life's been awfully wonderful."

She let go, and he crept out into shadow and moon patches.

The faint glow they had noted from the outside guided him. It outlined an entrance into the foundation. The vibration was stronger. He worked his way toward the crumbling outer wall, at times grazing the invisible force-barrier. Darkness covered him as he swung back toward the several solid-brick structures in the court. He paused, listening and scenting the incense fumes which permeated the area. He caught the smell of wood smoke, of cooking oil, of spices.

Li Fong had lost his hat in crossing the barrier. Garments hanging on a wash-line near the kitchen stirred in the breeze. These were monks' robes. Although his head was not shaved, it would make him less conspicuous if he wore one of those symbolically patched outfits. Thus, half disguised, he let sound guide him through a dark passageway.

The impact of concussion instruments began to shake him, jar him, hammer at him. Dismay quickly approached terror when he realized that his breathing had begun to accord with the rhythm. His heart, instead of rising to choke him, was slowing down, obeying the cadence of music and of chanting. The effort to resist was an exhausting struggle. Soon it had him sweating and tired and twitching. He was isolated, cut off from all being. He began to wish that Meilan were with him. He fought his urge for her presence, lest she sense his feeling and come to join him. He thought of Mei Ling and how she must be affected by that diabolic cadence beating at her hour after hour after hour.

There were moments of desperation during which he wanted to yell and rush crazily about, flailing his sword, slashing everyone he met—anything to break the enervating, the compulsive music of the massed adepts.

He fought his ruinous urge. Save that frenzy for the final moment! Hold your own! They don't know you're here, he told himself. You do know. Meet them, and then be like Meilan and her chopper.

He had new confidence, but hard-won, precariously balanced, and all of a flutter . . .


## CHAPTER XXXIX

EMERGING from a passageway, Li Fong looked into the spacious chamber ahead of him. This must be the center of the foundation. The walls were pierced by openings leading to further crypts. Vibration came from every direction, and so from no direction whatsoever. He faced taper-lighted emptiness—and the lights indicated that, at any time, one or more of Shen Hui's crew would be moving through what must be the crossroads of the foundation.

Keyed for sword strokes, he faced nothing at all. He had to guess which passage should first be probed. Either this or retreat and explore the perimeter of the terrace to find a fresh approach. He groped for decision. Meilan's serpent-intuition might guide him to the heart of the maze, to the operational center rather than to the architectural core, and thus to the area where Mei Ling was facing Mirror Magic. The painful throbbing at his temples left him muddled, incapable of thought.

Finally the helplessness, the stupor which had cost him so many minutes, brought compensation. A man emerged from the opening at Li Fong's right. He wore a black robe and wedge-shaped Taoist hat. The face was familiar. Images flickered through Li Fong's memory. Then came recognition; this was the man who, as a coolie, had delivered the ransom demand.

He moved deliberately, yet in the way of one going with a purpose.

The dead air stirred. There came a cooler current, fresh and without incense flavor. The newcomer went toward the source of the breeze. As he stepped into the darkness of an opening, Li Fong came from cover. Barefooted, he made no sound.

He entered the gloom of a cell. A narrow cleft in the farther wall opened on a court. Moonlight silvered the upper reaches of the brick-walled enclosure. Taper light gilded the tiles.

A man was asking, "Any trouble getting through?"

"That's why I'm late! I thought I'd never sound the *dharani* the way you taught me to sound it. Couldn't get the tone just right. Maybe I was too tired."

Li Fong risked a peep. Chang Lu was sitting on a cushion against the wall. The messenger continued, "Have they missed the Abbot?"

Chang Lu chuckled. "Not at all! I persuaded him to tell his crowd that he was going into retreat to build up his powers. He did better than I expected. He really did need a rest—pretty well worn out from battling that female devil. Anyway, he told them that he was not to be disturbed, and Hing is at the door, to make sure nobody interrupts his meditation."

The courier chuckled appreciatively.

Another, who sat beyond Li Fong's narrow range of peeping, cut in impatiently. "We've been tending to our business. What have you been doing? You took long enough about it."

"Tai Ching," came the biting retort, "you should have gone in my place. To do things well and quickly. But then you would not have been here, to make sure everything went perfectly."

Li Fong began to estimate the odds. A sword was part of Tai Ching's regalia, even when he was selling herbs. The best move might be to stalk them, and pick them off with the strangler's cord, one by one—after he had learned where Mei Ling was imprisoned.

"Well, what did happen?" Chang Lu demanded. "No time for wrangling!"

"I delivered the message. Got into different clothes, came back to watch the house. Followed Li Fong to a couple of brokers and money lenders, till I was sure he was busy with it."

"You came back and followed him? You didn't lose much time changing and getting back."

"He had to do some thinking before he made the rounds. And talk to the women and tell them he had news of the Number One Lady."

"Then what? Did he raise the silver?"

"I didn't see him. I talked to his concubine, Madame Meilan. If you ask me, he'd be crazy to go any further. He should settle for her and keep his hundred thousand."

"Stick to the point," Tai Ching grumbled. "Your taste in women doesn't interest me a bit."

"All right, you tell the story."

"Carry on," Chang Lu said smoothly. "Don't interrupt him."

"Madame Meilan said that the master had come back an hour ago and was so worried that he took some Indian sleeping potion and couldn't be roused even with hot irons. She said for us to take good care of Madame Mei Ling. The silver would be ready, maybe tomorrow, maybe the next day."

The so-called coolie, considerably different-looking simply because of a change of clothes, had returned for information and then hurried back to the pagoda. This, Li Fong told himself, indicated that Chang Lu did not have many accomplices. This was good to know. Good, also, to know that Ming Ta had a convincing story for every situation.

And then a voice tore all Li Fong's plans to shreds. Mei Ling was taking part in the parley. "Chang Lu, are you sure you have the Abbot under control? How long can you keep his monks from suspecting that he's a prisoner and not, by any means, in a retreat? That last face-to-face contest nearly finished me."

"That's something he didn't suspect. He took quite a beating. You nearly had *him* finished," Chang Lu assured her. "When he realizes he's a prisoner, he'll spend most of his power getting himself liberated. I'll help you get built up for the next duel, if there is one."

For Li Fong there would never be a moment better than this. He had only one armed man to cut down. The others, if agile, might escape with their lives. He edged through the slot. The swish of sword clearing scabbard was the first warning of his presence. The gleam of steel by moonlight and taper light, the spectacle of one in a monk's yellow robe, crouched behind a presented blade, shocked them.

"Woman, come here and out of my way!"

Tai Ching's gasp was hoarse, guttural, as he jerked to his feet.

Chang Lu remained seated.

The courier whirled about, recoiled, stopped in front of Tai Ching, at once blocking him and protecting him. Mei Ling came out of the corner which had concealed her. She moved swiftly along the wall to Li Fong.

He made two short, flashing-quick steps, shuffle-steps, bare feet slapping the tiles. The sound was as sharp as hand claps. The long-practiced menace-step jarred the three who faced him—the mincing step, the crisp impact, often disconcerted a seasoned swordsman if the timing were just right. Attack—no attack—not yet—*now!* The staccato question, the suspense, the change of pace—the slash—

Tai Ching's first reach for the sword beneath his robe ended in a jerk, his hand back to his side. He had read death and he knew that he could not draw in time to defend himself. Fury blazed in his eyes. His teeth gleamed in that familiar snarl. His brows bristled. He recoiled before the one-two shuffle-slap.

The courier leaped sidewise. That Tai Ching had not drawn his blade threw Li Fong off balance. He was a novice. A seasoned fighting man would instantly cut down an empty-handed enemy, purely as a matter of instinct and the need for security.

Chang Lu alone sat, not shaken. Li Fong's glance covered the trio, swept them. He was heartened by the effect of his long-practiced footwork.

Exaltation, like wine-dizziness, gave Li Fong a queer, floating feeling which went beyond reality and unreality alike. He knew now that when the instant came, instinct would prompt him. A ripping thrust for Tai Ching. Fling-topple him against Chang Lu. Then—

"Not yet," Mei Ling whispered. "Not yet."

Chang Lu asked, "How will you get out of here?"

Mei Ling said, "The same way he came in. Better think of those who won't live to leave."

Chang Lu's face changed. This encouraged Li Fong. Even an instant's revelation of disturbance had meaning. Getting out would not be simple. Meilan had barely grazed through with him. How would three fugitives fare?

And how many hidden enemies, armed men, did the pagoda conceal? In this short space, could Meilan have revitalized the peachwood sword? These and other questions needed more than a quick blade to answer.

Better be guided by Mei Ling's counsel.

Killing exaltation faded. Shen Hui was the real enemy. These Taoists were only ransom gougers who had saved Mei Ling for this moment. As nearly as he could reckon, they had saved her from the Abbot.

Chang Lu got to his feet and thrust Tai Ching aside. Smiling, he asked, "How did you get through? This is interesting."

"Come and I'll show you," Li Fong answered. "First, try guessing how many came with me."

His power was coming back. From the corner of his eye, he caught Tai Ching's apprehensive facial twitch.

Mei Ling said, "I'm watching the entrance. You watch these three."

Tai Ching said fiercely, "This devil is bad joss."

"Easy," Chang Lu countered. "There's an answer for all this. Hing—" He indicated the courier. "Madame Meilan convinced him that Master Li Fong was in an opium stupor. Also, she's in charge of the house and knows all about this business.

"Put up your sword, Master Li Fong. Stay with us until your concubine gets the ransom. Then go free with your wife." He smiled winningly. He was so very genuine. "Instead of killing and the risk of being killed—many of those you have not seen tonight are not peaceful Buddhists—it would be better to give us a gratitude gift. We've protected her against the Abbot's magic. We can do as much for you."

The Middle Way—the Way of the Sages—the awareness that in his heart he was not truly a man-slayer, appealed to Li Fong. This must have been the knowledge which had moved Mei Ling to check his moment-of-killing urge.

Mei Ling interposed, "A gratitude gift, perhaps ten thousand *taels*? I promise you this, before gods and spirits, before Heaven and Earth. But we leave now."

"You can't!" Tai Ching shouted. "Ten thousand! For all our work, all we did to protect her against being flung back into the serpent-world!"

"You don't know who or what or how many came through with me," Li Fong retorted. "I join her in the promise of a gratitude gift. Those who'll help kill all of you will ask me for a larger gift."

Tai Ching was scowling, sweating. Chang Lu's face hinted that he was busily flicking the balls of his mental abacus. He proposed, "Make your gratitude gift generous enough for *my* helpers. There's always a balance, a rightness, in things. Remember the teachings of the Great Men of Old."

Li Fong said, "The first time you and I met, I was bad joss. I brought a silver serpent to settle you. The next time, your friend Tai Ching found that I was bad joss, for him and for you. I've never brought you good luck. But this time, perhaps I will."

"How, Master Li Fong?"

"Simply that I'm here should mean much. Either accept a gift or push your luck too far, and see what the Son of Heaven does for you."

No need to speak of beheading, or impalement, or slicing. Such possibilities had lived with every Taoist ever since the Emperor had expelled them from the palace.

Mei Ling cried a warning.

Li Fong's glance shifted. He heard the *slip-slap* of footfalls from the larger chamber and a mumble of voices, echoed and re-echoed. Too late! Li Fong knew that he faced living men who should by now, and could by now, be dead men. Mei Ling had failed—no, he himself had failed, being a talking scholar instead of a man-slayer, as he should have been.

# CHAPTER XL

CHANG LU yelled, the startling shout, the lung-blast, fierce, trumpetlike, disconcerting, of the *kung fu* fighter. Rage whipped to flame by bad joss moved him. Empty-handed, he took his chance against a startled swordsman. Tai Ching, shocked into action by that same explosion of sound, drew and slashed. Li Fong, caught off balance by his own overlong bargaining, went into action, but not as he would have, not as he could have if he'd responded to his moment of exaltation, of killing ecstasy.

Tai Ching's blow failed, but it struck the sword from Li Fong's grasp. The courier, Hing, snatched a bamboo staff.

Chang Lu's charge brought him afoul of his ally. He missed his mark. The enemy he had sought to disarm was empty-handed, but not where he should have been. Nearly falling, Chang Lu lost an instant in recovering.

Mei Ling thrust a bamboo staff into Li Fong's hand as he twisted, evading Tai Ching's scramble to regain footing and close in with his sword. There was no chance for Li Fong to retrieve the blade, which had skated across the tiles. He had to meet steel with a quarterstaff and make what he could of stick fighting.

From the far corner of the court came a scream of pure fury, a cry of killing mania, the high, shrilling pitch of ultimate despair, ultimate and reckless resolve. Meilan had dropped from the crown of the wall and into the cushioning shrubs near the pool. She hurled the loaded truncheon. It smashed full into the face of the foremost of the two who bounded into the court. They came from the farther chamber.

She flung the peachwood sword to Li Fong. It slid along the tiles, and within his reach, as he and Mei Ling bounded back into the far corner. With his quarterstaff, he clouted and dropped the second of the new-comers, Taoists who shouted something which no one could understand. A third needed no smash across the head, no slash across the face, no thrust to the stomach.

Whatever he might have tried to say came only as a yell of terror.

Mei Ling outcried him. "Don't! *No—don't!*"

The agony which made her voice painful to hear checked the three in the farther corner. Tai Ching screeched, lowered his blade. Li Fong, moving like an automaton, plied his staff and struck a glancing blow. The last of those who raced in from the outer chamber stumbled and rolled across the tiles, thrown by the prostrate bodies of their predecessors in meeting madness.

Li Fong risked a glance through the slot. All was clear from the side, but there were three in the corner. Hing, the courier, was scrambling for the blade which had been knocked from Li Fong's grasp. Nasty odds, two swords against him.

Mei Ling wailed, a shuddering cry of despair. "*Aiieeyah . . .*"

Her voice and the faces of the enemies in the corner compelled Li Fong to risk a glance from his immediate front. Then he knew why his wife had dipped to the very bottom of misery.

Instead of Meilan, there was a serpent with emerald-gleaming scales. Seven yards of terrible beauty, moving with eye-tricking speed, cleared the lotus pool. Mumbling newcomers, recovering from cloutings and stumblings, choked and gasped, appalled by what they'd fallen into.

Hing quit scrambling for Li Fong's sword. He didn't know which way to run. Chang Lu's footwork failed him. He crashed against Hing. He recovered, but *kung fu* was no defense against the gleaming green monster which whipped about him. From knee to shoulder, the remorseless coils tightened.

There was no sound now except an agonized wheeze . . . the *crack . . . crack . . . crack . . .* of snapping bones. This was deliberate, measured . . . as if the serpent savored each moment. The green, gleaming head extended farther and farther from the cozy nuzzling, nestling against Chang Lu's throat and chin. His body was becoming thinner, ever thinner as the coils tightened and ribs cracked.

Mei Ling's wail of despair battered Li Fong. The splendor and the horror of Meilan's transformation shocked him. Stupefied, moving like a marionette, he clouted a man who knelt, gasping. Stupefied, he picked up the peachwood sword, as if it would be better than the quarterstaff he had plied so effectively.

"Sister—Sister—" Mei Ling wailed in misery.

Li Fong, beyond thinking, could only feel—until he became incapable of any feeling. He was one with those enemies, with all except Tai Ching.

Tai Ching, Taoist magician, *feng shui* man, the clown, the bungler who always made the wrong move, was the only one able to act during those dreadful moments in which the serpent wrath had squeezed Chang Lu from human stature to something so slender that it could be swallowed by a python of good size.

Numbed wits. Numbed body. Then Li Fong's yell, which released him. He bounded, peachwood sword advanced. He could not move fast enough. No one could. Again he yelled—

Tai Ching's blade flickered. He had said once to

209

Chang Lu that he understood serpent-folk. He did. He struck. The serpent head dropped to the tiles. The remains of Chang Lu toppled, thumped, and lay twitching within the gleaming green coils of the woman who had so long wondered whether wrath, or desire, or love could produce instant change.

Li Fong charged, wood against steel.

Tai Ching whirled to meet him. When he saw that he faced a spirit-sword in the hands of the man who had once blasted him with fire, he screamed. He dropped his blade. Panic drove him. He bounded, lunged, crashing against the masonry of the narrow slot. He could not check himself to turn and get through. There was a sound as of an overripe melon dropped to hard earth. He collapsed, an instant before Li Fong splintered the spirit-sword across his back. There had been no fire in the peachwood. There had not been time for Meilan to charge it. The terror of memory made it as deadly as if she had remained at her task and completed it.

Mei Ling caught her husband by the shoulder. "You can't hurt the dead. I heard, I felt, I know."

Li Fong recovered his blade of steel. He glanced at the green serpent and shuddered. He looked at his half-conscious enemies, lying on the tiles. His hand twitched. The sword twinkled, shimmered.

"I'll send them after her, to be her coolies—"

Mei Ling checked him. "They'd be poor slaves. Sending our love to her in shadow-land would be better. You have others to deal with, any minute now. And we must get out—quickly!"

They heard footsteps. The echoes were confusing. "Maybe no more than one or two," Li Fong said, cocking his head and gesturing to Mei Ling. "Over here—might be more—catch them from the side—"

After a moment, a man raced in. "The Abbot got loose!" he shouted, and then recoiled from what he saw.

"Get the old fool, quick, and you may live longer."

Mei Ling clung to her husband. "Sister, you didn't have to, you didn't have to," she wailed. And then she caught Li Fong's arms in time to keep him from slashing at one who was trying to regain his feet.

They went into the central chamber.

Abbot Shen Hui came hobbling to meet them. He was bent, haggard, and bewildered. He halted, shocked by the sight of Li Fong, sword in hand.

Mei Ling said, "Lord Abbot, no magic. He'd cut you in half before you made a *mudra*. He'd eat your liver."

Her bitter voice touched him as a whiplash. His face posed questions which his mouth could not shape.

Mei Ling continued, "Go into that court. See the killing that your good works produced. You and I have battled in magic. Each time you lost because your Taoist friends were double-dealing. They were holding me for ransom, always blocking you before you could beat me and send me back through time and space.

"Your crew of adepts doesn't know what we've done to Chang Lu. They're still at work, keeping up the force-barrier. It was not very good. My sister and my husband broke through. It wasn't my magic that beat you; it was your own conceit, your passion for being a savior, a Boddhisattva.

"Stop your magicians and let the barrier fall."

Shen Hui began to recover. He straightened. His magnificent old head and square face radiated power, dignity. "This is far from settled," he asserted. "It is just beginning."

"Go into the court and see the killings you caused. Do as I say!"

"Devil-woman, who are you to command me?"

"I'm one who has a magic you've never had. I'm going to call the Lords of Fire. I'll give you time to get your people well away from the pagoda, well out into the woods. Go, get the living, if you won't see the dead. My sister—Chang Lu—Tai Ching—and the wounded—get them out before they die in the fire. Quickly! I'll show you an enchantment such as you've never dreamed."

The Abbot said to his one-time guard, "Go, tell them."

"Venerable Sir, who'd believe me? You'll have to tell them."

"Lord Abbot," Mei Ling said, "my husband and I will wait at the barrier. If we have to wait too long I'll set to work; whoever is destroyed in the fire, it will be charged to you, your fault, your stubbornness."

They left Shen Hui to do what pleased him.

As they made their way out of the crypts, Mei Ling said, "Younger Sister wondered many a time whether any of the serpent-folk could be killed by material weapons. Now she knows! *O-mi-to-fu!* Now she knows!"

Li Fong guided his wife from the refectory into the open court.

"Meilan knew that she wouldn't be coming back with us. The way she hated Chang Lu, the one man she always wanted to kill . . . Whatever it costs, a desire fulfilled leaves one free from that desire; it's buried in the graveyard of desires."

They looked up at the moon. The drumming, the trumpeting, the chanting, all had lapsed into silence. It was strange and lovely to hear crickets and night birds again. Mei Ling went with her husband toward the little wicket. There was no longer any force-wall.

"*Tai-tai*, there was a moment when I could have killed the three, and Younger Sister wouldn't have died," he said as they stood against great bamboo stalks. "I was weak, stupid. I'll be sad all my life."

"*Taijen*, she had the desire for killing. It was in her soul. At last the craving is satisfied. She's liberated from it. Or she can be, if she has finally seen through it and really knows. You didn't have any such passion, or you'd have finished them in a flash, no matter what I said. Look—here they come!"

Monks in gray robes, monks in yellow robes, followed Shen Hui.

They hailed him. He said, "It is not fitting to leave the dead as they are."

Mei Ling said, "Lord Abbot, you still don't understand. Is every living creature out of the pagoda?"

"Yes, the well and the wounded are out. Only the dead remain."

"Buddhist and Taoist? Those who betrayed you? No one in the cells, asleep?"

"Buddhist and Taoist, yes. Those who hated me, yes. No one is asleep."

"Then come to the far edge of this bamboo stand, and you will get the fullness of knowledge." And as they edged and squirmed their way among the tall stalks, she said, "You'll see what I could have used against you at any time, and against Chang Lu and Tai Ching."

"Your final magic, Madame Mei Ling?"

"Only the gods can use it a second time. I and my kind use it only at the cost of all powers, all magic beyond ordinary humans."

The Abbot muttered, halted, looked up, as he waited at the far edge of the grove and saw his followers and his betrayers come into the openness of the forest.

"You will become fully human, then?"

"I won't know until I've looked into a mirror."

Mei Ling raised her arms. She stood silently for endless moments. Then she began to make a droning, keening sound, without ever shaping a word. It was a sound which rose and fell, with all the many modulations of *pip'a* and flute, and many another instrument, stringed and wind. This was neither *dharani* nor *mantram*; it was basic sound, which went beyond words, beyond ideas, beyond concepts.

Chills raced up and down Li Fong's spine. For a while, he heard the Abbot's hoarse breathing and he knew how the old man must feel in the presence of someone, something, so far beyond him, above him.

Great wings blotted out the moon, and shifted, and circled the pagoda. Dark wings, dragon shapes, swooping, soaring, down to the terrace and up again. As they swerved, the wings and scaled bodies began to shimmer and glow, until iridescence became radiant and outreaching. The soaring, circling dragon shapes came ever closer together, until they made a spiral veil which hid all but the peak of the Rainbow Pagoda and its nine stages.

Ruddy . . . orange . . . golden . . . finally, blue-white, blinding! Then the dragons winged away, leaving the pagoda a column of fire. Flame gushing up the tall hollow shaft roared like a typhoon. Tiles exploded in scintillant flashes. The masonry of the terrace became a white-hot, lambent pool from which sparks erupted.

Li Fong gasped, snatched the Abbot's shoulder, and pointed. "She goes to the Fire Dragons, the Great Lords. Look!"

The column of fire such as he had never imagined became rose and lavender. From it emerged a human shape, a figure all flame-colored, made all of fire, yet as clear and lovely as Meilan herself had ever been. She raised arms in an embracing gesture and she smiled and called words he could not hear. He knew that those were happy words, triumphant—a farewell in which joy went beyond the sadness that rules all partings.

Li Fong lurched forward, burying his face in the leaves and the grass between his palms. "First Woman, First Woman! *O-mi-to-fu!*" he cried. "You knew when we started out—*you knew*—"

A hand touched his shoulder. Mei Ling knelt beside him. He looked up. The apparition had vanished. The flames were subsiding. Only fluid masonry remained, turning from white to gold and then to sullen red.

Mei Ling said to the Abbot, "I could have included you in all this, as a sacrifice to give Younger Sister a fitting funeral."

He stood, looking at her. Understanding began to grow; it showed in his haggard face. "Is there peace between us?"

Mei Ling sighed. "The only peace for you to seek is within yourself."

He knelt, spread out his hands. Before he could touch his forehead to the ground, Mei Ling knelt and took his hands. He rose with her, and then she said, "We're all bound to the wheel of Life and Death, she and you and I and all these other creatures. Go, and with my good will."

Mei Ling turned to Li Fong. "Let's go home and uncover my mirror, to see what face it reflects."

"I know already," said Li Fong as they picked their way to the wagon track leading back to Soochow. And then he told her how Meilan had taken leave of Ming Ta, wife of the apprentice, and later of him, as they had approached the pagoda.

"She knew," he concluded when they came to the rutted road, "that she would never return with us. She went out of love of you, to pay what she called her debt from that night you two won human form. There's nothing left for you to pay Fate, and you've been released from the karma."

At last they came to a small stream which wound out into open moonlight. Mei Ling stepped toward the bank, then drew back and nudged Li Fong. "You drink, Old Master. I'm not thirsty."

"Lovely Mei Ling—Tien Yuk—Jade Lady—that pool is a mirror, and I can't wait till we're home. Let's look."

"Old Master, I'm afraid. In the pagoda pool, my reflection—I didn't like it—it wasn't human."

He gave her a gentle push. "Go alone, look alone."

He watched her slowly, hesitantly, approaching, kneeling. He said, "I don't care—Heavenly Jewel, Jade Lady—" And he bounded to her side and knelt.

There was no serpent image mirrored in the water. All he saw was the human loveliness of that morning near West Lake by the willows. Li Fong laid a hand on her shoulder and slowly traced the elegant curve all the way to her hip. He said finally, "Your good karma, *tai-tai*. You said, in the pagoda court where I found you, that the image was not like this one. You saved some lives, I think, and kept me from being a mankiller when I would have sliced a few apart to send them with Meilan to be her coolies."

Li Fong had half turned to face her as they knelt. Mei Ling clutched his arm, gasped, "Look—my reflected face changes—"

"*O-mi-to-fu!* I don't care what it is!" He turned to see the water-mirrored image. "It's still changing!"

Bit by bit, the reflection, which was neither that of his wife nor that of Meilan, became ever more like that of the First Woman he would never again see in this incarnation. But when it finally ceased changing, it was the face of a Meilan neither he nor Mei Ling had ever seen.

Li Fong gave her his hand. Eyes gleaming, Mei Ling regarded him through large tears which trickled slowly

215

along her cheeks. "Lover, that was the face of her next birth. Maybe she didn't gain merit, crushing Chang Lu to death, but she'll be human, really totally human, her next birth."

## ABOUT THE AUTHOR

E. HOFFMANN PRICE (1898–present) soldiered in the Philippines and France during World War I. At war's end he was appointed to the United States Military Academy, where he entered intercollegiate pistol and fencing competition. He was graduated in 1923 and commissioned in the Coast Artillery Corps. His first fiction sale was March 1924, to *Droll Stories*. By 1932, he was writing full time—fantasy, adventure, westerns, detective. When the pulps folded, he earned grog, gasoline and groceries by holding two jobs and by filming weddings and practicing astrology in his spare time. Thanks to his incessant motoring, he met and made enduring friendships with Farnsworth Wright, Hugh Rankin, Otis Adelbert Kline, Lovecraft, Howard, W. K. Mashburn, Clark Ashton Smith, Edmond Hamilton, Seabury Quinn, Jack Williamson, Robert Spencer Carr, Leigh Brackett, C. L. Moore, and a comparable number in the non-fantasy fields.

During the past sixteen years, Price has been known in San Francisco's Chinatown as Tao Fa, the *dharma* name conferred by Venerable Yen Pei of Singapore, and he is mentioned in prayers every new moon and full moon in two Taoist-Buddhist temples. As a gourmet, he cooks shark fin soup, sautées *bêche-de-mer* with black mushrooms, and steams "tea-smoked" duck. He declares that in addition to silk, gunpowder, and the magnetic compass, beautiful women were invented in China. Doubters are invited to meet him at dawn, on horse or afoot, with sword or pistol.